LEGENDS

MARVEL®

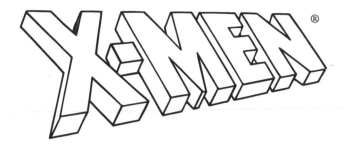

LEGENDS

Stan Lee, Editor

ILLUSTRATIONS BY MIKE ZECK

MARVEL®

BP BOOKS, INC.
NEW YORK

BERKLEY BOULEVARD BOOKS, NEW YORK

Special thanks to Ginjer Buchanan, John Morgan, Keith R.A. DeCandido, Dwight Jon Zimmerman, Steven A. Roman, Ursula Ward, Mike Thomas, and Steve Behling.

X-MEN LEGENDS

A Berkley Boulevard Book
A BP Books, Inc. Book

This is a work of fiction. Names, characters, places, and incidents are either the product of the authors' imaginations or are used fictitiously, and any resemblance to actual persons, living or dead, business establishments, events, or locales is entirely coincidental.

PRINTING HISTORY
Berkley Boulevard trade paperback edition / June 2000

All rights reserved.
Copyright © 2000 Marvel Characters, Inc.
Cover art by Vince Evans.
Cover design by Claude Goodwin.
Book design by Michael Mendelsohn.
This book may not be reproduced in whole or in part, by mimeograph or any other means, without permission.
For information address: BP Books, Inc.,
24 West 25th Street, New York, New York 10010.

The Penguin Putnam Inc. World Wide Web site address is
http://www.penguinputnam.com

Check out the Ace Science Fiction/Fantasy newsletter, and much more,
at Club PPI!

ISBN: 0-425-17082-9

BERKLEY BOULEVARD
Berkley Boulevard Books are published by The Berkley Publishing Group, a division of Penguin Putnam Inc., 375 Hudson Street, New York, New York 10014. BERKLEY BOULEVARD and its logo are trademarks belonging to Penguin Putnam Inc.

PRINTED IN THE UNITED STATES OF AMERICA

10 9 8 7 6 5 4 3 2

Contents

Introduction

Stan Lee

I DON'T THINK ANYONE KNOWS!

No matter how big a fan you may be, I'll bet you don't know how many X-Men heroes and villains there have been since the series started. Remember, in order to start counting, you've got to go back to the early 1960s—also, you've gotta decide how many times to count those characters who died and then came back again. It would keep me awake all night just trying to figure out what to do about Phoenix.

But the purpose of this long-winded intro isn't merely to provide a new guessing game for you. No, my motive is far more devious. I merely wanted to pique your interest, to stimulate your curiosity, and now that I have your attention, I wanna talk about my favorite subject—me.

I cannot count the number of times that people have asked how I dreamt up the concept of the X-Men. After hundreds of explanations (some of which might actually have been true), it occurred to me to put the answer in print, once and for all, to satisfy the intellectual hunger of countless frantic fans.

But before we begin, I have a big favor to ask of you, which is—don't grow impatient. I promise I'll soon clue you in to some of the literary magic from the stories on the pages ahead, but like moster mothers always say, "You can't have dessert until you finish your vegetables!" Well, at this particular moment in time, I'm your vegetables. You can't get to the good stuff on the pages that follow until you've waded through my introduction. And I suggest you read it carefully—there may be a quiz!

Y'know, Professor Xavier and his merry mélange of mixed-up mutants have taken the world by storm to such a degree that it's hard to believe that they haven't been around forever. But, though I know it's a frightening thought, just try to imagine a world without the X-Men. Picture, if you can, no Danger Room, no Professor X, no Magneto, no good mutants battling evil mutants while the rest of humanity is battling them all. Well, that's the world in which I found myself in the beginning of 1963.

At that time, Marvel had already bequeathed to an understandably

3

grateful world such titles as *Fantastic Four*, *The Incredible Hulk*, *The Amazing Spider-Man*, *The Avengers*, *Daredevil*—you get the idea. But now it was time for us to introduce a brand-new title, the like of which nobody had ever seen before. And so we begin our little footnote to literary history.

I decided to create an entire group rather than a single hero because we already had more single heroes than groups, and I kinda like keeping things symmetrical. But then I ran into my biggest stumbling block, the problem I knew I'd have to face sooner or later . . .

The problem was—we already had a group of heroes who had gotten their super powers due to cosmic rays. We had another hero who had been bitten by a radioactive spider, and another who had been unceremoniously zapped by gamma rays. That was when I realized we were in danger of running out of new ways for our heroes to get their super powers. I mean, how many different kinds of rays could an unscientific guy like me dream up? Of course, there were always X-rays and Sugar Rays (sorry, Mr. Leonard!), but I knew I'd be in deep doo-doo unless I could invent some new ways whereby our heroes and villains could obtain their colorful super powers.

And then it hit me! The answer was as clear as the whiskers on Wolverine's face. There was no need for me to spend countless hours dreaming up a new origin for each new super character. All I needed was a formula, an excuse for all of them to have the same origin—and the formula was the simplest one of all.

We could forget about cosmic rays, gamma rays, radioactive spider-bites, and all the other clever, carefully constructed reasons for normal people to develop super powers. All we needed was one simple word, one all-encompassing word that could apply to an infinite number of heroes and villains; one word that readers would accept without question because it's scientifically sound; one word that would make my hero-creating life a lot easier forevermore.

That word, of course, was—mutation!

We all know that mutations are a fact of life. They occur spontaneously, unexpectedly, and inexplicably. They're just as apt to occur in human life as in animal or plant life; and, most importantly, they can assume any shape and any qualities.

So that was it. I had my answer. All I had to do was create any type of super-powered characters I desired and I could simply attribute their powers to the fact that they were mutants. Nobody could argue with that. Nobody could deny it. Nobody could claim it wasn't possible. Face it, a mutation could occur anywhere, any time and in any way. I was home free!

And that's the reason our beloved X-Men are a bunch of mixed-up mutants. It's also the reason we can keep adding new ones just as fast as we can dream them up—because we don't have to explain how they got the way they are. Hey, they're mutants, right? 'Nuff said!

Now that we've laid that weighty matter to rest and historians of the future can ponder the social significance of our mutant philosophy, it's time to tackle the heavy stuff—namely, the cornucopia of exciting legends that await you on the pages ahead. I can't tell you everything about the thirteen great stories that are about to enflame your emotions and mangle your mind, but I'll try to give you a tantalizing taste for the wonderment in store.

To keep up the suspense, I won't name the titles or the authors of our stories, nor will I list them in the order in which they appear in the book. You can have fun trying to guess which ones I'm referring to. So, if you're game, here they are:

This one stars our own Miss Alive-Again, Dead-Again, Alive-Again. Why does Phoenix have nightmares about being present at the bombing of Pearl Harbor? And, even more mystifying, how can she and her new husband, Cyclops, find the startling explanation before it shatters her mind?

Here's a two-for-oner. It features both Nightcrawler and Sprite, who decide to take some time off and have a relaxing evening at the circus. But how relaxing can it be when the Blob and Unus the Untouchable show up? If you're expecting a ton of fireworks, I've a hunch you won't be disappointed.

Have you ever wondered what life was like for Warren Worthington III before he joined the X-Men and became the high-flying Angel? Well, here's your chance to find out as we take you back to the early years when Warren was attending prep school and became involved with a strange, murderous creature.

This one has enough plot twists and turns to satisfy the most critical reader. It's a tale that's been hidden from the unsuspecting public for years: a tale of Madrox the Multiple Man and the time he helped the X-Men face off against none other than the seemingly invincible Super Adaptoid.

How about a yarn wherein something goes horribly wrong when Wolverine's innocent attempt to give Jean Grey a gift ends up in a life-and-death battle as the deadly ninjas known as the Hand attack Jean's roommate, private detective Misty Knight!

Being a teenager, it's only natural for Jubilee to have lots of new obsessions. But when she turns on to figure skating, it starts a pulse-pounding chain of events wherein she learns that her new idol is himself a mutant—and no one but Jubilee herself has the power to save him.

Gambit has long been one of our most popular X-Men as far as female readers are concerned. Now, both men and women alike can get a new perspective on the charismatic Cajun as we go back to the time, shortly after he joined the X-Men, when he's strangely tempted by his dark past as a New Orleans thief.

One of my own favorite characters has always been Professor Xavier. I'm intrigued by the fact that he is both the physically weakest and the mentally strongest of the X-Men. But, though he's more than a match for almost any other mutant, what chance does he have against a psychic vampire?

At last, here's the full, unvarnished story of the one man who dared to impersonate Professor X. Why did this super-powered villian, known to humanity as the Changeling, suddenly decide to help his enemy and die a hero's death?

The beautiful Rogue arguably possesses the most tragic super power of all. This memorable tale takes us to the time when she shared her consciousness with Carol Danvers. We have a chance to look inside our heroine's tortured soul and learn of the torment suffered by both females.

Have you ever wondered what really happened after Colossus came out of his Mutant Massacre-induced coma on Muir Island—before he rejoined the X-Men? And what about Callisto? What sinister and deadly role did the former leader of the Morlocks really play? This one has all the answers.

Know what I like about the Beast? Savage-looking as he is, he's the most erudite of all the X-Men except for Professor X, and I love going against type. To learn more about him, we give you a twenty-questions interview with Hank McCoy, conducted by the bestselling *Now Magazine*.

It happened after Banshee left the X-Men and before Peter Wisdom joined Excalibur. The Englishman and the Irishman had to contend with the evil and dangerous Justin Hammer and a new breed of Sentinels. You're sure to enjoy this clash of character, personality, and wills in a dramatic adventure you'll long remember.

And there you have it. Enough great thrills, suspense, and surprises to satisfy the most critical super hero savant and fantasy fan. Now that you've finished your vegetables, you've earned your dessert. I wish you, as ever, happy reading!

Excelsior!

Stan

Stan Lee

Every Time a Bell Rings

Brian K. Vaughan

"It's not the fall that kills you . . . it's the landing." Is that how the old joke goes? Weird, I had always heard that your life flashes before your eyes right before you die. As I fell thousands of feet from the midnight sky to my rapidly approaching death below, the only thing *I* could think about were bad puns I heard in first grade and the way that year's teacher, Mrs. Chinchar, smelled like strawberries and Elmer's glue.

My name is Warren Worthington III (Dad forces me use the embarrassing "third"), and I can fly. That's right, *fly*. Not metaphorically, mind you. Or with the assistance of some kind of aircraft. Nope, I can fly.

I know a lot of people would give anything for this ability, but trust me, looking back at idiotically practicing my first high-altitude barrel role at the tender age of fifteen (with the vast wisdom that comes with now being sixteen), I realize that flying just makes life hell.

The problems began a few years ago when I noticed two small lumps on my back, just below my shoulders. Eventually a couple of, and I swear this is true, *feathers* pierced through my skin. At first, they were just an itchy annoyance, but over time, they grew. By the time I was fourteen, I had full-blown, soft, white plumage and a twelve-foot wingspan.

Thankfully they were incredibly flexible, so I could hide them somewhat comfortably underneath a normal dress shirt using one of my father's large leather belts bound around my chest to hold them down.

I know, I know. Why bother hiding them? Why not show everyone my amazing "gift"? Well, sorry, but I had no interest in joining a carnival sideshow or becoming some sort of religious icon. Having come from a long line of men and women who had always valued sameness (see: Warren Worthington and Warren Worthington Jr.), I knew that most people fear and hate the things that make us different.

Besides, sprouting new appendages was a lot more terrifying than I probably made it out to be. I mean, I know that puberty isn't easy for any kid, but *molting* wasn't exactly something they covered in health class. Lots of kids refuse to take group showers, but I somehow suspect that my reasons for doing so were a tad more unique than the rest of the guys in gym class, you know?

I was so confused by the things that it was another year before I even considered that maybe they were actually functional. After several experimental jumps off of staircases, I gradually worked my way up to the roof of Worthington Manor and, eventually, to the huge oak in our backyard. For just a second, after stepping off that old tree's tallest branch and gliding under the moonlight, all of the hardship that my wings had brought me almost seemed worthwhile.

Almost.

Anyway, none of this was going to matter in ten seconds or so, as I was about to become a feathered pancake on the soccer field that belongs to St. Ignatius, the exclusive all-boys preparatory school I still attend (in the grand tradition of all Worthington men). As I struggled to keep my eyes open against the whipping wind, I thought of my mother and how proud she was when I got accepted. I thought about how she looked when she wore her hair down for sad occasions, and tried to imagine which black dress she would put on for my funeral.

And I suddenly realized that I wasn't going to die that day.

Pull it together, Warren! My own cruel inner voice sounded like my father's familiar screaming, and the sudden shock of recognition that came with the memory snapped me to attention.

Yaw, roll and . . . Come on . . .

Flying is a lot harder that you would imagine. Birds don't have to read countless books on Bernoulli's principles of air pressure; but then again, birds were *designed* to fly. Teenage boys weren't. We're heavy, awkward, and like Icarus (I had a mythology paper due on Mr. Thomas's desk the next day), I assumed that we all paid for our arrogance in the end.

Yaw, roll and . . .

Inches away from kissing the ill-kept sports field, I kicked out my legs, hugged the tiniest current hidden in the still air, and forced all twelve feet of my limp wings open and taut.

Pitch!

Narrowly missing slamming into one of the soccer field's rusty goal boxes, I banked up hard and slowed to a stop, clumsily somersaulting onto the hard earth. Digging my fingers into the warm, wonderful soil, I collapsed in exhaustion and promptly vomited up that evening's chicken-fried steak.

See what I mean about flying?

By the dim light of the moon, I did my best to clean up, and carefully bound my wings together. Replacing my uniform shirt, I noticed the large stack of Wright brothers biographies and books on barometric pressure I had brought with me to the field.

I kicked them as hard as I could, destroying their fragile bindings. Loose pages wafted to the earth more gently that I ever could.

I felt ridiculous. I was no good at flying and I clearly wasn't meant to do it. I didn't *want* to do it. Right then and there, I made a solemn vow to visit the school nurse the very next morning to ask how the stupid growths could be removed before—

"Hey, War'!" a voice cried from the darkness. "Warren? Warren!"

Suddenly, a squat figure appeared. It was Benny Yorkes, my roommate, lab partner and best friend. With large, wide teeth that looked like Scrabble pieces, predictably thick-rimmed glasses, and a constellation of acne covering his face, Benny knew what it was like to be a social outcast much more than my tall, blond, rich, traditionally handsome self ever could. I was closer to him than I had ever been to any other human being in the world.

"God, I've been searching all over for you, Warren!" Benny said, looking even worse than usual. He was sweating, shaking.

"Slow down, Benny. What's going on?"

"It's Sullivan. He's dead."

"What?"

I had no idea how to react to this. Dan Sullivan was a bright kid with a big, dopey smile and a penchant for causing trouble, whether it was letting ferrets loose in the halls of our sister school or sealing Headmaster White's car doors shut with a new polymer bond he made in science class. He wasn't a friend, barely an acquaintance really, but Sullivan was still my classmate. My eighty-four-year-old Grandpa's passing had been a shock, but the death of a fellow fifteen-year-old seemed . . . unreal, I guess.

"They . . . they said he was murdered, War'. Somebody killed him."

"Who? Who would—"

"I don't know, but when I went back to the room to tell you, you weren't there, and I thought that, I thought . . ."

Suddenly, Benny grabbed my hands.

Slowly, I raised my hand and patted him reassuringly. "I'm fine, Benny. I'm fine."

We awkwardly pulled ourselves apart as Benny stammered, "The priests are checking up on the rest of us to make sure we're okay. They think whoever killed Sullivan might still be out here. We have to get back to the dorm right now!"

Hastily picking up what remained of my tattered aviation books, I said, "Sure. Of course. I—"

Impatient, Benny knelt down to help me collect my belongings, looking at the texts with confusion. "What are you, studying to be a pilot or something?"

"No, Benny. If God had wanted us to fly . . ."

"Yeah, yeah, yeah. Come on, let's get out of here!"

Dismembered flight books in hand, Benny Yorkes and I ran through the darkness, thinking of our fallen classmate.

High above the funeral of Daniel T. Sullivan, blackbirds circled. They didn't seem disrespectful, but they didn't seem reverent either, really. They just circled.

It wasn't raining like it always does at funerals in movies. Thick off-white clouds hung low in the sky, sunlight occasionally breaking through their ragged edges.

Mrs. Sullivan wasn't crying, but Mr. Sullivan was. This surprised me, I suppose. My parents sent their condolences to the family, unable to make it out to St. Ignatius for the funeral because of "pressing business concerns."

"I heard they had to have a closed casket because he was . . . torn open and, and, gutted. Could that be true, War'?" Benny whispered while squirming in his ill-fitting maroon blazer. The two of us stood together at the very back of the sea of identical brownish-red jackets.

"Don't know. Nobody's saying anything about the actual murder."

"Well, who do *you* think did it?"

"I don't know, Benny. Some psychopath, probably."

"I think it was someone here," he said nervously, "I bet someone from the school killed him."

"Like who, Ben?"

"Him," he muttered, subtly pointing to Hallahan, our resident spooky groundskeeper (trust me, every private school has one). A veteran of the war, Hallahan was a victim of mustard gas, an attack that left him without tear ducts. Every few seconds, he had to lick his thumb and eerily drag it across his eyeballs.

"Well . . . I wouldn't want to be caught in a room alone with him, but that doesn't mean Hallahan is a murderer."

"He's the one who found the body. Said that he thinks he saw some kind of 'animal' attacking Sullivan. Pretty convenient, huh? Look at him! That creepshow's not going to be shedding any tears for Sullivan, that's for sure."

As the funeral drew to a close and Daniel's parents departed arm in arm, Father White, the stern headmaster of St. Ignatius and Sullivan's archenemy, gathered us together in a small circle. The priest's thick, black eyebrows danced wildly underneath his incompatible white hair as he lectured us loudly, "Boys, a great evil has visited St. Ignatius . . ."

Benny looked at me and rolled his eyes.

"As you all know," White continued, softly now, "Mr. Sullivan was a very . . . troubled child. Satan held a powerful influence over him. He was not strong enough to fight for his own salvation, and in the end, he paid for his moral cowardice with his life. Pray for guidance, boys. Pray for salvation, lest such a fate befall you!"

The headmaster looked directly at Benny and me. "That is all."

Shocked but not surprised by his typically callous words, we slowly disassembled and headed for the dorms. Confidently, I turned to Benny and asked, "You know what I'm thinking, right?"

"Yep. White killed him."

"If he didn't, I don't know who did. I mean, he—"

Suddenly, Benny put out his arm and stopped me in my tracks. He pointed to a dying willow tree on the outskirts of the school's property. Sitting in its shade and smoking was one Chadwick von Stroheim, an antisocial new transfer student who loved to terrorize the younger boys. Spotting us, the hulking teenager shot an icy stare while casually blowing a geometrically perfect smoke ring.

Slowly, Benny and I turned to each other and nodded, silently acknowledging that this odd character was certainly responsible for the murder of Danny Sullivan.

* * *

"So, am I ever going to get back those aviation books I lent you, Mr. Worthington?" Father Timothy Ober asked with a knowing grin.

Ober (Father Tim to his older students) was St. Ignatius's impossibly thin biology professor and fencing instructor. The youngest of Ignatius's staff, this broomstick of a man was also the most approachable.

"Of course, Father," I said guiltily. "I'll, uh, have them back to you soon."

"No hurry, son. Making any headway on that science experiment of yours?"

"Some," I mumbled, slumping into one of the many identical desks in the vast science lab. I liked the way all of the perfectly arranged, unoccupied chairs looked in the mostly empty room. Calm, I guess.

Father Tim sat on the edge of an experiments table and slowly took off his glasses, his stock response for concern. "What's the matter, Warren? Is it Daniel? His . . . his death has been hard on all of us, you know. I was very close to him, too. He was a . . . a wonderful student."

"Sure," I said, tracing my finger thoughtlessly around the initials carved into the desk by students long since graduated. "But, to be honest, that's not what's really been bothering me."

"No?"

"No. Father, do you know anything about . . . I don't know quite how to phrase this. Do you know anything about people who are . . . different?"

He tapped one end of his folded glasses against his brow, closed his eyes and nodded. Choosing his words slowly and deliberately, he finally offered, "Warren, I think I've heard this line of questioning more times than you could imagine. Let me remind you that you are free to tell me absolutely anything in the very strictest of confidence."

"Do you know anything about people born with something . . . strange?"

Surprised, he instantly replaced his glasses and stared at me with confusion. "Strange? Why, you mean, birth defects or—"

"Not necessarily strange. Maybe I mean . . . extra."

"Ah," Father Tim exclaimed, leaping from the table and racing for his bookshelf. "Extra!"

Off of the top shelf, he grabbed a large hardbound book and cracked it open before me, saying, "I've been reading the most fascinating thesis by a brilliant geneticist named Charles . . ." He flipped the book over, searching for the author. "Xavier, that's it! He has pioneered remarkable research in just the kind of mutations I think you may be concerned about."

He looked at the heavy text for a moment before finally handing it to me, cautiously adding, "It's heady stuff, Warren. Try not to drown in it, now."

Graciously, I took the thesis, collected my blazer and backpack and headed for the door with, "Thank you, Father Tim. I can't tell you how much I appreciate it."

"Certainly, Mr. Worthington," he smiled. "Try to return *this* one before the end of the next millennium, eh?"

Inspired with the newfound hope of potential "normalcy" after reading Xavier's thesis, I decided to return to the soccer field that very evening to further explore what the author had referred to as my "mutant ability."

Waiting for Benny to finally begin his predictable snoring pattern, I quietly climbed out of our first-floor window and charged across St. Ignatius's immense property.

Suddenly noticing a single, glowing orange dot emanating from underneath the school's ancient willow tree, I stopped dead in my tracks.

"Chadwick," I said, watching the notorious bully calmly puff on his cigarette. "What are you doing out at this hour?"

"Just catching a smoke, Worthington." He exhaled. "Though I might ask the same of you."

I racked my brain for any plausible excuse at all, but before I could dream up an appropriate story, the overgrown transfer student flicked the flaming remnants of his cigarette in a blazing arc ending at my feet, and quietly walked away.

Standing there for some time, I watched Chadwick until he eventually disappeared in the campus' shadows. I tried to picture him ripping Danny Sullivan to pieces, but seeing those images in my head felt wrong. I sprinted for the soccer field, opening my mouth wide and letting the cold night air pour into me.

Inches from my makeshift "runway" at the soccer field, I heard the most terrible sound you could imagine.

I had seen the word *bloodcurdling* used in horror stories before, but it meant absolutely nothing to me until I listened to the shrill wail coming from the groundskeeper's quarters down by our football field.

Benny was right. Hallahan was the killer, and while I stood there motionless, he was probably taking the life of another student. I could have run for help, but I knew the deed would be finished by the time I made it back to the dorms. I like to think that it was bravery that drove me to run for Hallahan's quarters on my own, but it was probably just selfishness.

After Sullivan's, I never wanted to attend a classmate's funeral again.

Racing for the groundskeeper's small cabin, I found his front door open. Upon closer inspection, I learned that the door wasn't open, it was missing, torn from its hinges and casually discarded outside.

"Who's here? I . . . I heard screams!" Every heartbeat made my hands shake.

I fumbled in the darkness for a light switch. Finding it, I immediately wished I hadn't. Hard yellow light spilled out of a hanging overhead lamp. The swinging spotlight alternately revealed and concealed the lifeless body of Hallahan, still clutching the pair of gardening shears he unsuccessfully used to fend off his attacker.

His eyes were missing. The empty sockets were filled with shallow puddles of blood that rippled slightly as I cautiously stepped closer. The elderly man's body had been ripped open vertically along the ventral portion of the body (I think it was ventral anyway, we had done the same to fetal pigs the previous semester). The cuts were jagged, uneven, as if the claws of some wild animal had made them. I tried to vomit, but my body could only muster up dry, painful hacking.

Suddenly, I heard a noise amidst the silence. Heavy. Rhythmic. By the time I recognized it as breathing, it was right behind me.

With a deafening roar, the creature was on top of me. It was as large as a bear, though it clearly wasn't one. The bulk of its weight rested on its large, muscular hind legs. The beast had my shoulders pinned to the ground with rugged talons. This time, a childhood memory I had forgotten years ago, accidentally swimming into the forbidden deep end of our family pool, suddenly popped vividly into my head. Strange.

Somehow finding the courage to look up at my executioner, I saw only the silhouette of its long snout, which dripped warm, foamy saliva on my neck. As the low-hanging lamp swung directly overhead, I caught a single glimpse of its eyes. They looked almost human. Apologetic, maybe.

As I listened to the animal's jaws clack into their most open position, I desperately fingered for Hallahan's rusty shears. Just barely taking hold of a single handle, I swung the dull blades high in the air and plunged them deep into the beast's woolly neck.

As the creature let out a howl of clear agony, I rolled free of its grasp, bolted to my feet and ran as fast as I ever have or probably ever will.

Charging onto the football field outside, I frantically fought for my bearings as my eyes adjusted to the darkness. I heard the wounded monster stumbling to the groundskeeper's doorway. The faded white numbers painted on the field's grass told me that the thing was precisely fifty-two yards away from me.

Maybe it couldn't see me.

A few steps later, I finally admitted to myself that I wasn't going to be that lucky. Wasting the time to look behind me, I could see that it was now only forty yards away. The thing was closing on me at an unbelievable pace.

Thirty yards.

Recognizing that there was no way that I could outrun him, I realized that I still had one chance to out*distance* him. I frantically began tearing at the buttons of my shirt.

Twenty yards.

I could smell the stench of Hallahan's insides on the monster. Ripping my last three buttons off, I discarded the garment and went to work on the thick leather belt around my chest. As my feet pumped and my trembling hands fumbled at the buckle, my restless wings fought hopelessly to free themselves.

Ten yards.

"Our Father who art in Heaven!" I yelled—instinctively, I suppose. Directly behind me, I could hear the animal's staccato galloping. Panicked, I finally opened the belt . . . only to have the buckle catch on the strap's final hole. Screaming, I raised my arms, and tore the belt off over my head. Gloriously, my beautiful, wonderful wings finally unfurled.

Five yards.

I poured on the speed, preparing for takeoff. I could feel its breath on my leg hair. My wings desperately searched for the lift they needed.

The creature pounced.

"Yes!" Finally, my throbbing wings found what they needed and my feet left the ground . . . just as the beast's paw grabbed for my ankle!

But it was too late.

I didn't dare look back. I had escaped within a millimeter of my life and my only plan was to flap my stupid wings as hard as I could until I made it back to the relative safety of school

Reaching the campus, I suddenly realized that my shirtless body would require a little more explanation than I was ready to give in one night, so I made the difficult decision to first return to my dorm room. I had absolutely no idea what I would tell my roomie when I saw him.

Arching my shoulders, my wings came together and shot straight up behind me as I rocketed through my room's open window and landed with a resounding thump on the dusty floorboards. After all, I figured there was no harm in making my revelation a little dramatic for—

"Benny?" I looked around, only to find my roommate's bed unoccupied.

"No . . ." I whispered. What if that thing had gotten to other students as well? I collapsed my wings and threw on a baggy sweatshirt seconds before the door to my room slammed open.

Terrified, I swung around . . . only to see a frantic Benny at the doorway.

"Benny! Are you okay?"

"I'm fine," he said breathlessly. "Where have you *been*, you moron? I heard screaming out in the fields and woke up . . . and, and you were gone. I went to see if you were with Father Tim, but he wasn't in his quarters either. God, I thought you were dead, Warren! What were you *doing* out there?"

"Benny, I'm fine! I couldn't sleep, so I went out to . . . to run some laps," I lied unconvincingly. "We have to go get Headmaster White! Benny, I saw Hallahan get murdered! Something . . . something attacked him."

"Something?" he asked, staring at me with equal parts horror and confusion. "Was it . . . what, an animal?"

"No," I whispered. "It was human, but different. It had something . . . extra."

EVERY TIME A BELL RINGS

* * *

After answering questions as best I could for doubtful police officers, I walked across campus with Father Tim. Following Hallahan's murder, no student could leave his room without being accompanied by a teacher. All classes were temporarily cancelled and "the Green," as we referred to the big field that connected St. Ignatius's various buildings, was abnormally silent. Our school's ancient bell tower, located in the dead center of the Green, cast a long dark shadow over the two of us as we walked.

We strolled in silence for a while before I finally said, "Father Tim, this sounds stupid, but . . . Do you think God makes some people better than others? Does he make some worse?"

He was polite enough to pause and consider this even though he doubtlessly had an answer prepared already. "Well, Warren . . . God makes us all in His image. None of us are made better or worse than anyone else. We're just different."

"But what about what those men were saying?" I asked. "About how maybe these murders could have been done by a . . . by a mutant? Does God make mutants? Are they good or evil?"

The pause seemed genuine this time. "Well, yes, I suppose even these mutations are God's children, Warren. Whether they're good or evil is up to them. God's gift of free will is a glorious and terrifying thing. But if this mutant chooses to do evil—"

Suddenly, a dark figure appeared from behind one of Grounds-keeper Hallahan's untrimmed, orphan hedges. Father Tim and I simultaneously leapt back in shock, only partially relieved to find out that it was actually Headmaster White.

"What in God's name are you putting into this boy's head, Timothy?"

"Good morning, Father. I—"

"You heard what the detectives said! These mutants are the devil's children! They are abominations in the eyes of God and must be destroyed!"

"I beg your pardon, Father White," Tim said sternly, boldly stepping closer to the headmaster. "But I do believe God's only son would take issue with your stance!"

As the men continued to argue dogma and stuff, I slowly slipped

21

away and headed for the peace and quiet of my room. Upon arrival, I found anything but.

"Chadwick von Stroheim is some kind of werewolf!" Benny said, as I kicked off my shoes and collapsed onto my unmade bed.

"Good night, Benny. Please."

"Trust me on this one, Warren," he pleaded. "That psycho must turn into some kind of monster at night. And then he kills his enemies!"

"Sure," I offered, pulling down the blinds to shut out the harsh morning sun.

"I think he knows I'm onto him, too! War', you should have seen the way he was looking at me at roll call this morning!" Benny's words faded into the void as I promptly fell asleep.

For the first time in ages, I didn't dream of flying.

I kind of wish I had.

Those bloodcurdling screams returned as I was shocked awake by a sound that, surprisingly, didn't come from my dreams. I pressed the snooze button on top of my alarm clock as a pathetic little light barely illuminated the time: 12:32 A.M.

Slowly returning to alertness, I was horrified to see that Benny wasn't in his bed. As a matter of fact, he wasn't anywhere in the room. The screams continued.

Forcing my shoes on, I darted into the hallway and saw another door to one of the dorm rooms open. It was Chadwick's single, and it was empty. Benny had been right. Somehow, the transfer student was *becoming* the creature that killed Sullivan and Hallahan.

Following the screams, I charged out onto the Green. Why wasn't anyone else outside? How could they all sleep through the terrible noise? I spun around until I was dizzy, searching everywhere for the nearby yelling. The shouting was clearly audible, but there was no sign of Benny or the creature anywhere.

Finally, I looked up. Five stories above, I saw two figures struggling at the top of St. Ignatius's ancient bell tower.

I knew Benny would be dead by the time I made it up the eighty-four stairs (being forced to run up them was a freshmen tradition), so I did the only thing I could. I pulled my sweatshirt off, feeling the cold night air against my chest as I ascended toward the top of the tower.

Bobbing slowly in a holding pattern just outside the open-air section surrounding the huge dome-shamed bell, I saw something more horrible than even the groundskeeper's mutilated body. Chadwick von Stroheim . . . was inches away from being murdered by Benny Yorkes.

The hulking Chadwick, having run up the entire tower in an apparent attempt to escape my changing friend, promptly fainted at the sight of my silhouette against the sliver moon. A now-fanged Benny looked at me with tear-filled eyes. I noticed new fur dancing and materializing on his swelling body.

"Get away, Warren! I don't want to have to hurt you!"

"Is that what you told Sullivan?" I cautiously circled the tower, drawing Benny's attention with each flap.

"I never wanted to kill him, Warren! You have to believe me! The hunger! The hunger made me do it," he said, his voice deepening to a low rumble.

"You have to stop, Benny. I can help you. Just try to stay calm and . . ."

"I don't know what's happening to me! It just started one night! I thought it would end after Sullivan, but what if Hallahan knew it was me?" He grabbed Chadwick's neck. "What if this kid saw me last night? I don't know how to stop!"

"Just put him down," I begged, watching him inch closer to Chadwick's limp body. "You don't have to hurt anyone."

"I do!" he screamed, nearly fully transformed now. "It's what I am now! Why did God do this to me? I . . . ggggrrrRRAAAARRR!"

Before I could tell him how much I sympathized with his condition, my transfigured friend leapt off the edge of the bell tower, his talons aimed directly at my throat.

Stunned by how heavy Benny was in his new form, my wings fell slack and we immediately began pinwheeling downwards. Somehow, I managed to straighten my entire wingspan and catch an updraft, impressed by the unbelievable weight my wings could apparently handle. As I pulled out of our fall, Benny began snapping at my throat. Out of the frying pan . . .

Lumbering through the airspace directly above the school, I banked hard through the canyons between buildings, using everything I learned in my months of study in a desperate attempt to shake the vicious beast.

"Benny!" I cried against the rush of gale force wind. "I'm your friend! You'll kill us both!"

With a deafening roar, Benny clawed at my bare back. I screamed in pain and promptly went into a hard tailspin in a final attempt to shake him before he tore me to pieces. With the creature still clinging to my aching body, I began to accept the fact that neither of us would likely make it out of the dogfight alive.

Pushing my tired body harder than I ever had before, I shifted my wings to a ninety-degree angle and pushed myself straight at the moon, directly overhead. I flapped so hard that my wings smashed into each other in an explosion of loose feathers with every beat.

Still, Benny held on.

Flying directly up is like climbing to the top of the Empire State Building while being forced to increase your speed with each and every step. Higher and higher, faster and faster, it wasn't long before we were skimming clouds. My vision became blurry and my head throbbed in pain as we entered an altitude where the air was impossibly thin. Thankfully, Benny's grunting became a distant gurgling and his grasp weakened.

A hundred feet later, seconds before I would have passed out, Benny finally let go. I rocketed skyward for a moment as my wings were suddenly freed of their extra cargo. Quickly slowing to a halt, I listened as Benny's plummeting howl became a fading high-pitched whine. I shifted my center of gravity and dove straight down.

No matter what he had done, you have to understand that there was no way I could let Benny Yorkes, my roommate, my lab partner, my best friend, fall to his death.

Tucking my wings under my arms, I straightened my body and entered a devastating nosedive. I aimed myself like a rocket directly at Benny, whose bulky frame thankfully created enough drag to narrow the distance between us.

Less than fifty feet from smashing into the Green, I positioned myself away from Benny and prepared to attempt a feat that I had failed at countless times before.

Yaw, roll and . . . Come on! And . . .

For just a moment, the world became a blurry, beautiful Impressionist painting.

Pitch! "Benny, take my hand!"

Executing my premiere flawless barrel roll, I nabbed Benny's arm and cautiously slowed his momentum by swinging his heavy body gently upwards. I looked down at my almost fully reverted friend and said, "It's over, Benny. Let's go home."

As we soared back into the still air high above St. Ignatius, he stared into my eyes, shaking his head sadly.

"I'm sorry, Warren." With a single swipe of what remained of his talons, Benny sliced at my tired arms. While I hung there helplessly, my blood fell with him.

I don't remember what I screamed as I watched his fragile body tumble for what seemed like hours before it finally smashed on the schoolyard below.

This time, it did rain.

I stood at the back of the funeral, alone. My parents sent their condolences to Benny's parents, again unable to make it out to St. Ignatius for the funeral because of more "pressing business concerns." I wanted to go to the Yorkeses and offer some sort of explanation for their child's death, but what would I have told them that would have made it any easier?

For a long while after that terrible night, I convinced myself that Benny must have somehow "caught" his mutation from me. No matter what Xavier's book said, there didn't seem to be any other believable way to explain how two of these rare beings ended up being so close. Eventually though, I guess I came to accept the fact that, when Benny and I chose each other as roommates, we did so because we each recognized our own fear and confusion in the other. That's what I have to tell myself to keep going, anyway.

At the homily, Headmaster White asked us to pray for the repose of the soul of our dearly departed classmate, "Who must have thrown himself from the bell tower in a fit of stress-induced insanity." White assured the surprised students that God was wondrous and could forgive anything, even the terrible mistakes of our friend.

The headmaster's change of heart was doubtlessly influenced by the masked Avenging Angel who visited his window the previous night and delivered a stern message "from God Himself." Rumors raced throughout the campus about this mythical angel, whom the now sociable Chadwick von Stroheim claimed saved him from Benny's insane rampage.

After the service, I strolled into Father Tim's office and apologetically laid down several taped-together aviation books on his desk. "Thank you, Father. I'm done with these now."

His glasses already off, Tim simply leaned back in his well-worn leather chair. "Warren, you know you're welcome to them as long as you—"

"No. Thank you. I'm done."

"I'm disappointed, Warren. You're one of the most extraordinary students I've ever had."

"I don't want to be extraordinary anymore," I said, looking at my tarnished shoes. "I just want to be like everyone else."

"Of course," he nodded, standing to walk me to the door. "I understand, Warren. But I want you to know that I'm always here for you. And so is the Lord."

I thanked him halfheartedly and walked out to the empty Green. Staring up at the empty sky, I made a solemn vow never again to use my wings. Still, as the church bells echoed in the distance, feathers rustled impatiently underneath my faded maroon blazer.

Diary of a False Man

Keith R.A. DeCandido

PROFESSOR XAVIER WAS DEAD.

That, at least, was what Jean Grey had to pretend was the case.

She couldn't imagine how things had gone so wrong.

The man they had buried was not truly Charles Francis Xavier, Ph.D., world-renowned geneticist, headmaster of Xavier's School for Gifted Youngsters, and, more secretly, powerful telepath and mentor to the team of teenaged super heroes, the X-Men. Xavier was, in fact, presently in a sealed bunker beneath the school grounds, preparing for an invasion by an alien race known as the Z'Nox.

Jean Grey was the only one of the X-Men who knew that he wasn't really dead, but she could not reveal the truth to anyone.

After she and her four teammates—Scott Summers, Hank McCoy, Bobby Drake, and Warren Worthington III—had returned from the funeral to the mansion that housed the school, they played the message that "Xavier" had left for them in the event he was killed. Jean pretended to be surprised by it, even though she knew that the Professor recorded such messages before any kind of mission. He was always prepared for the eventuality of his own death. The man who took his place had felt obligated to do the same.

To Jean's horror, she realized she didn't even know the man's real name.

He had been called the Changeling, and he first encountered the X-Men as the second-in-command of the terrorist organization Factor Three. In the end, though, he had helped the X-Men defeat Factor Three's so-called "Mutant Master." Then, in secret, he had taken the place of Professor Xavier. Just a few days ago, he died fighting Grotesk, a sacrifice that saved billions of lives.

The recording of the Changeling-as-Xavier included a warning that Magneto might return soon—as indeed he had days earlier, facing the Avengers—and then came to an end with the words: "*And now, farewell, my X-Men. The torch has been passed, and I know you shall be worthy of it.*"

The tears that ran down Jean's cheeks and dampened her yellow face mask were genuine as she cried, "No, no! That can't be the end—it can't!" And the words were not lies, though the other X-Men probably took a much different meaning from them. The careful plan that she, the Professor, and the Changeling had worked out had not taken the latter's death into account as a possibility.

"It won't be, Jean," Hank said, tears also staining his mask, "as the Professor himself recognized. We must now carry on, and make a new beginning."

Hank McCoy was right, of course. He usually was. She squeezed her teammate's oversized hand and smiled.

Then she turned to the team leader—and also the man she loved, though she'd never dared to say so. "Scott, if it's okay, I'd—I'd like to be the one to go through the Professor's things and pack them up."

"Of course, Jean," Scott said stoically. "You knew him longer than any of us."

She couldn't read his face—that was nigh impossible at the best of times, especially with the ruby quartz glasses that completely covered his eyes—but she didn't need to. She could feel his grief and pain. And she could feel that he was trying desperately to shut those feelings out, to carry on as leader of the X-Men and not allow the grief to cripple him—especially with Magneto on the loose again. So having someone else do the onerous task of sorting through Xavier's effects would be fine with the X-Men's field leader.

Besides which, Scott spoke the truth. Unlike the boys, who were recruited to the X-Men out of high school, Jean first met Charles Xavier when she was ten years old. Her best friend Annie Richardson had been run over by a car, and Jean had felt Annie die in her mind. The Professor had brought her out of the ensuing depression telepathically and also closed off her psionic abilities until she was ready to deal with them.

That time had come just before Xavier had been replaced by the Changeling.

Removing her mask, she went upstairs to the Professor's study.

His papers and computer files were very well organized. Anything personal, she put in a separate pile, to be placed in storage—perhaps in the attic. The school paperwork would also have to be dealt with, though Jean had no idea by whom.

As she went through a pile of papers, files, and books, she realized that she probably needed to alert the school's lawyer, Michael Ramsey, about the situation. *Or maybe*, she thought, *I can just not say anything.* Then she chastised herself. *Right, Jean, just hope Mr. Ramsey doesn't notice that his client is dead until he "comes back" from the dead in a few months. That'll work.*

Then there was the domestic staff. All the paperwork related to the running of the school that she didn't even pretend to understand. Who was going to deal with all that? Xavier's only family was a half brother who despised him. Perhaps Mr. Ramsey could deal with it, but how could she explain the situation to him?

Clenching her fist, she resisted an urge to pound on the desk. This wasn't how things were supposed to go. The plan was that the Changeling would pretend to be Xavier for a few months, then Xavier would resurface from the bunker, they'd stop the Z'Nox, and the Changeling would go on with his life, having done something to help the world that he, as a member of Factor Three, had almost destroyed. When Jean, the Professor, and the Changeling had discussed and planned this, it had all seemed so sensible. And during those first weeks, it went very well.

But then the shapechanger had to go and get himself killed. And Xavier was now in the bunker, completely unreachable, leaving Jean alone. The Professor had made it clear that, until he was ready, he could not leave the bunker. To emphasize the point, he'd coded the lock so that it could only be opened from the inside. Even if she wanted to, Jean could not reach Xavier until he chose to come out.

So she had to maintain the charade and pretend that Charles Xavier was dead.

Suddenly, she felt less like the mature woman, the valued teammate, the person in whom the Professor had placed his trust, and a lot more like the frightened eighteen-year-old girl she really was.

She didn't know what to do, and the one man who could help her couldn't be reached.

At that moment, she hated the Changeling. Hated him for putting her in this position. Hated him for dying when she needed him to be alive.

Maybe I should just tell the boys everything. They'll understand.

Maybe we can break into the bunker and get the Professor out. Bobby could freeze the lock, or maybe Scott could blast it down, or . . .

Suddenly, she broke into tears. *I can't handle this.* She didn't care that the Professor had been explicit in his instructions. She didn't care that he'd locked the bunker. She didn't care about how important it was that he be prepared for the Z'Nox's eventual arrival.

She just wanted the Professor back to make it all better.

After a minute, she composed herself. She was almost done going through the pile. She would finish what she started, then go tell Scott and the others the truth. They deserved that. The world could go to hell, for all she cared. She would *not* carry this burden alone.

The last item in the pile was a book that Jean recognized as the Professor's journal.

She opened it to the back. Although she had no intention of reading it, she was curious as to when he last put in an entry.

To her surprise, the last entry was dated only five days previous—the morning of the day the Changeling died. Flipping through the pages, she realized that he had maintained the journal. His skills as a forger, she realized, were as good as he had boasted weeks earlier. Skimming through it, Jean could not tell where the Professor's handwriting ended and the Changeling's began.

Closing the journal, she placed it in the box she'd labeled PERSONAL. Then she used her telekinesis to lift some of the administrative files into the air, and tried to open one of the file cabinet drawers the same way. But the drawer wouldn't budge. At first Jean thought it was because she was splitting her concentration between the drawer and the files, but she soon realized that the drawer was physically stuck.

Placing the files back on the desk, she concentrated harder on the drawer. She mentally "felt" something physically blocking the tracks. Gently removing the object, she then took the drawer all the way out, and moved the files into it.

Then she pulled out the item itself: it was a small book. The cover had a lovely marble paper design, but no text. After replacing the drawer, she opened the book. The cream-colored pages had text written in very neat handwriting with what seemed to be a simple ballpoint pen. *Another journal of the Professor's?* she wondered. But no, the handwriting was different.

She read the first page:

I've had many names in my life: Charles Sage, Werner Reiman, Jack Bolton, John Askegren, Francisco Zerrilli, Martina Johanssen—and, most recently, Charles Xavier.

But there's a difference with that last one. The guy who was born with it is still using it. He asked me to take his place, to become him while he went off to do something else.

Part of being Charles Xavier is to keep a journal. Keeping his has made me decide to keep one of my own. I don't have long for this world (the doctor said the cancer would take me in six to nine months) so I figured I should leave some kind of legacy. Especially since, if everything goes the way it's supposed to, only two people are going to know what I did at the end: Xavier himself, and Jean Grey. Hell, only they and the X-Men and a few others are even going to know who I am.

So I figure Xavier or Grey will someday read this journal, and then people will know just who this guy was.

Jean felt her jaw fall open. *He had cancer. He only had a few months to live.* That explained why the Changeling had kept asking Xavier, "You won't be down for more than six months, right?" The Professor had assured him that he wouldn't.

It also explained something that hadn't made any sense to Jean at the time. As he lay dying in Warren's arms, the Changeling had said that he was dying "of an illness even I could not cure." At the time, Scott had thought that was why "the Professor" had been pushing the X-Men so hard, because he needed to get the training in before he died. In fact, the Changeling was simply following Xavier's instructions to work the X-Men as hard as possible in preparation for the Z'Nox invasion. Instead, the Changeling let them believe that Xavier was dying in any case.

Perhaps it was to take the sting out of his death at the hands of Grotesk—the knowledge that he would have died here long—or perhaps it was simply so someone would know that he was dying of cancer. Jean would never be sure. She had closed her mind off from the Changeling's when he died. She only recently started using her telepathic powers; she didn't think she could handle feeling someone die in her head again.

I shouldn't read this, she thought. *It's his private diary. Besides, I have to go tell the boys the truth.*

But he'd intended it to be found after he died. Just because that death happened several months ahead of schedule didn't change the intent.

And suddenly, she was consumed with a great desire to put off telling her teammates the truth. *Not the day of the funeral*, she rationalized. *Give it a day or two.*

She sat down in one of the the leather guest chairs—the wheelchair-bound Xavier had never placed a chair behind the desk itself, of course—and turned to the second page.

August 19, 11:45 P.M.

It's pretty late. Most of the X-Men have gone to bed, exhausted after the battle with the Frankenstein monster. And Xavier has locked himself in his bunker.

For the last week or two, Xavier and I have both been acting as the X-Men's mentor. He was the one who found out that the Frankenstein monster was real (which threw *me* for a loop, I don't mind saying). I was the one who told the X-Men about the mission initially, but he was the one who stopped the monster and wiped that boat crew's memory of the incident. This was his way of easing the transition, having each of us play the role of Xavier alternately. It seems to have worked, and now he's gone down in his bunker.

Leaving me with the X-Men.

Since I didn't go on the mission to stop the Frankenstein android, I'm not as exhausted as the kids are. So I figured I'd start this journal for real.

"Begin at the beginning," the Queen of Hearts said in *Alice in Wonderland*, and that's probably where it makes the most sense.

For me, the beginning was St. Julian's Orphanage for Boys in Central City, California, or, as I like to call it, hell. My first memory is getting beaten up by Johnny Brill, one of the older boys. So are most of the other memories. I was a scrawny, sickly, ugly little kid. I didn't have a real name. The nuns had me listed as Charles Sage, but they made that name up. When I was older, I broke into St. Julian's records, and found out that I'd been left at the orphanage as an infant, with a note saying, and I quote, "Tak kare of the boy." All I know about my parents is that they didn't want me, and they couldn't spell.

But that came later. After puberty. Before that, I was just Johnny's designated victim.

That changed one night when I was fourteen. I had a weird dream, then I woke up. I went into the bathroom, and some tall, muscular kid with a good-looking face stared back at me in the mirror. Took me a few minutes to realize it was me.

Took me half a day to realize I could change myself back.

But I didn't. To this day, I've never gone back to looking like what I looked like before. Why should I? The scrawny, ugly, sickly kid that the nuns called Charles Sage was a miserable little twerp whose main purpose in life was to be Johnny Brill's punching bag. I didn't need to be him anymore.

The nuns didn't recognize me, assumed I was a trespasser, and threw me out.

At first, I thought everything would be great. Freedom, away from Johnny and the nuns!

What I forgot is that St. Julian's, whatever its flaws (and believe me, it had plenty) also fed me three squares a day and put a roof over my head. I was in Southern California, so sleeping outside wasn't as much of a chore as it might've been. But I was still a fourteen-year-old kid with the clothes on my back and not a hell of a lot else.

I noticed the beggars on the street. I started watching them, and realized the ones that looked crummy but not *really* awful were the ones who did the best. So I changed to look like one of those and panhandled for a few days. That at least got me enough to buy some lousy food.

Then I went back to St. Julian's. I knew my way around the place (years of hiding from bullies had taught me all the hidey-holes, and I knew the security routine) so breaking in proved pretty easy. That was when I read my file.

And then I went after Johnny.

And I beat the holy crap out of him.

It was the greatest moment of my life up to that point.

Pathetic. All I'd lived for was to do to Johnny what he'd been doing to me for ten years. But when I was done, I didn't know what else to do. I didn't even know who or what to be. All I'd known was the orphanage.

That, and panhandling. So I went back onto the street and joined the ever-growing ranks of the homeless.

Then Werner Reiman came along. Werner was a retired guy who apparently was bored, so he'd wander out and check out the homeless. He didn't want to give them money, he just wanted to lecture them on how they should make something of their lives like he did. "Worked at Consolidated for forty-seven years. Took a job right out of high school, retired at sixty-five. Made me a nice little nest egg. Never heard me beggin' for no handout, nosireebob." For the better part of a week, I heard him use this spiel on various homeless guys.

When he tried it on me, I told him to go away. It was easy for him to say, "Get a job." He had a name. He had an identity. All I had was a sickly kid named Charles Sage that I swore never to be again. That left me with nothing.

Undaunted, Werner went to bother the colonel.

He wasn't really a colonel, of course, but he did serve in the Army. I got a look at his dog tags once when he was sleeping—he'd been a corporal. What war he served in changed depending on the time of day, and he had so much hair on his head and face that you couldn't tell what his age was.

Nobody messed with the colonel for two reasons. One was that he carried a pistol. The other was that he was as nutty as a fruitcake.

But nobody told Werner Reiman either of these things. So old Werner was pretty surprised when the colonel shot him.

Realizing what he'd done, the colonel ran off. So did the other local homeless guys.

I didn't. What I was missing was a name, an identity. Werner Reiman had both, but he wasn't going to need them much longer.

As the life bled out of Werner, I removed his clothes. I studied his face and his skin tone, looked for birthmarks, everything. It didn't take long, since I have a photographic memory. Or, at least, I have since the day I discovered my powers. I'm not sure now if it's a part of my mutant abilities, or if I just don't *want* to remember the days before I stopped being Charles Sage. Ultimately, it doesn't matter. One look up and down Werner Reiman's body was enough for me to remember every detail of it.

Then I became him. I now had his face, his ID, his wallet, his credit cards, his car keys, and his "nice little nest egg." I didn't have his fingerprints—I can't manage that—but that never turned out to be an issue.

Werner Reiman was my ticket off the street.

Getting tired. Going to get some sleep. I'm surprised at how good it feels to get all this down. Been a while since I even thought about life in Central City—so much has happened since then.

I'll probably do more tomorrow.

August 20, 7:30 P.M.

Pretty routine day today. Ran the X-Men through a training session, then through a more traditional day in the classroom. Good thing Xavier prepared detailed lesson plans, since teaching is a bit out of my league. I had thought "Xavier's School for Gifted Youngsters" was just a front, but this place really is a school, and these five kids *are* gifted. Especially McCoy. If he has any brains (and he's got plenty), he'll get out of the hero racket and become a scientist or something. He's got the talent.

Anyhow, I just updated Xavier's journal, and I figured I'd do it for mine, also. I left off at Werner Reiman yesterday.

Werner's driver's license had his address, so I went there, changed into less bloody clothes, and then started to *become* Werner.

The hardest part at first was duplicating his handwriting. After all, having his credit cards wouldn't do any good if I couldn't sign his name. Though the nuns always gave me bad penmanship marks, I was always good at copying things. Whenever they'd given us tracing paper and a drawing and told us to reproduce it on the paper, I had never bothered putting the tracing paper on the picture. I just looked at it and copied it over, and I always did better than the other kids. (The other kids, goaded by Johnny, usually used that as another excuse to beat me up, of course.)

So it didn't take long to hone my talent for forgery.

I always wondered about that. Was the affinity for forgery a by-product of the fact that I was a shapechanger? Did my ability to copy things as a little kid have some kind of effect on what my mutant power would be? Or was it part of the telepathic talent I didn't even know I had until Xavier, Grey, and I concocted this plan? I wondered the same thing about being eidetic, for that matter.

Yeah, I know, it's all philosophical and you can't answer it, but hell, it's my journal. If you can't be philosophical in your own journal, where can you be?

Anyway, it took a couple of months, but I finally got Werner's handwriting down.

Luckily, Werner was single, retired, and weird. He had a couple of relatives, but they didn't call that often, and I blew them off. They told me I was acting immature, which in retrospect was absolutely true. I mean, I was a fourteen-year-old passing myself off as sixty-five. Werner was cranky. I was whiny. People didn't notice the difference.

So now I had some money, a home, an identity.

I was bored to tears.

The problem was that Werner's "nice little nest egg" was fine for an old man, but it wasn't enough for a teenager who'd never had anything.

One day, I came up with an idea on the spur of the moment. I'd gone to the corner deli to pick up a sandwich. As I was paying, I heard the owner in the back telling one of the kids who worked there, "Remember, Marty, come back at eleven to take the till to the bank. That's *eleven*, not a quarter after or half past, *eleven*."

I followed Marty for about eight blocks after he left, making sure I knew his facial features and the clothes he was wearing. Then I went back to the store right at eleven, having changed myself to be Marty. There was no sign of the genuine article. I figured from his conversation that he was always late. Sure enough, the owner made some noise about being stunned that I was on time for a change, gave me a canvas bag full of money, and I left.

It wasn't much money—a couple hundred, or so—but it was a start.

By the time I hit my eighteenth birthday, I'd amassed a ton of cash.

I was bored to tears. Again.

You see, once I got the hang of it, using my powers to be a thief got boring. I mean, it was too easy.

Also, honestly, I was really starting to hate being Werner Reiman.

So I started doing other forging. God knows there was a market for it. And I never did two jobs with the same face, and I never used Werner's face for any of them. This was a good thing, as I didn't do such a great job covering my tracks in the beginning. There were probably about twelve APBs for guys fitting my "description." Luckily, those guys would never be found.

I also taught myself how to use computers. By the time I hit nineteen, I'd slowly created enough documentation—both physically and online—to establish another identity. This was a young good-looking guy of thirty named Jack Bolton. I slowly drained Werner's bank accounts and deposited it all into one I created for Jack, and moved all my stuff to an apartment in the upscale part of Central City. Then I pretended to be a neighbor of Werner's and called his cousin Myrtle, saying nobody had seen Werner in days, and he left the TV on really loud.

Then I turned on the TV really loud, left Werner's apartment, and never came back.

As Jack, I invested some money, and I lucked out. A couple of investments turned out great, and I was suddenly rolling in it.

But I was still bored. I kept Jack around, this time, for whenever I felt like hobnobbing with the rich and stupid, but I went ahead and created a few more identities: master forger John Askegren, mob enforcer Francisco Zerrilli, even a female pool hustler named Martina Johanssen. I dropped Askegren when the heat was on after an insurance scam, but the other two worked just fine. Not that I needed the money. But breaking up the routine—one day forging, one day hustling pool, one day beating up store owners, one day having lunch with my stockbroker—kept the boredom from setting in.

Fire alarm just went off. Better go check it out. I'll do more tomorrow.

Jean actually laughed at that. She remembered that night. Warren had been making one of his periodic—and laughable—attempts at cooking. The result, as usual, was inedibly burnt food, the fire alarm going off, and the X-Men assembling in the kitchen ready to face some menace or other, and being confronted with a contrite Warren and ruined pots.

And the Changeling had come down and given Warren a stern talking-to that could just as easily have come from the Professor himself.

He was good at what he did, she thought. *Maybe too good*, she added, thinking of Johnny Brill and Werner Reiman—not to mention Marty, that poor store clerk, who was probably blamed for the theft of the till.

To her surprise, the next entry was dated two weeks later.

September 3, 9:20 P.M.

Haven't even thought about this journal in a while. Been busy putting the X-Men through their paces. I'm actually starting to like this. I'm used to running things, but it's nice to do it from a position of respect instead of power or fear. When I was running the day-to-day of Factor Three, the troops followed my orders because they were afraid of me and the Mutant Master. But the X-Men follow Xavier's orders because they respect him and care about him and *believe* in him. I didn't realize just how hollow what I did for Factor Three was until I became Xavier. And I have to say I like this better. A lot better.

Anyway, the details of my life in the last entry were starting to get dull, and you probably don't care about it. The interesting thing happened around when I hit thirty. As Zerrilli, I got introduced to a new bag man: Johnny Brill.

I almost didn't recognize him. It *had* been fifteen years, and his nose hadn't been set properly after I broke it way back when, so it looked different. And, of course, his voice had changed.

But *he* hadn't changed. He was still a bully.

This really really annoyed me. I mean, I'd gone to all the trouble to teach him a lesson fifteen years earlier, and he didn't even have the brains to learn it.

At first, I decided to try teaching him the lesson again. I had lots of ways of doing it. I could frame him for a crime, I could ruin him financially, I could destroy his marriage. I could even do all three. I had the power to do it.

And that was the big thing. I realized that I had the power. So why was I wasting it on Johnny Brill? He was nothing. A stupid low-life bag man for the Central City mob. This was worth getting worked up over? He was only human.

That was the kicker. He was human. I wasn't. I was better.

A lot happened after that. A big "4" showed up in the sky on the same day that a burning man was sighted flying through the sky and a rocky monster tore up the street. Soon after, we found out that that was the Fantastic Four, right before their first battle against the Mole Man.

There was more. A big gray monster near a southwest Air Force base. A man with long blond hair claiming to be a Norse god. Guys in New York dressed like spiders and devils.

And a man claiming to be the forerunner of a new race of humans taking over Cape Citadel, being stopped by a group of teenagers in matching black-and-yellow costumes.

He called himself a mutant. Soon, the news was full of people talking about mutants. I finally knew what I was.

The question was, what to do about it.

I can sense Grey walking toward the study. Better put this away.

11:35 P.M.

Grey just had some administrative stuff to take care of, and we also set up a time to work on our telepathy tomorrow. She's been fantastic. We're both new to having telepathic powers. Xavier had repressed her psi abilities when she was a kid, and only took those blocks off recently. As for me, I had minor psionic talents all along. It helped make my shapechanging more convincing, allowed me to telepathically influence people into seeing what they expected. Xavier boosted that ability tenfold when I took over as him. But it's taken some getting used to. Grey and I have been kind of encouraging each other. Under other circumstances, I might try making a play for her.

No, scratch that. She's *way* too young for me. I keep forgetting that she's only eighteen years old. She carries herself better than most women I've known, but she really is still just a girl.

Besides, it's patently obvious that she has the hots for Summers, only he's too into the brooding thing to realize it.

It's getting late. I have an early session with the X-Men tomorrow. I've got to keep working them hard. We're all going to need to be in tip-top shape when the Z'Nox finally get here.

Jean's head spun. She wasn't sure what disturbed her more, that the Changeling was attracted to her, if only a little, that he thought so highly of her, or that her feelings for Scott were so transparent to him.

Every time she wanted to hate the man, she found that she couldn't bring herself to do so. But every time she wanted to like him, she'd learn of another despicable act he'd performed.

September 6, 8:15 P.M.

I was going through some old files of Xavier's today. Found a couple of newspaper clippings. One in particular caught my eye. An old New York *Daily Globe* front-page item: MUTANT MENACE! DR. BOLIVAR TRASK, NOTED SCIENTIST AND RESEARCHER, WARNS OF A MUTANT PLOT AGAINST U.S.

I remember the first time I saw that headline. It was probably the second most important day of my life, after the day I woke up with a new face when I was fourteen.

While I maintained apartments for Zerrilli in the Heights and Johanssen in the projects (I'd dumped the Askegren persona at this point), I spent most of my time at Jack Bolton's large house in the Central City suburbs. One night, I went home to find someone in my living room.

First off, just that someone *was* in my living room was pretty spooky, since I had a state-of-the-art security system that hadn't been messed with *at all*. The intruder got past it without tripping it.

He stood in the middle of the living room. He was wearing a large, black, billowing cloak with a hood that covered most of his face. And what the hood didn't cover was taken care of by a metal mask. I basically had no idea what he looked like.

"Who are you?"

"Greetings, Mr. Bolton," he said in an electronically filtered voice. "Or should I say Mr. Askegren. Perhaps, Mr. Zerrilli? Ms. Johanssen? Mr. Reiman? Or shall I follow the lead of St. Julian's Orphanage and call you Mr. Sage? Such a multifaceted little changeling you are."

Suddenly I was very very scared. More scared than I'd been since any time after I left the orphanage. In fact, it was the *first* time I'd been scared since then. There was no way anyone could connect me to *all* those names. One or two, maybe, *maybe*, but not all of them.

"Who the hell *are* you?"

"My real name is unimportant. You see, my dear changeling, while you are a mutant, I am the *master* of mutants. And I have a proposition for you."

I didn't know what this guy could do, but I figured it was more than I could, if he could break in here so easily. So I said, "I'm listening."

A gloved hand emerged from the folds of his cloak. It held a newspaper. "Have you seen this?" he asked.

It was the same *Globe* headline about Trask. "No," I said. It didn't take long to get the gist of it. Trask, an anthropologist, was claiming that mutants had a "secret agenda" to take over the United States, and would enslave normal humans in labor camps.

"Sensationalist hogwash," I said, tossing the paper aside. "What does it have to do with me?"

"Oh, Trask is doing more than what you see there. The public doesn't know of it yet, but he has been developing Sentinels. Giant robots that will seek out mutants and stop them."

Another type of fear gripped me. "Stop them how? And how do you know this?"

"The same way I know who you are, changeling. I am the Mutant Master. And Trask's Sentinels will fail."

"How do you know *that*?"

"Because Trask is an anthropologist, not a roboticist. His Sentinels are flawed. They were ineptly conceived and incompetently constructed. I have every faith that they will fail in their intended task."

"Then why show me this article?" I asked. I was completely confused by the entire conversation, and I was still waiting for the proposition the Mutant Master had promised.

"Because Trask raises an excellent point. Mutants are the next step in evolution, and by rights, we *should* take over the world. My proposition, changeling, is to form the very conspiracy that Trask imagines. I have already begun to construct this organization, which I have christened Factor Three, but I need a second-in-command. Someone who can handle the day-to-day operations. Someone who can combine his shapechanging abilities with the resources at my disposal to seek out and recruit allies and gather information on enemies. You are ideally suited to this task."

I thought about Johnny Brill. I thought about how easily I had manipulated humans to gain money and power. And yet, what kind of power was it, really? I was three different false people. The Mutant Master was giving me an opportunity to be someone.

That someone would be the Changeling.

I not only accepted the Mutant Master's proposition, I also offered to provide funding for Factor Three. He declined that, saying it wasn't an issue, and said, "I'll be in touch."

And then he just disappeared. Which, if nothing else, explained how he got past my security system.

Over the next few months, we put Factor Three together. I sought out and recruited a variety of mutants. These were grown men who called themselves "the Vanisher," "Unus the Untouchable," "the Blob," and "Mastermind." I have to admit, I've never understood the need for such colorful names. I mean, yes, I call myself "the Changeling," but that's due to a lack of alternatives. But when you've got a perfectly good name like Fred J. Dukes, why on Earth would you prefer to be named after a stupid movie monster?

Not all our recruits came willingly, of course. While Dukes and the other three seemed eager to further our cause, Sean Cassidy, a former Interpol agent, was more reluctant. But I was able to put him under our control using the amazing technology the Mutant Master had at his disposal. (With all the gadgetry he had, it was no wonder he turned down my offer of funding.)

The long term plan was to start a third World War by convincing each super power that the other side had launched a strike. When the two powers wiped each other out, the third factor (us) would take over. Mutants would finally rule.

It started to unravel when we kidnapped Xavier and I began doing surveillance on the X-Men. For one thing, the Mutant Master was getting more and more unstable. He started firing laser blasts at me to keep me in line, and gave ever-more eccentric orders.

But more to the point, I saw something in the X-Men. They were fighting to save humanity. And Dukes and the other mutants we had gathered were all just in it for themselves. They didn't care about the destiny of the human race, they were just thugs who wanted revenge on the X-Men for past indignities.

Finally, I realized what was happening. The war we were trying to start wouldn't just wipe out most humans. It would wipe out everything. I checked the Mutant Master's computer, and it confirmed what I was starting to suspect. My boss was trying to kill *everyone*, mutant and human alike. And that's when

I realized why he had access to such amazing technology. The "Mutant Master" was an alien trying to destroy the Earth.

The X-Men had managed to stop the missles from being fired, and had returned to Factor Three's base to stop us. Dukes and the others prepared to defend the base. Disguising myself as Xavier, I convinced the X-Men to stop fighting their fellow mutants, but rather focus their attention on Factor Three itself. I also sowed enough doubt in Factor Three's enforcers about their boss's true motives to make the "Mutant Master" panic and attack everyone. That did my work for me. Between the X-Men and the Factor Three enforcers, the Mutant Master was defeated, his alien nature revealed.

In the end, the alien committed suicide when he realized he had failed. The X-Men let everyone go, including me. After all, they're not like the Avengers. They had no authority to arrest us, no facility to imprison us.

At first, I returned to Jack Bolton's house in Central City. But I couldn't go back to that life. Seeing the X-Men in action, seeing these kids risking everything to make the world a better place, opened my eyes even more than realizing I was above petty revenge against Johnny Brill.

I needed to do something worthwhile for the world I'd almost destroyed.

Then the pains started. A trip to the emergency room confirmed that I had cancer. Best guess was that I got it shortly after I started working for Factor Three. It had gone too far to be operable, and chemotherapy wound up doing no good whatsoever. (The joys of being a mutant, probably—our kind tend to have an increased resistance to radiation.)

So I went to the one person who would understand a mutant wanting to leave the world a better place than it was when he came in: Xavier.

I didn't expect him to ask me to take over as him. But it was something I figured I could handle. I even got to learn something about myself: that I was a telepath, too. In some ways, I was glad I didn't find that out until after Factor Three. If I was even close to being on a par with Xavier then, things might've turned out a lot differently.

I just read over what I wrote. Wow. I can see why people do this now. It feels kinda good to get it all down on paper like this. Kind of liberating, you know?

I'm not sure what anyone's supposed to get out of my life story. I mean, let's face it, "If you're a shapechanger, don't hire on as the second-in-command of a terrorist organization led by an alien out to destroy the planet," isn't exactly universally applicable advice.

Still, maybe it'll do somebody some good some time.

Maybe that somebody'll be me.

September 7, 6:00 A.M.

Had a strange dream last night. A woman was asking me my name, and I couldn't tell her what it was.

And what would I tell someone who asked me that now? Charles Sage is a name some nuns made up. Jack Bolton, John Askegren, Francisco Zerrilli, and Martina Johanssen were names *I* made up. Werner Reiman and Charles Xavier are really other people. Even "the Changeling" is a nickname an alien had for me that I took as a cutesy moniker.

What will they put on my headstone when I die?

I have no idea.

I don't even have a proper will. Whose will would it be? Jack Bolton's? He's not real, and any competent lawyer would tear it to ribbons.

What kind of legacy am I going to leave?

Dear God in heaven, I'm dying, and no one will know who I was . . .

10:20 A.M.

What maudlin garbage I wrote before. Oh, well.

I let McCoy and Drake head into the city for dates with their girlfriends. Meanwhile, Worthington, Summers, and Grey have a session this afternoon.

Jean shuddered. That was the day that Hank and Bobby first encountered Grotesk in the subway. What happened that day would lead to the Changeling's death.

She wasn't sure she wanted to keep reading.

But I've come this far.

I just read over what I wrote this morning. And I started thinking about the X-Men. Most of the world doesn't appreciate what they've done. The news is always talking about the Avengers and the Fantastic Four—but never about the X-Men. Or if they do, it's to follow Trask's route and declare them a menace out to destroy humanity. They've saved the world more than once, including from my own organization, and nobody knows. Nobody appreciates them.

And yet they keep doing it, anyhow. If they all died tomorrow fighting Magneto or Mastermind, it probably wouldn't even make the inner pages of the newspapers. They *know* this, but it doesn't stop them. They keep laying it on the line.

Even if it is a lie, I'm supposed to be their mentor. I can do no less.

Maybe they won't know who I am when I die. But I'll know. I'm the Changeling, and I helped save the world. Nobody can take that from me.

11:30 P.M.

Not been a good day. I didn't deal with the X-Men very well at all. I think that dream had me more flamboozled than I thought.

Or maybe it's this journal. My emotions have been all churned up, and it's not allowing me to focus.

From what I've been able to read in McCoy's and Drake's thoughts, they fought a nasty mutant who called himself Grotesk. To make matters worse, Xavier's mutant-hunting computer, Cerebro, has detected Magneto. We may have to deal with him.

I need to go get a full report from the X-Men.

September 8, 1:05 A.M.

The situation with Grotesk is worse than I thought. He's too much for these kids to handle. They've got the heart for it, but I don't think they have the skill.

Not that I'm sure I do, either, but Grotesk is going to destroy the entire planet. I can't let him do that. I almost destroyed this world once. I'm sure as hell not going to let it die now.

I have a plan that *should* work, but it's risky. I'm recording another one of Xavier's "play this if I die" messages, just in case. He's apparently recorded one of these every time the X-Men are involved in something dangerous. This is the first time I've had to do one. And I'd better tell them about Magneto, too. Again, just in case.

And I still can't get that question out of my head:

What will they put on my headstone when I die?

That was the final entry.

Of course, what they put on his headstone was somebody else's name, she thought sadly.

She felt Bobby Drake approach the room, and she quickly put the Changeling's journal under the desk.

Do I tell them? she asked herself.

Then she thought about what the Changeling wrote in his journal about sacrificing his life even if nobody knew.

He faced his death with his eyes open. And so do we, every day. Because we believe in what the Professor taught us. I have to believe in him now.

"Jeannie?" the youngest X-Man said as he poked his head into the study. "Scott's used Cerebro to track Magneto down, and he's come up with another one of his cunning plans to stop him. He, ah, wants us downstairs."

"Of course, Bobby."

"You okay, Jean?"

Wiping the tears from her eyes, Jean said, "I'll be fine, Bobby. I'll be fine."

Welcome to the X-Men, Madrox

Steve Lyons

ONE OF THE FOUR MEN had drawn the curtains tight against the early moonlight. Two more had maneuvered the heavy wooden chest until it barricaded the door. The fourth had turned off the light, as if to spare them all from having to see this tiny, unfamiliar room.

And then they had turned on the television set and, for a while, had been able to forget where they were. They lost themselves in the two-dimensional fantasy world that had been their sole source of comfort for six long years.

The men's names—all four of them—were James Arthur Madrox. And Jamie had become, quite literally, used to his own company.

"Jamie?" The call came from outside the room. It was accompanied by an insistent knocking. Jamie—the original Jamie—scowled. One of his duplicates turned up the volume on the television set. They all leaned closer to the screen, determined that the canned laughter of its insipid sitcom should drown out the intrusion.

Jamie. This time, the voice was inside his head, where he could not ignore it. *Jamie, how long do you intend to hide in there? I would like you to meet my students.*

He remembered how the inhabitants of New York City had stared at him and run from him; how their heroes, the Fantastic Four, had attacked him, when he had only wanted to find help. Jamie wasn't used to dealing with people. They frightened him.

There is nothing to be afraid of, Jamie. We are your friends.

Could it be true? Through the mists of time and hurt, Jamie remembered Professor Charles Xavier. He had seen him at the farmhouse, talking to his parents. Before the tragedy. Before the freak tornado that had made him an orphan.

Xavier had saved Jamie from the Fantastic Four. He had brought him here, to the mansion that housed his School for Gifted Youngsters. He had introduced him to a man called Doctor McCoy (like the character from *Star Trek*), who had blue fur. McCoy had repaired Jamie's malfunctioning containment suit so that it no longer caused him pain. In fact, he had made it better than before. Now, instead of repressing Jamie's special ability, it gave him control over it.

James Arthur Madrox didn't have to be alone again.

Very well, Jamie, sent Professor Xavier, with a telepathic sigh. *We shall be waiting, whenever you are ready to talk to us.*

Jamie at last ventured from his room the following morning. Hunger and the pleasant aroma of fresh coffee tempted him to the head of the stairs. He looked down into the hallway and strained to hear the voices that came from the direction of the kitchen. Were they talking about him?

"Hello," came a voice from behind him. Jamie turned, startled, to find himself facing a beautiful redhead. She smiled, as if to show she posed no threat—but Jamie remembered how the female member of the Fantastic Four had hurt him invisibly.

"You're Jamie, aren't you? I'm Jean." She held out a hand, which Jamie stared at uncertainly. "Smells good, doesn't it? You must be starved. Did you eat anything at all yesterday?"

He shook his head.

"Looks like you'd better come with me, then." Jean took Jamie's arm firmly, and led him downstairs. "Scott's doing the honors today and he tosses a mean pancake."

Jamie didn't feel he could refuse. Even so, as Jean took him into the bustling kitchen, he was reassured to see the familiar face of Professor Xavier.

"Ah, Jamie," said the Professor, beaming up at the new arrivals from his wheelchair, "I am glad you could join us."

"Orange juice?" offered a young man with mousy brown hair. He thrust a glass into Jamie's hand, then grinned mischievously. "Cool as you like." An ice cube appeared at his fingertips, and dropped into the drink. Jamie was disconcerted. What had he just seen—some sort of sleight-of-hand?

"Please," said Xavier, "take a seat and allow me to introduce my students. You've already met Jean, I see."

Jamie sat, and a blond man with extraordinarily broad shoulders placed a cup and a plate before him. According to Xavier, his name was Warren. Scott was cooking—although Jamie wondered how he could see at all through his opaque red glasses. Also present was Scott's younger brother, another blond, named Alex. He was sitting beside Lorna, who, oddly had green hair. Jamie had never seen that before. The guy with the ice trick was called Bobby.

"Coffee, Jamie?" Jamie started as the coffeepot rose into the air and glided toward him. But nobody else seemed concerned, and he realized that, somehow, it was Jean's doing. He nodded dumbly, and the pot tipped, filling his cup.

"Do you have any plans for today?" asked Xavier.

Jamie shook his head.

"Alex and I are heading into Salem Center, if you want to come with us," said Lorna.

"Or, if you want a bit more fun," said Bobby, with a glint in his eye, "you could come and watch our training session downstairs."

"I don't think Jamie's ready for that yet, Bobby," said Jean.

"Hey, he wants to find out what the X-Men are all about, doesn't he? What better way?"

"Bobby has a point, Jean," said Scott, as he tipped a pile of fresh pancakes onto Jamie's plate. "Jamie's a mutant. He deserves to know what that means."

Mutant. Jamie had heard that word before. It related, in some way, to his special ability. He wondered if everybody here had a special ability too. The floating coffeepot seemed to indicate that.

"Well," said Xavier, "it's your choice, Jamie. What would you like to do?"

Back in his room, Jamie mulled over his options. Xavier's students seemed nice enough, and he guessed he would have to learn about their world sometime. But he was nervous. What if he dared to trust somebody and they betrayed him? What if something went wrong? What if he ended up under attack again, unable to think?

Then an idea occurred to him.

He clapped his hands together and the air around him shimmered. Suddenly, another Jamie Madrox stood beside him. Jamie clapped again, and a second copy of himself sprang into existence. He considered for a moment, before creating a third.

"Okay," said the most recent duplicate, "who gets to do what?"

"I'll go with Alex and Lorna," the first duplicate offered.

"Why are there three of us?" asked the second. He shared his progenitor's memories only up to the point at which he had split from him; therefore, he had no knowledge of Jamie's subsequent decision.

"We thought I could explore the mansion," explained the third dupe.

The second dupe shrugged. "That leaves me with the training session."

Jamie smiled to himself as the three duplicates filed out of the room. It was the perfect solution. When his dupes returned to him, he would absorb their memories of the day. In the meantime, nobody would even know that the real Jamie had not left his room.

He would be safe.

It had been a cruel winter, and the streets of Salem Center were treacherous with ice. The sun made a valiant attempt to share its light, but it was doomed to failure. Of course, it had often been cold on the farm, so Jamie was used to that.

Even so, Lorna had dug out a heavy coat, a scarf and a hat for him, insisting that he ought to wrap up warmly. Alex had added something about the garments hiding his conspicuous green and yellow containment suit.

Within minutes, though, Jamie had forgotten his discomfort. Salem Center was not a huge city, like those he had seen on television, but its shops still offered all manner of goods. He was mesmerized by stereo equipment and video machines, by novelty ornaments and toys such as he had never seen, and by clothes in all shapes, colors, and sizes. Each window seemed to call to him, to offer him warmth and opportunity, even friendship.

Alex and Lorna did their best to indulge his childlike fascination, but they had their own concerns too. Jamie hopped impatiently from foot to foot as they stood for what seemed like an age, staring at details of apartments in a realty agent's window.

"Are you sure it's the right thing to do?" asked Lorna.

Alex shrugged. "I don't know. Professor Xavier has been good to us, but I've never felt as if we belonged with the X-Men. I can control my powers now—I want to try living a normal life."

Lorna smiled demurely. "Are you sure you're not just trying to get me away from Bobby?"

Her attempt at humor was lost on Alex, who scowled. "I've seen the way he still looks at you. He was doing it over breakfast, when he thought I wasn't watching."

Lorna sighed. "You know, you are one of the most insecure men I have ever met."

As Alex and Lorna settled into the easy banter of lovers, Jamie began to wonder if they would ever move on. He guessed they might not be pleased if he wandered off on his own, but there were so many temptations. Surely they wouldn't miss him for a few minutes?

A thought occurred to him. He didn't have to leave his guides. A mere dupe he may be, but he could duplicate himself just as easily as could the real Jamie Madrox.

He clapped his hands.

Alex and Lorna failed to notice as a second Jamie appeared behind them. With an eager grin, the first ran past them and followed the siren calls of the windows further down the street.

If he saw the shocked expressions of passersby, then they didn't register in his excited mind.

Meanwhile, a different Jamie sat with Bobby in a small control booth, overlooking a vast room in a subbasement of Xavier's school. He hardly believed what he was seeing.

Warren had shed his shirt to reveal that, rather than broad shoulders, he possessed a pair of beautiful feathered wings. He was exercising them now, negotiating a complicated obstacle course of poles and hoops whilst pursued by faceless silver drones.

And he was wearing a costume: a spandex suit of blue and white.

Jamie was reminded of the Fantastic Four, and of other super heroes whom he had seen on television. Was that what being a mutant meant? The thought that he could have anything in common with someone who could do what Warren was doing was plain weird.

When Jamie commented that Warren looked like an angel, Bobby laughed. Bobby himself wore only a pair of trunks. He didn't seem bothered by the cold.

Warren reached his objective: a large, red button on one wall of what he and Bobby had referred to as the Danger Room. He let out a whoop of triumph as he hit it. The drones fell, like marionettes with their strings cut, and the obstacles retracted into the ceiling and floor.

"Hey, well done pal," said Bobby, leaning over a microphone, which presumably broadcast his voice into the room below. "You shaved almost a second off your record. Of course, you're still a good one-point-four behind mine."

Warren took to the air again. He hovered on the other side of the Plexiglas window, a grin spread across his face. "Yeah, sure. Don't think I don't know how you crank up those drones when I'm not looking."

Bobby feigned an air of injured innocence.

"Get down here, Drake. Let's take them on together—we'll see how good you really are."

"I've got a better idea," said Bobby, punching buttons on the main instrument bank. "Let's give the room a real workout, show Jamie here what being an X-Man is really about."

As Bobby kicked back his chair and stood up, the air around him crackled. To Jamie's alarm, ice seemed to form around his body. Incredibly, Bobby could still move.

Appearing not to have noticed his companion's reaction, Bobby pointed to two controls in quick succession. "Okay, Jamie, press that one to start the program when I give the word. And that's the emergency shut-down button, for if Warren here gets out of his depth."

And then, with a wink of a frosted eyelid, he was gone, leaving Jamie to shiver with a chill that was not entirely caused by the slight drop in temperature.

Not too far away, another Jamie felt a similar chill of trepidation, as he took his first step outside of the school. More than ever, he felt alone in a huge and intimidating world.

The air was still, but for the occasional breath of wind. Tendrils of frost had left silver patterns on the grass. The grounds of the mansion were surprisingly tranquil. Jamie began to feel safe, deciding that the solitude of this place precluded any sort of danger.

Then he heard something moving, just a little, behind a bush to his left.

Startled, he whirled to face the source of the disturbance. He discerned the outline of a man.

"Who are you?" he called, backing away. "What do you want?"

The man was still for a moment. Then he stepped slowly out from his hiding place. His hands were raised, and he looked as scared as Jamie felt. "Please," he bleated, "don't hurt me."

Jamie relaxed a little. The man was slight of build, and he appeared to pose no threat. His hair was neat and brown, and his features were . . . bland.

Somehow, that was the only word that fitted him. The man had unremarkable eyes, an even mouth, a perfectly straight nose—no distinguishing characteristics at all. Even his clothes were gray and shapeless.

"Do you live here too?" asked Jamie.

The stranger blinked as if confused. "I don't know. I don't think so. But I have been here before. This is where the beings with powers reside, is it not?"

Jamie looked at him blankly. The stranger took a step toward him and cocked his head to one side. "You have power." He concentrated for a moment, then flinched away. "No. Power flows through you, but you are not its source. You cannot help me."

"I don't know what you mean—I don't know what you want."

"It is so difficult to recall. There was one here before—one who hurt me—one who had the powers of the others combined."

"I haven't seen anyone like that," offered Jamie.

"No. No, I have been watching. No sign of that one. No sign. So difficult . . ."

"Why don't you come inside?" asked Jamie nervously. "I'm sure one of the others could help you—the Professor, maybe. I don't know what to do."

"Yes, yes, they can help me. The ones who have powers, they can help me."

The stranger reached out a hand toward Jamie. Jamie backed away from it quickly. "Come on," he mumbled awkwardly. He walked back to the mansion rather more quickly than he had walked from it. He prayed he was doing the right thing.

The stranger followed, gratefully.

"Hey, you! Freak!"

At first, it didn't occur to Jamie that the words were directed at him.

"Hey, freak!"

He looked up and saw four faces reflected in the glass of the shop window. The nearest belonged to a young man with a shaven head, a stud in his nose and a sadistic leer. Puzzled, Jamie turned to face him—and moved into a punch. Caught unawares, he was knocked back into the glass, head ringing. He slid halfway to the ground before regaining control of his legs.

The containment suit was working. A few days ago, the force of the blow would have automatically created a dupe.

The stranger swore, and drew back his fist to aim another punch. This time, though, Jamie was prepared. The thug's fist landed on his jaw, but Jamie was unhurt. He had absorbed its kinetic energy. Absorbed it—and used it.

Another Jamie appeared beside him.

"You were right, Baz," cried one of his attacker's three friends. "He's a mutie—a dirty, freaking mutant!"

"Get him!"

Suddenly, all four of the youths were running at Jamie. For an instant, he panicked, remembering the four who had fought him in New York. But, this time, he was faced with only brawn and bravado—and he had control now.

As each punch and kick landed, Jamie stole its energy and used it to duplicate himself. The fight was furious but brief. Within seconds, the thugs were outnumbered two to one, and their expressions changed from anger to confusion to outright fear. One by one, they withdrew, nursing bloodied noses and cut lips. But, if Jamie thought that was the end of the matter, he was wrong.

"Help," yelled Baz, "somebody help, this psycho's laying into us!"

"He's a mutant! Look—look what he can do!"

"Somebody call the Avengers!"

A crowd had begun to gather, although no one had the courage to draw too close to Jamie and his dupes. Jamie recoiled at the terror and loathing in their expressions. "No, please, they attacked me. I was just . . ." His voice trailed off as he saw that it was having no effect. The minds of the onlookers had been made up.

A short, heavyset, middle-aged man stepped forward. "Come on, let's take 'em! Doesn't matter how many people he can turn into— there's enough of us!"

And, for a moment, it looked as if mob mentality might rule.

Then somebody cried out, "More of them!" and there was an explosion in the street.

The crowd was scattered by a burst of white energy. A female voice ordered, "Back, everybody back!" And two costumed figures—a man and a woman—raced into view.

Super heroes. Jamie felt cold. This was going to be like New York, all over again.

Then he saw himself—or rather, the dupe who had stayed behind with Alex and Lorna—straggling behind the newcomers, and he looked again. He saw that the woman had green hair, and he recognized Lorna's face behind a mask that concealed only part of it. So, the black-clad man with white circles on his chest had to be Alex.

"You were right, Havok," said Lorna. "Jamie is at the center of all this."

"What possessed you to use your powers here?" Alex berated him.

Jamie didn't know what to say. What was wrong with using his special ability anyway?

"Never mind that now," said Lorna. "Jamie, absorb your duplicates. We've got to get out of here, before things turn even nastier."

A collective gasp rose from the onlookers, as Jamie's dupes laid their hands upon him and were reintegrated, as if they had never been.

"Yeah, go on!" somebody shouted, as the trio fled the scene. "Get outta here, ya lousy, no-good mutie scum!"

But nobody dared to follow them.

One wall of the Danger Room exploded.

A second earlier, Bobby and Warren had been exercising their powers against the room's faceless drones. Now, they whirled to face an attack from three unexpected intruders. From the control booth, Jamie watched in horror.

The foremost of the three was resplendent in a billowing red cape and a bucket helmet. "Ah, more of Xavier's whelps, I see. You will fall before the power of Magneto, Unus and the Blob—the Brotherhood of Evil Mutants!"

"In a pig's eye, mister!" retorted Bobby. He flexed his fingers and released a barrage of snow.

Another red-clad figure intercepted it; the snow fell to the floor around him, without touching him. "Why don't you try your tricks on me, Iceman?"

"Hey, why not make me an offer I *can* refuse?"

Magneto gestured, and the wreckage of a defeated drone levitated into the air. Warren twisted and turned as shards of metal darted toward him and attempted to encircle him, to bind him.

"Nice try, Maggie—but I could dodge these things in my sleep!"

"It doesn't matter how 'untouchable' you are, Unus," Bobby crowed, creating a dome of ice around his opponent. "I can still wrap you up nice and snug in an ice shell!"

Warren swooped toward Magneto, plucked the villain's helmet from his head and landed a solid blow to his jaw. "Infidel!" Magneto squawked. "You will pay for this affront!"

Then Warren cried out, as the huge man who could only have been the Blob shot out a pudgy hand and seized his ankle. "Came too low, fly-boy!" The Blob tugged Warren out of the sky, and flipped him hard onto his back.

Magneto was freed to concentrate on his other foe. As Bobby was floored by an invisible bolt of force, Jamie overcame his paralysis and ran. There were other people in the building—people with powers. They could help. On his own, he could do nothing. "Help," he shouted, as he ran along the corridors of the mansion. "Help!"

He had hoped to find peace here. But men in costumes had found him again. Was he never to be left alone?

Then he heard somebody behind him, and a voice called his name. His heart leapt. Had the men in costumes come for him?

He turned. To his relief, he saw only Warren and Bobby. They must have witnessed his abrupt departure, must have followed him.

"Jamie," Warren called again. "Wait! Where are you going? What's wrong?"

"Magneto," he stammered breathlessly. "The Brotherhood . . ."

"Take it easy, pal! They're holograms, that's all. They were part of Bobby's program."

"Holograms?"

"Like the TV," added Bobby, "only three-dimensional."

"Didn't Bobby explain?"

"Hey, I didn't know he'd freak out, did I?"

"But—but why?" asked Jamie. "Why would you want to create those people?"

Warren sighed. "Because it's our job to fight them, Jamie," he said gently. "That's what we were training for."

"But they said they were—" Jamie struggled for the word—"mutants. Aren't they like us?"

Bobby turned to Warren with a wry grin. "Are you going to explain, or should I?"

As Jamie approached Professor Xavier's study, he heard voices within. He hesitated, feeling as if he was interrupting something. The bland stranger came to a halt beside him. He seemed much calmer than before, and happy to wait.

Jamie crept a little closer to the half-open door, and listened.

"I don't understand why you felt you couldn't trust us," complained a familiar male voice.

"It had nothing to do with trust, Scott," insisted Xavier. "I didn't feel it was the right time to put the X-Men back into the public eye."

"So, you sent us off on a wild-goose chase after Bobby, and called in the Defenders to deal with the Brotherhood instead?"

"You could at least have told us your plans, Professor." Jamie recognized Jean's voice, calm and reasonable.

"But then you might have insisted on facing the Brotherhood yourselves. I couldn't take that risk."

"What risk?" said Scott. "I don't understand why we're still keeping a low profile anyway."

Xavier sighed. "We have discussed this before."

"But it hasn't worked, Professor. Listen to the news. People fear and hate mutants as much as ever. We need to be out there, doing something about it, not hiding away."

Jamie was beginning to feel that he was intruding. He shouldn't be here.

He turned to the stranger—and gave an involuntary yell.

The stranger's appearance had changed. He seemed to have grown a little taller and more muscular. His body had taken on a green hue. He was wearing a pair of spectacles, like Scott's, only green instead of red.

"Yes," the stranger hissed, in a voice full of malice. "Yes, I remember now."

Jamie shrank away from him in terror. He felt the door behind him and pushed back against it. He almost fell into Xavier's office.

The room's occupants had already been alerted by his cry. As one,

Scott and Jean pushed Jamie behind them, protectively, as they raced toward the hallway.

They leapt for cover as a bolt of green power slammed into the floor between them.

Jamie—the original Jamie—had turned off the television set.

He stood at his window, looking out at the skeletal trees that swayed in a gentle breeze. Perhaps, he thought, he had made a mistake, sending his duplicates out into the world in his stead. He was bored, and impatient to assimilate what they had learned.

He thought about leaving the room and exploring the mansion himself. But he was too afraid.

Then Jamie was startled by a sudden, tremendous crash.

For a second he sat paralyzed, cold sweat beading his forehead. The sound had come from downstairs.

Part of him didn't want to know what was happening. Another, larger part knew that his flimsy door would provide no protection against any serious threat.

He ran from the room and toward the top of the staircase, his legs becoming heavier and less willing to move with each step.

There was a green man in the hallway. He stood in the doorway of Professor Xavier's study, glaring at somebody or something within. A second later, the man took a step back and turned, as Warren flew—literally—along the hall toward him.

"Another with power?" said the green man. "Come—let me feast!"

He lifted his green spectacles, and an energy beam erupted from his eyes. With astonishing agility, Warren twisted in mid-flight to avoid the attack. But the cramped confines of the hall gave him little room for maneuvering. He hit one wall and spun out of control.

"Looks to me like somebody needs to cool off!"

The voice was Bobby's, although Jamie was astonished by the appearance of Xavier's youngest student. All encased in ice, he achieved a terrific speed by surfing through the air on a self-created ice slide.

Bobby gestured, and an avalanche of snow descended toward the green man. Too late—he had already flown out of its way.

Yes, flown. For Jamie saw now that the green man had green wings, although he had not possessed them a second earlier. They seemed to have just sprouted from his back.

"Bobby, keep away from him—he'll copy your powers!"

The warning came from Scott. He and Jean had appeared in the doorway to the study. Mirroring the green man's earlier action, Scott lifted his glasses a fraction. His power beam was red, but no less destructive. But the green man shared Warren's agility: the blast barely singed his feathers. The green man swung one arm, and Scott was hurled backwards as if struck. Jamie remembered how Jean had demonstrated her telekinesis at breakfast.

"I remember everything," the green man roared. "It was beings like you, super heroes, who melted me down. You thought me destroyed—but I cannot be destroyed! I was created to adapt."

Bobby had taken Scott's advice and withdrawn, but too late. The green man demonstrated that he already had the youngster's powers, by showering his enemies with frozen spikes. His left arm had taken on the appearance of green ice.

Aloft again, Warren wove his way through the onslaught and landed a solid blow to the intruder's chin. The green man fell to the ground, and, though the impact must have knocked the breath out of him, his angry words buzzed in Jamie's head: *You are nothing without the one called Mimic!*

"Of course," gasped Jean. "Scott, this must be the Super-Adaptoid!"

"Agreed," rapped Scott, "and he has the Professor's powers too. Hit him hard and fast, team—and remember, he's not alive. He's an android!"

"Your puny efforts are as nothing," the Super-Adaptoid scoffed. "I have defeated you before and I shall do so again. I shall take your powers from you, and then I shall turn them against the accursed Captain America and fulfill my programming."

Scott was the first to fall, as the Super-Adaptoid created a localized blizzard and buried him beneath a snowdrift. Warren and Bobby were next, as the android merely gestured and altered the flight path of the former so that he collided heavily with his friend. Jean concentrated and telekinetically lifted a pair of tables, which she hurled at her foe. For a second, it seemed she had the upper hand. But the Super-Adaptoid employed Scott's optic blast in a wide-angled beam to destroy the makeshift missiles, before winging Jean with a more concentrated burst.

Fortunately, reinforcements had arrived.

"What's going on?" cried Alex, appearing at the main entrance door. The question was a rhetorical one. An intruder was standing over the unconscious bodies of four of his friends. As it turned toward him, he extended both hands toward it. Crackling, white energy radiated from him in concentric circles. The energy shredded his shirt, and Jamie caught a glimpse of a black costume beneath. "Who are you?" Alex bellowed, as his energy struck its target with devastating force.

The Super-Adaptoid was unmoved. Indeed, it threw back its head and laughed. "You ask who I am?" it boomed. "I am the first of a new generation. Once Captain America has fallen, then you will all become as I am. You will look to me as your leader."

Alex stood for a second, dumbfounded by the failure of his attack. Fortunately, Lorna was behind him. "Look out, Alex!" she yelled, launching herself at her partner and knocking him out of the way as, with Jean's powers, the Super-Adaptoid gathered up the pulverized remains of the tables and flung them at him.

In the meantime, Scott had recovered and dug his way to freedom. Jamie crossed his fingers hopefully. "It doesn't matter how many powers you adapt," shouted Scott as he let loose with a tightly focused beam, "there's only one of you—you can't fight all of us at once!"

To Jamie's joy, the beam struck its target squarely on the back of its head.

It had no effect.

The android turned slowly, as if Scott had merely tickled it. "Your attack comes too late," it scoffed. "I have completed a pantographic tracing of your teammate. I have absorbed his immunity to your power, as I absorbed yours to his." Jamie saw that, on the Super-Adaptoid's chest, a pattern of concentric circles had formed.

A look of alarm crossed Scott's face. He leapt and rolled and avoided another shower of ice, coming to rest beside Alex and Lorna.

"He's an android, Lorna," he gasped, "can't you take him apart?"

"I've tried. There's no metal in him."

"Your magnetic powers might not affect me," crowed the Super-Adaptoid, "but now I have them too, and I can certainly use them against you!"

Lorna fell to her knees and clutched at her throat.

"Scott," cried Alex, "her necklace! The Super-Adaptoid's making it contract—it'll choke her!"

Scott and Alex hit their foe with simultaneous blasts, to no avail.

Lorna gasped with relief as her necklace snapped into two pieces and flew from her neck. She must have employed her own ability, Jamie realized. She took a deep breath, tried to stand—and the Super-Adaptoid felled her with Alex's white energy.

Left with no other recourse, Scott tried to tackle the intruder physically. The Super-Adaptoid flew upwards, out of his way. It halted Scott in midair and telekinetically flung him into the wall. He slid to the floor in an unconscious heap. Alex fell beside him: Jamie didn't see what had happened to him, but for a second he had felt an uncomfortable pressure inside his skull.

There was nobody left to fight the Super-Adaptoid now. Jamie felt a suicidal impulse to race down the stairs and confront it himself—but what could he do against it?

Another thought occurred to him: what if it came for him next?

Hold! I will not allow you to do this to my students.

Professor Xavier had appeared in his doorway. Even confined to his wheelchair, he exuded power and authority. But what shocked Jamie most of all was the identity of the figure who stood at Xavier's shoulder: himself.

The android turned to face its new enemy, and froze, as did Xavier himself. For long seconds, nothing seemed to happen. But the pressure in Jamie's skull returned, and he knew instinctively that a mighty battle was raging beyond the scope of conventional senses.

Sweat formed on Xavier's brow, but he was not the first to stagger. For a moment, Jamie had hope—but only for a moment.

"Your experience gives you the edge on the psychic plane," the Super-Adaptoid growled, "but I have the powers of all your X-Men." It formed a gigantic spike of ice, which hovered in midair and twisted slowly, taking aim at Xavier's heart. Still locked in psychic battle, the Professor could do no more than stare at the weapon, wide-eyed.

Jamie knew then that he had to do something—but it was too late. He was too far away.

"No!"

With a scream of defiance, Jamie's duplicate leapt into the hallway and tackled the Super-Adaptoid. Distracted by Xavier's invisible onslaught, the android actually toppled. But it recovered quickly and brushed off its attacker. "The power within you is diluted—you are nothing!"

Jamie held his breath. His duplicate had been sent sprawling—but might the distraction have turned the tide? The Super-Adaptoid was almost doubled over, its hands to its temples—but now it could return its attention to the source of its pain.

This time, perhaps in desperation, it chose a quicker way of dealing with Xavier. Its emerald copy of Scott's force beam cannoned into the Professor, knocking his chair backwards at the same time as a magnetic field caused one wheel to buckle. The chair overturned, throwing Xavier to the floor. He grunted once and didn't move again.

The pressure in Jamie's head relented, as the Super-Adaptoid drew itself up to its full height and savored its victory.

Then the dupe from the study attacked it again. And from the main entrance door, came another angry Jamie, who duplicated himself as he ran. His actions were mirrored by a third Jamie, who appeared from the back of the mansion.

What were they doing?

Jamie knew the answer already. His dupes were doing what he dearly wanted to do. They were helping, fighting to protect the lives of their new friends.

Of course, they were only duplicates. They weren't risking much. Even if they died, Jamie Madrox would live on.

But no. Much as it would have helped him to think like that, he couldn't. Jamie had reabsorbed many dupes over the past few days, and he retained their memories. He knew that each one considered itself— himself—a living, thinking human being. He knew that each one feared harm or death as much as he did. They just weren't letting it stop them.

Jamie knew what he had to do then. He had known all along. The dupes had shown him that there was courage within him. All he had to do was find it.

By the time Jamie reached the foot of the stairs, the hallway was swarming with copies of himself. He couldn't even see the Super-Adaptoid beneath them. Perhaps, he thought, despite their lack of strength and training, the dupes could win through sheer force of numbers.

But, then, the Super-Adaptoid scattered its attackers with a combination of force blast and telekinesis. It clambered to its feet, angrily, and saw the real Jamie. It froze and stared at him.

Then it smiled malevolently.

"Ah! At last, the source of this power comes to me."

Jamie was rooted by the Super-Adaptoid's glare. Even his duplicates fell silent, as if sensing that something terrible was about to happen.

Suddenly, there was a second Super-Adaptoid beside the first.

"Yes, yes," the original crowed, "with this ability, I can accelerate my plans a hundredfold. The Avengers could not have stood against one Super-Adaptoid with the combined powers of the X-Men—how can they hope to prevail against an army of such?"

Jamie felt sick. He should have anticipated this. He should have stayed hidden.

Now there were four Super-Adaptoids. Now eight, and now sixteen . . .

And Jamie was struck by a desperate idea.

"Hit them!" he shouted. He threw a punch at the nearest android. It glanced off ineffectually, but it did what Jamie had hoped for. One Super-Adaptoid became two. "Hit them!" he repeated to his startled dupes. "It doesn't matter how hard—just hit as many as possible, as often as you can."

Seeing Jamie's plan, the dupes began to copy his actions. Each time they struck one of the Super-Adaptoids, it was duplicated. It could not control itself.

The hallway filled up quickly. Jamie lashed out, almost blindly, in all directions, landing punch after punch against his ever-multiplying foes. Dupes were falling all around him, struck down by blasts or blizzards or telekinetic attacks—but he could not allow himself to think about that.

There must have been a hundred Super-Adaptoids by now. Several had taken to the air, to avoid being crushed. Jamie found himself sandwiched between four green bodies.

Then the Super-Adaptoids reeled, and put their hands to their heads in pain and confusion.

Jamie thought of New York and the Fantastic Four, and he knew how they felt.

And then there was just one—and no longer did it resemble a monstrous amalgam of Xavier's students. It had become a gray humanoid, slight of build and featureless.

Over a field of fallen X-Men and duplicates, Jamie came face to face with the android, in its true form, for just a second.

Then it turned and fled through the open door.

An hour later, Jamie sat in Professor Xavier's study. Having reabsorbed his duplicates, he was coping with the memories of having been defeated by the Super-Adaptoid many times over. But he had won once, and that was what counted.

"It is fortunate indeed that you were here," said Xavier. "Our enemy, it seems, made a fatal miscalculation. It adapted Scott's ruby quartz spectacles and Alex's costume because it recognized them as means of controlling their incredible powers—but, in your case, it neglected to see the need for your containment suit. It didn't appreciate how quickly your unique ability could spiral out of control. Its must have been strained beyond the point of endurance—until, evidently, its only option was to purge its systems and retreat."

From the hallway, Jamie could hear sounds of movement and the occasional crash, as the X-Men cleaned up the mess left by the battle. There was talking and laughter too. He wondered how they could so quickly have recovered from an attack that had almost left them dead.

"I wish I could tell you this sort of thing happens rarely," said Xavier with a humorless smile. "Unfortunately, life here can be unpredictable and dangerous. In the weeks to come, it may become more so." A pensive and distant look crossed his face.

Jamie squirmed in his seat, impatiently, but didn't interrupt.

At last, the Professor seemed to remember him—and to make a decision. "I am aware that you overheard my discussion with Scott and Jean earlier. You know I have chosen to avoid the public eye of late. Alas, circumstances have changed. I now find myself questioning that decision."

Jamie looked at him blankly, and said nothing.

"All over the world, new mutants are appearing. I have been monitoring several of them, planning for the day when I might gather a new, larger and more proactive team of X-Men. Perhaps they can make a better life for themselves—or perhaps they would be happier not knowing some of the problems that might stem from the accidents of their births."

Jamie thought that he, for one, would have been better off not knowing.

"Yes," said Xavier softly, as if he had read Jamie's mind—and he probably had, thought Jamie, uncomfortably—"I do realize that you would have preferred to stay where you were, at least for now—but, in your case, events forced my hand. With your containment suit repaired, you could, of course, return home, or live wherever you wish—but I would like to make you an offer first."

Jamie guessed what was coming. He wasn't sure how he felt about it. Nervously, mostly.

"I can give you a home here," said Xavier. "I can teach you how to use your powers for the benefit of all. I can do my best to protect you. I would like you to become the first of my new generation of X-Men."

As that cold evening turned into night, Jamie sat in his room alone and looked at the television set without really watching it.

His mind was too full of thoughts to concentrate on the drama unfolding before him. He thought about Professor Xavier's offer and about all he had learned from his duplicates—the terrible experiences that now seemed like his own.

He had seen how Xavier's students, his X-Men, were reviled and feared by humanity. And yet, they were hated no less by some of their own kind. They fought to do the right thing—but even this noble desire made them targets for such villains as those who had created the Super-Adaptoid. He had had a taste of the difficult choices faced by the X-Men daily. He had felt the responsibility that they bore to make the world a better place.

Jamie had learned something today, and he had learned it four times over. Life with the X-Men could only be harder and, in some ways, more lonely than the life he had left behind. It made him feel like a coward, but he had to admit that he was not yet ready to face such a life. He had other, more basic, obstacles to surmount first.

Tomorrow, he decided, he would see the Professor. He would thank him for his kind offer, but explain why he felt he would have to decline it, this time. Xavier would understand.

For now, James Arthur Madrox drew his curtains tight, tried to empty his mind of all the ways in which his life had just changed, and looked for solace in the flickering patterns of the television screen.

Peace Offering

Michael Stewart

A STEADY RAIN WAS FALLING out of the night sky over New York City. The streets below were soaked, but the downpour wasn't enough to wash them clean—it just got the grime wet. On the fifth floor of a Greenwich Village brownstone, a pair of boots smudged some of that grime into the white shag carpet in Jean Grey's living room. The man who had broken into the place wasn't ordinarily the sort to leave tracks, but it was no ordinary night.

The prowler moved quietly through the apartment. By Manhattan standards it was gigantic, a full floor through, with thirty-foot ceilings. Large arched windows took up most of the front and back walls. A raised loft level overlooked one side of the main room, with the kitchen, bath, and bedrooms underneath.

Stopping in the center of the apartment, the prowler looked around slowly. It was dark, the only illumination coming from the streetlamps below. Yet in the half-light the man somehow took in every detail around him, his attention lingering on the placement of personal items: an open book on the dinner table, a jacket draped casually over a chair by the door, a pair of sunglasses on the kitchen counter. As he scanned the room, the back of his right hand absently stroked the thick, coffee-colored velour upholstery of one of the living room's big sofas. His left hand, hanging straight at his side, was clenched tight around the wooden handle of a small metal cage.

From an end table, the prowler picked up a framed photograph. In it, a smiling Jean Grey stood with friends in the library of Professor Xavier's School for Gifted Youngsters. He recognized them all: Hank McCoy, Bobby Drake, Warren Worthington III, and, standing closest to Jean, Scott Summers. They were the original X-Men, all gone their separate ways now, except for Scott—and Jean.

Staring at the photo, he could almost hear her voice, imagine the characteristic sounds of her movements replacing the night noises in the apartment. Then, looking up, he was struck by his own pained expression reflected dimly in a mirror above the table. He contemplated the face for a moment. His name was Logan, but Jean didn't know that.

Almost no one did. She knew him as Wolverine, her teammate in the second group of X-Men. And she, or anyone else on the team, would have found the expression on his face that night—anxious, vulnerable—a strikingly unfamiliar one to say the least.

Logan moved slowly toward the side of the apartment. The first bedroom was Jean's. He stopped at the threshold and looked inside, suddenly aware that his mouth was dry, tasted of ashes. The room was heavy with her scent. A normal man would not have noticed it, but to Logan, a mutant whose senses were many times more acute than any human's, it was overpowering.

He let the scent draw him into the room and he stood there a moment, delighting in the complex beauty of it. There was a whole range of perception to be found in nature that people were simply oblivious to, entire levels of sensation reserved for "lower" animals—and him. Here was a part of Jean that no one else had the capacity to understand, to appreciate as thoroughly as he did—least of all Scott Summers.

So acutely focused on this reverie were Logan's senses that he was unaware there was another person in the room until the barrel of a thirty-eight special reached a point very close to the side of his head. He wasn't ordinarily the type to be taken by surprise but, truly, this was no ordinary night.

Instinct jolted him into action. From the top of his right fist slid three metal blades, and without a thought, he'd spun a quarter turn and brought their points to the throat of the figure holding the gun on him.

That Logan managed to neatly stop his strike the instant he perceived the identity of his target was a tribute to his keen reflexes. That he had been caught flatfooted in the first place was, to him, an inexcusable failure. The first rule in his line of work, he would tell you, was to never, ever let your guard down. It could get you killed. At the very least it could get you caught standing in some frail's bedroom, looking like a fool.

The woman holding a gun to his head, as Logan had abruptly realized, was Misty Knight—tall, dark skinned, an ex-cop, and Jean Grey's roommate. She hadn't been home when he first arrived. Obviously she was back, and in no mood for visitors. He peered over the barrel of her pistol, down her extended left arm, and into her wide brown eyes. It was clear they recognized each other, but for a time neither moved.

They stood frozen there—his claws at her throat, her gun to his head. In that enduring moment, each knew the other was capable and even willing to bring violence, but didn't. The dangerous fascination of that instant's unrealized potential held them fast: two strong egos suspended in confrontation.

In the end, it was the compromised nature of his position which forced Logan to break the face-off. He was an intruder in Knight's apartment. She had found him in Jean Grey's bedroom. Once the initial shock of the encounter was over, he began to feel a rising embarrassment.

Slowly, Logan retracted the metal claws and pulled his hand away, palm open. "No need to get violent here," he said evenly.

Knight's thumb snapped back the hammer of her pistol. "Who says, sucker?"

Doubt flickered in Logan's mind. Knight was a hard case, but he didn't think she would gun down a man she knew in her own apartment. Still, what did he know about her state of mind? Normally he could trust his instincts about people, but lately he didn't trust anything.

"Lady, my noggin's laced with pure adamantium. You fire that thing, it's likely to bounce right back atcha."

Since Knight was Jean Grey's roommate and a private investigator who made it her business to stay well informed, Logan assumed she would know he was telling the truth, that his entire skeleton had been augmented with an unbreakable metal called adamantium, the same stuff his claws were made of.

"Let's see what happens if I put one through your eye socket," she said, shifting the barrel slightly.

Logan looked back at her blankly. The way he had been feeling tonight made him half willing to find out.

This unexpectedly indifferent reaction seemed to break through the edge of intensity that gripped Knight. She relaxed visibly, uncocked the hammer of her pistol, and lowered it to waist level. Logan could tell something had her keyed up, something besides his presence in her apartment.

"Just tell me what the hell you're doing here, Wolverine, and it better be good."

Before Logan could say anything, there came a soft rustling sound. They both looked down. Forgotten in his left hand was the small metal cage, and in it the source of the noise. He held the cage up so that she could just make out a dark shape moving within.

"Bird," he said simply. It was as good an answer as any.

A few minutes later, with the lights turned on and the tension further dissipated, Knight contemplated the small white bird cooing happily inside the bars of the cage, which Logan had set down in the living room.

"A dove? You're saying you busted into my apartment to drop this bird off?"

"Yeah, that's about it," Logan replied uneasily.

"And this dove required such covert measures because—"

Logan intently picked at a loose thread on his shirt. "It's a gift. You know, for Jeannie. Because o' the—ah—incident here a while back."

"I assume the incident you're referring to was when you and the rest of the X-Men trashed our apartment in some irrational attempt to beat the tar out of Iron Fist, who happens to be a friend of ours?"

"Yeah. I sorta jumped to conclusions there. Sometimes when us super-powered types come across each other spirits can run high; misunderstandings can happen." Logan scratched at the back of his neck uncomfortably. "Anyway, I didn't want Jeannie thinkin' I was some kinda jerk. I just figured I should give her something to show—how I feel."

"Uh-huh."

"It's kind of a—peace offering. Of course, I never expected to nearly get my flamin' head blown off deliverin' it."

"Next time knock," Knight replied coolly, pulling off the purple trench coat she was wearing. She presented a striking figure in low-slung leather pants and a charcoal gray turtleneck, over which was strapped a black leather shoulder holster that held the same police special she'd carried in the NYPD. Her full afro framed strong, elegant features. She smoothed her hair with one hand and took a long, hard look at Logan. Then she let out a short, throaty chuckle.

Logan bristled visibly. "What's so funny?"

"Come on. You, Wolverine, bring Jean Grey, Phoenix, a caged bird as a present? That's a hell of a loaded gesture, Jack."

"It ain't nothin' personal, lady."

"Bull."

"Well, it ain't any o' your concern either way," Logan snapped, his uncomfortableness with the subject turning into anger.

"It became my concern when I came home to find you prowling around in the dark. You're lucky I didn't shoot you. The case I'm on right now has me way out on the edge. I've got to be real careful—"

The strain in Knight's voice convinced Logan that she was in more trouble than she let on.

Then the apartment's large back window exploding inward, making it clear that they both were.

Glass, metal, and wood cascaded across the room. A score of armed figures burst out of the rainswept blackness through the empty window frame. Hooded, clad in dark, loose-fitting uniforms, and brandishing an assortment of edged weapons, they hurtled silently through the air toward their prey.

The first assassin's sword traced a deadly arc over his head as he dropped down on Logan. The mutant sidestepped the strike, gripped the killer's shirtfront, and propelled him hard across the living room into the bookshelves below the window. Popping the claws on both hands, Logan deflected the next two attackers' sword thrusts. Their momentum carried them forward and he let them in close, then disabled both with precise claw slashes.

Out of the corner of his eye, Logan was surprised to see Knight catch an assassin's sword in her bare right hand. She snapped the blade in two, chopped down on the assassin with the half she held, and rolled him into the strike of a second attacker. Logan caught her attention and she gave him a hard smile. It would be a night full of surprises.

The killers kept coming, swarming into the living room, dropping noiselessly out of the loft. In a fluid motion, Knight drew her thirty-eight and leapt backwards, narrowly eluding a sword cut. She landed on an easy chair, balanced one foot on the seat cushion and one foot behind her, then tipped the chair backwards, bringing the front end up to deflect her attacker's next blow. This maneuver left her gun hand free to fire round after round into the onrushing assassins.

Convinced Knight could hold her own for the moment, Logan threw himself into the thick of the assassins. "Heads up, boys, Wolverine's comin' at ya!" he barked with gusto.

They were the best killers in the world—silent, fast, and invariably deadly. Their training, refined for hundreds of years, had been perfect. But nothing could prepare them for a target like Logan. In addition to enhanced senses, his mutant physiology had the ability to heal his wounds very quickly. This gift, in addition to his claws and unbreakable skeleton, had led him to develop a uniquely effective fighting style.

The first swordsman Logan reached scored what should have been an incapacitating strike to the mutant's side. To the assassin's amazement, his target kept coming. Logan could, and would, casually sacrifice his body to overcome an opponent—it was all just meat to him. That gave him the edge.

Unprepared for the ferocious abandon of his attack, the assassins fell one after another, until sheer numbers inevitably began to turn the tide. Logan was barely able to block a double overhand sword blow to his head. Metal shrieked and sparked against metal as his claws stopped the blade inches from his face. The big assassin holding the sword bore down heavily on Logan, pushing the mutant's strength to the limit.

The killer muscled in close, glaring into the eyes of his opponent. As their numbers had been thinned, the assassins were losing their carefully cultivated air of detached professionalism. Honor was on the line. It was getting personal. "You are good, *gaijin*," the man whispered in Japanese.

"I'm the best," Logan hissed back in the same language.

"Not today," the killer countered, driving the point of a spiked knee pad up into Logan's thigh. The howl of pain that erupted from the mutant was so startling, so ill-suited to a human being, that it shook even this seasoned killer, and broke his composure. Before he could recover and press his advantage the assassin heard the crack of a gunshot and felt, simultaneously, the hard impact of a bullet in his shoulder spinning him away from his target.

That bullet had come from Knight. Though he was injured in several places and beginning to get tired, Logan was still annoyed that she had taken out his man. The clash with the assassins, murderous though it might be, was just what he needed. A good fight focused him like nothing else, and he craved that kind of focus.

Logan was tempted to change his mind about the holistic benefits of combat as a volley of arrows sliced down at him from the loft. One clipped his arm. Another buried itself in his shoulder. For the second time that night he howled in rage and pain.

Knight reacted to the new attack quickly. Pushing off from the side of the kitchen counter with one foot, she threw herself out into the room, and slid on her back across a section of bare wood floor. As she cleared the overhang of the loft, she pumped rounds from her pistol into the archers above.

Logan lunged over her as Knight rolled behind a couch to reload. He bounced off the bookshelves on the far side of the room and leaped up onto the loft level. He was mad now, and he needed a target.

With practiced speed, Knight thumbed shells into her weapon and snapped the cylinder back into position. Another assassin dropped over the couch at her, sword ready. She turned aside his killing blow with her right arm. But before she could raise her weapon, the assassin was leveled by the falling body of one of the archers. Both landed in a heap at the foot of the couch. They were quickly joined by a second and then a third archer, evicted from the loft by Logan.

Knight rolled sideways and came up on one knee behind the coffee table, pistol ready. This time, though, she had no target; nothing moved in the apartment.

The sudden quiet was broken by the beating of the dove's wings. Its cage had been smashed and it was lying in a puddle of rain beneath the broken window. Logan saw it struggling to free one blood-flecked wing caught in the twisted bars. He knelt beside it, pulling gently on the bent metal. The bird shook the water off its wings and fluttered unsteadily through the air over the living room, disappearing into the dark recesses of the high ceiling.

Logan watched it go.

After a quick sweep of the apartment to be sure they were alone, Knight brought bandages from the bathroom and began to bind Logan's arm, leg, and torso.

"You gonna be all right?" she asked.

"I'm used to this kinda thing." He nodded at her arm. Her shirtsleeve was slashed in several places. "I could ask you the same question."

She sat back and pulled up the sleeve. There were severe cuts, but no blood. Beneath the torn edges of her smooth, brown skin he could see the glint of metal. Suddenly self-conscious, Knight tugged the sleeve back down and let the arm fall to her side.

"The good Lord made the rest of me, but I have Stark International to thank for the arm."

"Bionic?"

"Yeah."

"Line o' duty?"

"Yeah." She sighed and looked around the wreckage of the apartment. "I was working the Twelfth Precinct, day shift. There was some kind of disturbance at a bank. I answered the call. This nut throws a satchel—had to be a bomb. I caught the fool thing—instinct I guess. Then, boom. Made a mess out of the place—and my arm.

"I got a commendation and a desk job. That's not what I joined the force for, so I quit. The boys at Stark heard the story. They had a mechanical arm they wanted to test. I signed up and the rest, as they say, is history."

"Well, seems like we sorta got somethin' in common," Logan said, glancing at the trio of slots on the top of his hand. "I guess we all got a sad story to tell." He jerked his thumb over his shoulder. "What about the welcome wagon? You way behind on the rent?"

"I wish." Knight stepped over to the nearest of the assassins and began to search his clothing. "My partner Colleen Wing and I have been working on a case—crimes in New York committed by Japanese gangsters. We traced the jobs back to Japan. Colleen's working that end of the case now. Looks like it's all tied in to the emergence of a new figure in the Japanese underworld. I'd say these guys are a not-so-subtle warning that we're getting too close to whatever's going on."

"Yer right there. They're called the Hand, an ancient society o' Japanese assassins. I ain't run into them in a while."

Knight stood up and kicked the man she'd been searching. He didn't stir. "Maybe we can persuade one of these jokers to fill in a few details for us when they wake up."

"I don't think so, lady." Logan nodded at another of the assassins. A thick stream of vapor was beginning to rise off the man's body. When he nudged at the assassin with his foot, the body collapsed into a pile of empty clothes. The same transformation was occurring all around them. In a moment, the killers were all gone, reduced to smoke wafting out through the back window. As the last of the strange vapor dissipated, the dove flew down from the loft railing and settled on the floor near what was left of its cage.

"These guy's ain't the chatty types. If they miss their target, they're dust—do or die. The Hand tends to be real strict that way."

Logan winced at the pain in his side. Now, as the adrenaline rush of the fight subsided, his uneasy mood was returning. It was a mood he was getting sick of. The bird, the trip to the apartment, it was all supposed to be a nice gesture. As if by reaching out, making an honest effort to be kind, he would find some release from the anxiety in his mind—and his heart. Instead, what did he find? Another fight, pain, more death. Like there was no possible action he could take, nowhere on earth that he could run to escape the violence that filled his life.

Knight bent down, pushed aside some broken glass, and picked up a half-crushed pack of Kools from the floor. Leaning against the back of a sofa, she smoothed out one of the cigarettes, lit it, and took a long drag.

After exhaling a slow, gray cloud of smoke, she said, "Since we're having story time here, why don't we talk about you for a while?"

"Not exactly a fascinatin' subject."

"Let's start with how long you've had a thing for Jean."

"Yer crazy," Logan said in a measured voice.

"Don't try to snow me, Jack. I saw you mooning around her room all dewy eyed, remember? Now, come on, talk to me. I'm trying to be understanding here."

Logan searched her face for some sign she was mocking him. What he saw instead was a cool compassion that he responded to. As much as a show of earnest sympathy would have put him off, he was drawn in by the forthrightness he saw in Knight's eyes. Maybe she could understand what had brought him there that night. Besides, he was getting too tired for denials.

"I guess you might have somethin' there," he said finally.

"Ain't like there's something wrong with liking somebody, Wolverine. Happens to the best of us."

"Not to me. Not in a long time. I'm pretty much a loner. It suits me just fine—usually." Logan looked out the broken back window, up into the rain pouring out of the darkness above the building. He searched for words, unaccustomed to verbalizing his feelings.

"When I joined the X-Men—on a whim, really—one o' the things that kept me around was Jeannie. I could tell she was special. Then she died—"

Knight knew the story. "When the shuttle that brought you all back from the Starcore One space station crashed."

"Right. But she didn't really die. She was reborn out o' that crash as Phoenix. And it was like a part o' me was reborn then too. Like there was the way I was used to livin' my life before, and then there's my life now—with her in it. I haven't gotten used to the change. It's a tough thing for a guy like me to live with."

Knight stubbed out her cigarette thoughtfully. "What about Jean's boyfriend, Scott? He's your teammate too."

"I don't sweat him. Jeannie and me, I figure we're a lot alike, got the same kinda nature deep down in our guts, you know? She ain't got that with Summers."

Logan had drifted back into the living room and found himself standing close to Knight. He looked up at her as he finished speaking and they were both abruptly aware of the height difference between them. Without acknowledging it, Knight took a few steps back and leaned against the kitchen counter.

"So what's holding you back? What's the problem?" she asked.

"Look at me. I ain't exactly Prince Charmin' here." It was true—standing there in a bloodstained flannel shirt, bloody, torn jeans, wet from the rain, bandaged in several places, he looked more like a war refugee than someone's romantic ideal.

"You ain't really at your best right now. I'll give you that," Knight admitted.

"Problem is, this is the real me." Logan turned away from her and stared into the mirror over the end table. "I'm a scrapper—always have been. There's just a darkness inside o' me, something I ain't got no control over. 'Til recently, the only really strong emotion I ever felt on a regular basis was blind rage. I been tryin' my whole life to live with that—to live with honor. But what's honor to a savage? How could a woman like Jeannie love an animal?"

He edged back around and glanced at Knight cautiously, unsure how she would react to his confession. After pouring his heart out, the last thing that Logan was looking for was straight answers, but that was all she had for him.

"It sounds like you have serious issues to work out, Wolverine," she began, "and I sympathize. But if you really want to do the honorable thing here, you've got to get past the noble but unworthy routine. That ain't gonna cut it."

Logan winced, like he'd been slapped in the face, but Knight plowed on. "It's up to Jean to decide if you're worthy of her, not you. But you don't even have the respect to let her make that choice. Instead, you're creeping around, leaving secret gifts, pining away—anything just so you never have to face that moment of truth.

"I'd expect that kind of thing from a kid, Wolverine, not from you. Maybe instead of trying to be less like an animal, you just need to act more like an adult."

Logan glared at Knight. His face flushed. His emotions were racing so fast he couldn't react to any one of them. So he stood there fuming, unable to move or say a word until, at last, he got a hold on his temper. His whole body tense, he leaned toward Knight, a finger stabbing out accusingly.

"Listen, lady—"

His retort was interrupted by the sudden appearance of Jean Grey at the door to the apartment. She saw Logan, obviously agitated, squaring off with Knight, then took in the wreckage around the room.

"Oh, Wolverine, not again!" she cried.

At the sound of her voice, Logan turned and saw her framed there in the doorway. She was dressed in a green evening gown, a dark brown overcoat on her arm. Her hair was pinned up, with wispy red strands falling around her face. Her cheeks were flushed from the cold. She looked beautiful.

"Jeannie, it ain't what ya think—" he rasped.

The raw emotion in his voice caught Grey by surprise. "What are you—" she began, then stopped short, seeing the anguished look on Logan's face.

He suddenly felt calm as everything fell away but the two of them. "Never mind that, Jeannie. Nothin' matters except what I gotta say to you right now."

Logan knew Grey had never seen him as he stood before her then—open, humbled, reaching out to her as a woman. He could see in her eyes that she was responding, that he had touched a part of her nature that could understand what he felt.

"Jeannie, I—"

The dove suddenly fluttered into the air between them, breaking the intensity of the moment. They both realized too late that something was wrong. Logan would never finish that sentence.

The bird dropped to the floor, pierced by the silvery points of a *shuriken*. A half-dozen more of the throwing stars cut through the air around them. As one glanced off Knight's metallic right wrist, Logan threw himself toward Jean. He took stars in his chest and thigh, but was unable to stop a third. The *shuriken* struck Jean in the shoulder. Her startled expression said it all: Though she possessed powers on a cosmic scale, Jean Grey—Phoenix—was brought down by a tiny, spiked metal disk coated with poison.

Crouched on the ledge outside the empty back window of the apartment, the assassin who had thrown the *shuriken* surveyed the results of the attack.

"Gotcha," the slim, dark figure whispered in Japanese.

The front window shattered and fell away as Hand assassins poured in from both ends of the building. In the doorway, Logan was hunched over Jean's limp body, cradling her gently. Poison burned in both their veins. He would live. He wasn't sure about her.

Moving in front of them, Knight struck a wide stance, clenched her mechanical right hand into a tight fist, and drew her pistol.

"Let's do this," she said grimly.

From behind her came the distinct sound of Logan's claws extending. He took up a position at her back. The choked, guttural snarl under his breath sent a chill down Knight's spine. And then the Hand were on them.

Knight emptied her pistol into the rush and then assumed a defensive pose. Three of the assassins dropped down on her simultaneously. She caught the sword hand of the first, crushed it, and hurled the man into his partner. The third killer chopped down at her shoulder, and Knight only just managed to lean far enough over to take the cut metal on metal. Another few inches and she would have lost her mechanical arm. That was exactly what they had in mind, and Knight knew it as she smashed the butt of her pistol into the swordsman's face.

This time the assassins understood what they were up against. They had been prepared for their targets' special characteristics. It didn't matter. All the tactics in the world, all the different weapons, all the poison couldn't save them as Logan entered the fray. Berserk with rage, he cut them down savagely, relentlessly.

Logan threw himself into a shoulder roll toward Knight. She watched as he came up from the roll and two of the Hand suddenly dropped between them. The mutant's claws hamstrung both of the men neatly before they could hit the ground.

That moment's distraction cost Knight dearly. A blade slashed deep into her side. Ignoring the pain, she vaulted over the couch. A weighted chain snared her left leg in midair and upended her. She landed hard against the wall next to her desk. The opposite end of the chain was connected to a short, bladed weapon gripped by one of the Hand. He held it in attack position as he sailed over the couch toward her.

"Thanks a lot, chump," Knight said, ramming her right hand through the side of the heavy oak desk. When she pulled it out there was a forty-five-caliber automatic in her fist. The assassin saw the pistol too late. She jerked the trigger twice, knocking him out of the air.

At that point, Logan's free-roaming fury had become fixated on the shadowy figure in the back window. He waded into the last of the Hand, determined to carve a path through them to reach the one who had struck Jean down.

As the final assassin standing between Logan and his ultimate target fell, more shots rang out. Three bullets tore away chunks of the window casing as the slim, black form of the *shuriken* thrower cartwheeled smoothly out onto the ledge.

His enhanced senses were working perfectly now, and Logan was sure he heard the assassin laugh in the face of the gunfire. He bared his teeth and leaped across the room toward the window.

"Wolverine, wait!" Knight yelled after him.

He reached the opening, then hesitated.

"Jean needs our help," he heard Knight say.

Logan looked out the window. He could just make out a dark figure retreating across the rooftops.

"Call an ambulance," he grunted. And then he was gone, out into the night, on the hunt.

Twenty minutes later, Logan was pressed up against the cold stone wall of an alleyway. Red emergency lights from an ambulance parked in front of Jean Grey's apartment flashed across him as he watched paramedics emerge from the building carrying a stretcher.

The leader of the assassins had managed to lose him like he was a rank amateur. Given his injuries and the amount of poison in his system, it shouldn't have come as any surprise. The rest of the cadre had gone up in smoke by the time Logan's rage burned itself out somewhere on the Lower East Side. Afraid of what he might find if he went back, he had lingered on a rooftop there for a few minutes. At least it stopped raining.

Now, Logan watched silently as the two stretchers were loaded into the back of the ambulance. Knight was on one, conscious, and talking to the paramedics as she was loaded into the ambulance. Logan could just make out the exchange. Jean exhibited every sign of a severe reaction to poison, but the toxin seemed to have mysteriously burned itself out of her system. Knight claimed she could not account for this unusual reaction. She was relieved to hear that her roommate would recover in time.

Logan slumped against the wall. The enormous energies contained in Grey's body had saved her, as his own mutant healing ability had saved him—though just barely.

His relief dissolved quickly into shame and regret. All the strength drained out of his battered limbs. In his long, violent life, he could not remember ever being so completely exhausted.

The paramedics closed the doors of the ambulance and it pulled slowly out into the street. Logan looked on helplessly as it passed by the alley, splashing through a puddle at the curb. The spray of water spooked a group of pigeons on the sidewalk. They scattered, rising up in a cloud of fluttering wings while the red lights of the ambulance swept away, receding out of sight.

The silence that followed was broken only by the slow sound of Logan's breathing. He leaned his head back, and for a long time gazed numbly into the empty darkness overhead. Slowly at first, but then with increasing consistency, it started to rain.

He pushed away from the wall and steadied himself on his feet. As the shower became a downpour, he took a last look back at the apartment. Then, hunched over against the weather, Logan turned around and silently walked away down the alley.

The Worst Prison of All

C.J. Henderson

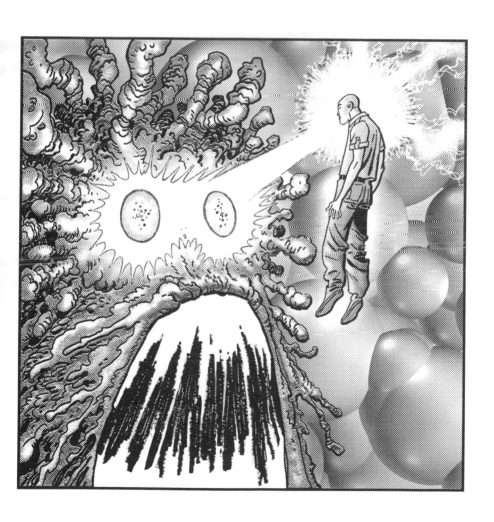

"THAT BALD CRIPPLE . . . HE'S THE ONE."

It was a whisper, low and dark and promising violence, a grim breath of air formed a thousand yards from the ears of the man it labeled. The speaker's intended target could not hear the words, of course. The noise of the street—people squawking over the price of vegetables, greeting friends, hailing jitneys, jostling and laughing their way through the dry and baking morning—reduced everyone's auditory range to mere inches. Luckily, the target did not need to rely on such a minor, inadequate sense as hearing.

His name was Charles Xavier. Bald and thin, a figure of powerful shoulders and bent, crushed legs, he had come to the city of Agadir in southern Morocco for the Moslem festival of Achoura. It was a day of fasting and honoring the dead marked by masked carnivals and fireworks. Being attacked by a half-dozen men, however, was not usually a part of the itinerary.

A smile—part curiosity, part pity—disrupted the normally straight line of Xavier's mouth. A segment of his brain filtered the different impulses swirling in the auras of the men waiting to pounce upon him. Although he could not see them, he could feel their presence quite clearly, their attention linked to the energies of the speaker, his attention still piercing the air, stabbing outward directly at what he only thought of as "the bald cripple."

Interesting, thought Xavier. *They do not even know who I am. Or why they are about to attack. This is not their idea.*

Intrigued, Xavier decided to take a moment from his passage through the colorfully festooned side streets of Agadir to investigate what was happening around him. Turning his wheelchair, he propelled himself straight toward his would-be attackers. His scan of their brains' motivational centers had found them devoid of purpose. They were being manipulated by some unseen force—one even Xavier could not sense clearly. Not yet.

I'll need a focal anchor, he thought, still wheeling himself toward those who would murder him. Scanning the simple forms of the third

89

dimension all about him with only his eyes, he found nothing that suited his need.

Buildings, merchant's stalls—too stationary, uncaring, cold. Cars, passersby—not stable, uninterested, transient. Then his eyes struck the little girl. And her toy.

"Let's go."

The half-dozen thugs stepped free of the shadows, out of their alley, their movements quick and precise—carefully guided by an extra hand.

Throw it.

The girl hurled her ball as ordered. The thick, hard rubber sphere rolled through the eighteen-and-a-half feet of space separating its owner from Xavier. He raised his hand to intercept the flying toy, positioning each finger carefully.

At the same time that one tiny segment of his brain occupied itself with catching the ball, another debated what to do about the men approaching him. They had dashed from the alley with the speed of hungry cats—their hands filled with blades and clubs, their eyes locked. Their wills were things of iron resolve. The cripple had to be destroyed. Killed. Beaten. Bloodied. Smashed. Annihilated.

But, Xavier again noted with interest, *they don't know why. They're not even actually aware that they're attacking.*

A thousand options lay before Xavier. Even as he had mentally commanded the girl to throw her ball, he realized he could do anything to the men he wished—reduce them to mental children, terrorize them by making them see monsters, send them to turn themselves in to the police, fry their neural circuits, cripple them with strokes—for one with the bald man's vast mental abilities, the list was virtually endless. But, knowing they were under the control of another, he merely threw forth a simple mental command into each of their brains.

The flying ball neared the zenith of its arc, hanging in the air in gravity-destroying triumph, resisting its inevitable capitulation.

The men stumbled into each other, their brains freed of the controlling fingers snaking into them from the unknown.

As the girl watched her ball, her unblinking stare still in its first second, as the men took control of their brains once more—the clouds blown clear from their minds—Xavier left his hand poised to catch the ball while he mentally threw himself outward through the depths of his fathomless consciousness.

The mental dagger he had launched at his attackers had neatly cleaved the ethereal binders linking the six to that which had possessed them. In a flash, Xavier's astral presence followed the severed strands back to their source. He found their owner waiting. It was a vast thing, stretching for miles through the twisting nether spiral.

"Well done, meat thing. Well done."

Xavier floated in the swirling fling of an unending dreamscape. The void pulsated, a limitless abyss of inexplicably colored twilight, one filled with locomotions determined not by gravities but through their relationships with the cacophony of discordant sound that leeched in from the edges of one's consciousness.

Xavier had been there before. Any of sufficient mental power could have traced the ethereal wisps of control back to the nowhere between the dimensions where he now faced his unknown foe. Over the millennia the pulsating emptiness had been known by many names—limbo, Erebus, Tophet, Gehenna, Avernus, a thousand more. It was, simply, that segment of eternity where those without power waited. And from where those with power struck.

"What are you?"

"I am Gol-shenthu, the Forgotten One. Which is my preferred condition."

"I asked not your label," said Xavier. "What syllables you attach to yourself are of no consequence to me. I asked '*what* are you?' Now answer."

The massive shape shifted, colors jumbling discordantly along its shimmering frame. Angles boiled along the surface of the thing, jutting, then recessing awkwardly. After a millisecond of eternities, the creature released a handful of words into the ether.

"I am known by many names to your like. The thought of me has shaken the logic of your realm, leaving those who would describe me lost in the contradiction of dreadful joy."

Xavier created a noise with his mind which translated in the silent world of sheer thought as a derisive sneer. The sound was a lie, however. The bald man could sense unimaginable power within the horrid bulk warping inward on itself before him. A score of different sections of his brain all analyzed the situation into which he had been drawn, instantly informing him that he had stumbled across a being of limitless strength.

"To know me is to die," said Gol-shenthu, "and yet, not to know me is to have never lived."

Feigning indifference to his host's posturing, Xavier told it his own theory. "Allow me to differ. You are nothing more than a common demon. Specifically, a vampire. Aggrandized by the ease with which you have snared your victims for so many years, you now think of yourself as some great and fearsome godling, instead of the licker of carrion that you are."

Xavier felt the void heat all about him. The irridescent, prolately spheroidal form of Gol-shenthu boiled, the chaotic geometry of it splintering and re-forming a thousand times. Crackling sound shattered against the color of the massive beast-thing. All the time, Xavier's astral form hung still in the great black nothing, waiting for the confrontation he could sense growing in dark waves.

"And I will tell you what *you* are, charlesxavier." The voice sliced cruelly through the bald man's brain.

(In the third dimension, the red rubber ball toppled past the zenith of its arc, hurtling forward toward Xavier's outstretched hand.)

"You are a tired and wretched creature," said Gol-shenthu. "You watch life while others live it. From the confines of your chair. Your feeble transport. Your prison."

Xavier smiled once more. "I float the cosmic fibers, as do you. I do not envy others any more than I would wish for them to envy me."

"You lie," insisted the pulsing maelstrom. "You have the ability to fuse with the In Between for a moment here or there, but this is not your home. Your home is disabled, a maimed and enfeebled sack of flesh and fluids that binds you to your self-propelled wheelbarrow. *I* live here, free and magnificent, grand and alive and immortal. But not you." The atmosphere shuddered. A blistering noise ran across Gol-shenthu's surface, a wet concordance feigning disinterest as it sneered, "You, despite the powers of your mind, can never be as long-lived as I. You will always remain a helpless prisoner of your lame flesh, forever hindered by your useless legs."

Xavier's mind split for a moment—part keeping a watch on his opponent, part slipping into memory. In the swiftest of moments, all the relevant portions of his life passed through his mind's eye in millisecond splinters, all of it tossed forth so that he might prove or disprove the horror's accusations.

THE WORST PRISON OF ALL

For a moment Xavier saw his parents again, Brian and Sharon. He saw himself playing ball with his father, running through the yard with his mother. He saw his college years, enriched by the cheers of his fellows as he brought his alma mater trophy after trophy. Running races, playing football, he was unbeatable, his considerable mental powers always allowing him to know what his opponents' next moves would be. His tour of duty as an infantryman had seemed charmed, again due to his heightened senses.

And even when he lost the use of his legs, he had been living life to the fullest he had ever known. Traveling in Tibet, he had reached a mysterious walled city in the shadow of the Himalayas. There he had encountered a terrible dictator known only as Lucifer. Leading local rebels through a secret tunnel his mental powers had discovered, Xavier had freed the local countryside from the grasp of the monster who had conquered it. Unfortunately, his reward for his efforts had been to end trapped beneath a massive slab of stone, dropped on him by the fleeing tyrant. The locals managed to free him, but not before his legs had been crushed and ruined beyond all hope of repair.

"I have preyed on the mental energies of your type for centuries," sneered the horrid bulk of the Forgotten One. "For ages I sustained myself on regular mortals. One brain at a time . . . so slow, so little return for my efforts. More energy was used to consume them than was gained in their consumption. But then, meat like you began to be born."

"Lucky you," answered Xavier.

"Yes, exactly so," the thing replied. "You mutants, bursting with energy, so much more delicious, so much more nourishing, satisfying . . ."

"We do our best," said the bald man, sarcastically.

"You do, indeed," the Forgotten One said. "And you—*you*, especially—you will be the best of all. Your mind is excellent, brimming with energy, enough to last me for centuries. My consumption of it will allow the time I have never had to find others like you, to build reserves of power so that I might finally rend the wall between our dimensions, that I might finally be able to feast in earnest."

"And, I'm just supposed to sit back and allow all of this?" asked Xavier in a measured tone. "You may remember, I dispatched your minions without any real effort."

93

"Of course you did," responded the boiling mass of ectoplasm hanging in the void before Xavier. "You were supposed to."

And then, the first obsidian tentacles wrapped themselves around the surprised mutant.

"They were but a tap on your shoulder to capture your attention, a signpost to bring you to me."

Xavier evolved his astral form, driving spikes outward from his form into Gol-shenthu's appendages. The thing noticed a moment of pain, but manipulated its tendrils so that they slid around its opponent's defenses. Xavier raised his body temperature to solar levels, but the creature instantly channeled the frigid atmosphere of the void between itself and its victim.

"To struggle is futile," admonished Gol-shenthu, its thick words ringing within Xavier's brain. "And besides, why would you even bother to? A captive to limiting flesh, locked in the terrible prison of your ruined body—why would you ignore the chance to free yourself, to join me as I first conquer all of this space, and then your own?"

"Never!" Xavier's thought echoed through the miles of Gol-shenthu, rattling the corpulent form violently enough to shake scales loose from its shimmering hide.

The mutant reached within himself, first steeling his astral form, then exploding it outward. His spirit form segmented into a thousand different sentient entities, all of them propelled at blinding speed throughout Gol-shenthu's form. The massive vampire barely seemed to notice the attack.

(The red rubber ball rolled onward through the air, still following its predetermined arc, hurtling ever onward toward the same out-stretched hand.)

"Foolish meat," whispered Gol-shenthu. Its essence congealed around the thousand bits of Xavier's astral self. "You have no choice. Give in, cripple. Spare yourself more of the pain you have lived with all your life. Give in."

Xavier's consciousness sharpened the edges of all his random aspects, slicing through his enemy's hardening body. At the same time, memory flooded him as well, admitting the truth in and yet also rejecting Gol-shenthu's words. The bald man remembered his life after he was freed from Lucifer's trap. For months after his return to America he had sulked and despaired, spending half his waking moments enraged, the other half in tears.

"Your premise comes close to reality," Xavier said, feeding the grasping thing surrounding him. "Before my accident I had been on top of the world—young, wealthy, gifted with powers beyond all reason. Whatever I desired became mine."

(The red rubber ball crawled nearer to the beckoning fingers. The blink the little girl had begun when she threw the ball finally finished itself, her eyelids slamming against one another, slamming their owner into darkness.)

"But then my golden life was stripped away. I was left crushed and broken—no longer a star, an attraction. The admiration that had flowed to me in rivers soured into pity. I could not run, walk along a wooded path, swim the oceans, climb the stairs. My life was over."

Xavier could sense his enemy's interest in his words. After a hundred thousand centuries of solitude, the peaks of the thing's ability to amuse itself had worn away to featureless planes. Splitting the tiny fragments of his astral self into even smaller sections, Xavier burrowed even further into the bulk of his foe.

"But then, I found that my legs had been holding me back, diverting me from my true destiny. As the joys of self-pity waned, I discovered the true power of my mind. Forced by fate into my prison, I effected my escape across the floodplane of dimensions outside my own."

(Less than a yard from the outstretched fingers, the ball rolled onward. The little girl's lashes began to separate.)

Gol-shenthu listened to Xavier's words, all the while grasping at the elusive motes of the bald man's astral form. The shining particles flashed from point to point within the pulsating horror's bulk, dodging wildly as the thing grasped at their enervating essence. By constantly shrinking the fragments' size, Xavier had been able to elude the Forgotten One's salivating grasp. But, the reductions had also reached a near subatomic size. Another subdivision would render him infinitesimal, incapable of ever escaping Gol-shenthu's personal gravity.

(Thirteen inches from the rigid hand, the red rubber sphere forced its way forward, shattering the air, streaming onward toward the desperate fingers.)

"There is no escape for you now, charlesxavier. In your fear you have digested yourself for me. You are mine."

"You overestimate yourself, monster," answered Xavier. His individual astral specks clawed frantically as the grasping geometry of Gol-shenthu cornered them one by one. Ignoring the impending doom surrounding him, the bald man blasted the monster with his words.

"You speak of prisons, but you are so blinded by your own inadequacies that you do not see the bars holding you in and down and back—bars far more capable of restraint than those of my mere 'meat prison.' "

(Ten inches—the red sphere continued to work its way forward.)

"You are a pitiful thing, a leeching coward afraid of life, afraid of kindness, afraid of joy and truth and anything that binds beings together instead of thrusting them apart."

Xavier felt the coldly burning touch of the Forgotten One gathering in bits of his astral form. The bald man had run out of time. Rapidly, Gol-shenthu sucked up the struggling whits of Xavier's essence, pulling them toward the central space within its bulk where it processed the energies it captured.

(Seven inches. The girl's eyes were open wide again. The ball flew onward.)

"Greed and sloth are all that propel you through your existence," snarled Xavier. "They are the prison that hold *you*, that keep you twisted and small and afraid. Too lazy to live, too grasping to die. How you must hate yourself."

More than half of Xavier's astral form had been gathered by his foe. He could feel himself being herded—one speck at a time—dragged to the heart of the pulsating horror.

"It matters not what you think," said Gol-shenthu. "Your voice will be silenced soon enough. You will not so much die, as fade away, one jot at a time. Your pride will dissolve into terror, and your chastisements will be rendered into pleas."

(Three inches. The fingers twitched. The girl smiled.)

"I think not," whispered Xavier. "You claimed to need my power to be able to reach my dimension, but like all of your life, those words are a lie."

A thin trace of a shudder folded its way through the Forgotten One's bulk. Trying to ignore the bald man's words, Gol-shenthu redoubled its efforts to drag together all the runaway flecks of Xavier's essence so that they might be processed.

"If I can travel across the dimensional rift," Xavier challenged, "then it is inconceivable that you cannot as well. You lurk in shadows and trick prey to within your grasp only because you are too cowardly to pursue it on your own."

(One inch. Less. The ball crossed into the jurisdiction of the gravity generated by the body in the wheelchair, increasing its speed. Dropping to Earth. Speeding toward the still waiting fingers. One millisecond more . . .)

Gol-shenthu dragged the last fragment of Xavier's astral form into his central core. Panicked triumph boiled in a sea of colors, sloshing their way across the Forgotten One's surface. Conic bursts of purple sound fried their way across its enormous bulk.

The thing laughed—vulgar echoes tarred the atmosphere.

Xavier waited. Praying.

The red rubber ball crashed against the waiting hand.

Instantly Xavier's consciousness responded to the anchor he had set, as planned.

The bald man's astral form was returned to his body, snapped back by the contact.

Instantly Gol-shenthu the Forgotten One, was dragged from its hiding place between realities and slammed into the dimension Charles Xavier called home.

The bald man's fingers closed around the red rubber ball. Without hesitation, he smiled widely, then tossed it back to its owner. The girl caught it, waved, then turned to rejoin her mother. The woman, staring at a feathered mask hanging in a sidewalk stall for the past few seconds, had not noticed her daughter's distraction.

As Gol-shenthu had been able to manipulate Xavier's essence within his own realm, the bald man had been able to do the reverse when his anchor had dragged them both back to the third dimension.

As Xavier had suspected, the Forgotten One was not really a city-sized creature. Like a blowfish, it had expanded out of all proportion, fear making it distort itself to ridiculous lengths so that it might frighten all who saw it.

The monster's smoldering remains were heaped in the alley from which his original dupes had first watched for Xavier's approach. Without hesitation, the bald man wheeled his chair forward, not bothering to turn his head to view the remains. His powerful mental senses had already told him what he needed to know—that Gol-shenthu was dead, its essence shattered, consumed when forced to substantiate itself into a thing of flesh and blood.

It feared mortality so much, thought Xavier as he made his way down the street. Then suddenly, he turned to look once more at the girl and her mother. Quietly, he watched the two of them move off down the street. They were oblivious to his observation—not caring that they would die some day, not concerned that they were not all-powerful, or that something beyond their control might enter their lives.

No, Xavier thought, *all they are concerned with is living their lives. As best they can, day by day. Without fear.*

The charred stench of Gol-shenthu's astral essence brushed past the bald man's consciousness.

And then, the bald man put his hands back to the wheels of his chair and moved once more into the crowd. The sun was on his shoulders and back, as it was on all about him. Fading into the crowd, Xavier opened himself to the busy life surrounding him, feeling its pulse, drinking in the dizzy energy of the simple love of life he felt all around him. Every person in the city of Agadir was making ready for the festival of Achoura. The day's fasting was over—soon would begin the masked carnivals and the fireworks.

Xavier thought one last time on his attacker. He shook his head involuntarily as he pondered the sad foolishness of such a wasted life. Then, he shoved the encounter from his mind. It had been, after all, only a minor confrontation, and he did have more important things to do.

Allowing himself the simple pleasure of feeling the sun on his back, Charles Xavier smiled, and then turned his attention to the task of picking a good restaurant for lunch. He paused for a moment, letting his senses range up and down the boulevard, then smiled.

Coffee, he thought. *And just the right blend. Life is good.*

By the time he had placed his order, Gol-shenthu had truly become "the Forgotten One."

Chasing Hairy

Glenn Hauman

HE BOUNCES FROM HIGHBROW intellectual discussions to low humor. He bounces from physics to genetics to chemistry. In conversation, he bounces from English to Latin to French. He bounces from blondes to brunettes to redheads. He bounced from the X-Men to the Avengers. And he bounces off the walls, the ceiling, and anything else. Small wonder he and everybody else call him the bouncing Beast.

Henry P. McCoy was born in Dunfee, Illinois. In high school, he combined all-state football playing and all-state academics. Shortly thereafter, he appeared with the X-Men to stop Magneto from taking over Cape Citadel. He stayed with the mutant team for a number of years, then joined the Avengers, sporting a new, furry appearance. This fresh look and his freewheeling style made him one of the most popular Avengers in history.

Now Magazine editor Carol Danvers conducted our Twenty Questions interview while following the Beast around for three days, and reports: "Two things absolutely amazed me; his energy level is off the scale. He ran me ragged following him from labratories to nightclubs to charity events—and the number of women who flock to his side wherever he goes is unreal. The man practically radiates a Women's Liberationist neutralization field."

1. Is it safe to hang out with you? I'm half expecting to be attacked any minute.

My dear, it's against my principles to make a pass at any member of the press until well after the interview is concluded, ever since that torrid night with Carl Bernstein, Herb Caen, Jimmy Breslin, and J. Jonah Jameson at the Stuckey's in Kansas City. I try to never offend anyone who buys ink by the gallon.

2. I meant attacked by the bad guys, giant robots, that sort of thing.

Oh, you wanted safety? You could be kidnapped by aliens on the way home, but you're more likely to be hit by lightning. Well, maybe not *you*, per se, you're a good abduction possibility—the Kree Empire needs women.

3. So how did you come to join the Avengers?

I did all the regional contests and was crowned Miss Congeniality, then took over when the paegent winner was unable to fulfill her duties. I still wear the swimsuit I wore in the competition, to keep me humble.

4. What was the final question you were asked in the paegant?

You're drivng a bus. At 1st Street, three men get on. At 2nd Street, four women get on and one man gets off. At 3rd Street, two men get on and the man who got off is slapped by the four women, who then leave the bus. At 4th Street, the bus is picked up and thrown crosstown by Magneto. What is the color of the bus driver's fur?

5. You have over three dozen patents to your name. What's the strangest thing you've patented?

There are so many weird things I've patented, many of them with single-usage applications, so most people have never heard of them. But probably the oddest one has to be a device I invented to open popcorn bags noiselessly in movie theaters. It took up three rows of the theater, so it never gained widespread acceptance amongst cinema owners—nowadays three rows *is* the theater. I've also patented my own musk, but I dare not release it on the general public, as it will make the wearer irresistible to women. It works too well. The world is not yet ready. I alone must bear the brunt of this terrible burden. All alone. [pause] Wanna comfort me in my half hour of loneliness, babe?

6. You were all-state in high school. How come we never see super heroes playing professional sports?

Who says we don't? Have you ever seen Michael Jordan play basketball? Jean-Paul Beaubier ski? The only one I know who wouldn't do it is Quicksilver, because he wouldn't be able to hold back enough to be convincing.

7. You're well known as a poker shark. Describe your strategies.

I am an absolute fiend for any game wherein, one, it's possible to win money, and two, a player can increase his chances of winning himself. Poker, blackjack, billiards, golf, Ping-Pong. Betting where you can outthink the other guy betting is fun—horse racing, football games, and the like—but unless I'm playing the game directly I'm often not entranced after I place the bet, and so I'm less cognizant of the actual participants and less likely to win. And games of pure chance bore me to tears very quickly.

That said, I tend to play outrageously, but keep very close counsel on the inside—I blow a few small pots intentionally and then clobber 'em on big hands. Except when I don't. Hey, you think I'm going to tell you how I play so everybody reading this can beat me? You're delusional. I will tell you that I always make it a habit to get no less than three of a kind on the opening deal, which helps immensely.

8. Do people treat you differently because you're blue?

No, I'm generally quite cheery to be around, I'm not depressed at all. Wait a minute. [looks at himself] I'm *blue*? Good Lord! [makes choking noise] You mean I'm color-blind, too? Noooooooo! It's too much to bear!

9. Are you self-conscious about your looks?

Hey, wouldn't you be, if you looked this great? Good thing I'm humble.

10. You have an image as a ladies' man. Why? What's your secret?

Some women think of me as a great big cuddly teddy bear. Some say I bring out the wild side in them. And a few have this thing about fairy-tale romances. And I'm immediately noticeable at a distance. I can be sitting on a bench in Central Park, just licking my eyebrows, and suddenly I'm surrounded by a dozen women. I mean, really. If a bouncing Beast can't go unnoticed in Central Park, what can he do? Go live in underground tunnels?

My real secret: these claws give the best backscratch in the tri-state area.

11. Is blue the natural color of your fur?

Only my hairdresser knows for sure.

12. Straight razor, disposable, electric, beard trimmer, or Nair?

Curry comb. I don't shave at all.

13. Give those of us who aren't multitalented some consolation: Give us an example of something you're lousy at.

I can't fit in any seat on an airplane, and people keep suggesting pet carriers. Most shoe boxes fit my feet better than most shoes. And my shower drain clogs with hair a lot more than yours does. Does that count?

14. Pretend they're making a movie about your life. What characteristics do you want for the person playing you?

The ability to emote whilst wearing a suit made out of cerulean blue carpet under hot lights. Good grooming habits are a must. The elocution of a Shakespearean actor while reciting dialogue out of *Star Trek* is a prerequisite. And I want script approval. But what I really want is to direct.

15. What untruths have come out about you in the press that you would like to correct?

I don't have fleas. They couldn't afford the rent, and had to move onto a dachshund. I'm a high-rent district. And I am not only not the president, I'm not even a client, so stop asking me how.

16. Mimes: what should be done with them?

Whatever else you may think of them, they can be a very important source of protein.

17. Describe the perfect night on the town for you.

I'm called away from a seven-course meal at Lutèce, right after dessert but before the check is delivered, to battle the Mad Thinker, who I demoralize into defeat by my incisive Jungian analysis of Proust's *Remembrance of Things Past* and my conclusive proof of the existence of an all-encompassing superior deity deduced from the implicate order. After depositing him with the authorities, where he promises to turn his Cosmic Whangdoodle into a source of clean power for the dolphins, I retire to Avengers Mansion sitting room with a snifter of Benedictine cognac and get into semantics with Dr. Porsche

Lipkind, associate professor of physics at Empire State University, and Bambi Abromowitz, a dental hygenist from Weehawken.

18. You have an impressive vocabulary, and are well known for using big words. Describe your fellow super heroes, one word apiece.

Iron Man: reflective. Captain America: iconic. Hawkeye: impassioned. Wonder Man: reluctant. The Vision: taut. Hercules: rambunctious. The Scarlet Witch: unpredictable. Quicksilver: impatient. Yellowjacket: married. Wasp: recherché. T'Challa: statesman. Cyclops: taciturn. Marvel Girl: fiery. Iceman: eager. Angel: prodigal. Spider-Man: exculpatable.

19. Can a super hero have close friends that aren't superpowered?

Oh, *mais oui.* I have so many diverse interests in specialized fields that I can share a kinship with colleagues who are more concerned about the charm of quarks than the charm of the Black Widow. That doesn't stop them from asking me to set them up with her, mind you, but it's not the first thing on their minds.

20. What was the most unexpected advice you ever got?

I'll always remember it. My uncle Fred came up to me at my graduation party and said, "Hank, I want you to remember one word—Croaton." I have no idea what he meant. But he came all the way from Levittown, Pennsylvania to tell me and if I can ever figure it out I'll be rich, I tell you, richer than Midas!

He also told me something very important: No matter where you go, no matter what you do, no matter what troubles you may encounter in life—there are nine hundred million people in China who really couldn't care less. So you might as well have a good time.

One Night Only

Sholly Fisch

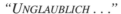

"UNGLAUBLICH . . ."

Kitty Pryde looked over at her companion with a smile. Even in the short time she'd been with the X-Men, the thirteen-year-old must have heard the word from Kurt Wagner's lips a hundred times. She'd heard it said in surprise, shock, and disbelief, but never with the sense of awe that she heard now. Tony Stark's image inducer might have changed the German-born mutant's appearance—at the moment, he bore a striking resemblance to Errol Flynn—but despite the illusion, there was no mistaking the childlike wonder in Kurt's openmouthed stare as he gaped upward toward the roof of the tent.

High above the center ring, a troupe of Chinese acrobats from the avant-garde Cirque de la Lune contorted their bodies slowly and gracefully with no apparent effort. Their synchrony of motion would have made the spectacle impressive in and of itself. What made the feat remarkable was the fact that each acrobat performed the act while balanced on the tip of a twenty-foot pole. What made the feat incredible was that the poles themselves were being held up by other members of the troupe.

Kitty leaned over to her companion and whispered, "Good present, huh?"

She waited a moment for an answer, but Kurt was too caught up in the performance to respond. "I'll take that as a yes," she decided. "Happy birthday, fuzzy-elf." Satisfied, she settled back into her seat.

Kitty could understand Kurt's reaction. After all, before joining the X-Men as Nightcrawler, Kurt had spent years performing in a traveling circus in the Bavarian Alps. The circus had been a perfect fit, both to Kurt's superhuman agility and to his flamboyant personality. More importantly, though, the circus was also one of the few settings in which a mutant with blue, furry skin and a prehensile tail could fit in comfortably.

Kitty didn't know how long it had been since Kurt had gone to see a circus—certainly, not since Kitty had joined up with the X-Men—but she was sure that it had to be bringing back all kinds of memories. And a postmodern circus like the Cirque de la Lune, where lasers and fog machines combined with haunting electronic music to create an atmosphere that would be more at home on Mars than here on the banks of New York's Hudson River ... well, Kitty was pretty sure he hadn't seen anything like this back in Bavaria. Tickets to the premiere performance had been hard to come by, but the expression on Kurt's face convinced Kitty that it had been worth the effort.

The acrobats wrapped up their act with a set of one-handed handstands—still on top of the poles. As she turned her attention back to the spectacle before her, Kitty couldn't help but marvel at the performers' skill. *Wonder how they'd manage in the Danger Room,* she thought with a grin. The fact that such feats could be performed by "mere humans" put the lie to all the Magnetos and evil mutants of the world, who considered humans to be their inferiors.

She watched the performers slide down their poles to land with a flourish. *Or* are *they really just human?* she wondered idly as she joined in the applause.

The big man sneered as the applause reached his ears in the deep shadows outside the tent. "Rubes," he muttered.

His partner, an even bigger man, nodded his assent. "Artsy wusses wouldn't know a *real* carny if it jumped up and bit 'em in the butt."

"Maybe," the first man said with a wicked grin, "but it didn't look like it hurt the take."

"Naw," the bigger man agreed. "C'mon. Let's go hit the box office."

"Whoa, whoa, stick to the plan," said the first man. He laid a hand on his partner's massive arm, his fingers sinking into folds of flesh. "It'd be too noisy now. Wait until the show's over and the rubes clear out. That's when we'll make our move."

The bigger man considered this for a moment, then nodded. "Yeah, okay. Guess we gotta be careful. Play this right, and we got us a chance to trash this farce and make a profit all at the same time."

The two exchanged a conspiratorial glance.

"I'll tell ya, Gunther," said the bigger man, "it don't get better'n this."

The applause died down as the synthesized music began to swell once again. A spotlight shone up into the darkness to illuminate the lone figure of a young woman standing upright on a trapeze, forty feet above the ground. Her long, blonde hair was pulled tight into a ponytail. It struck a contrast to her pale skin and royal blue leotard.

The awe in Kurt's eyes was slowly replaced by surprise. "Johanna?" he murmured.

The audience gasped as the attractive young acrobat suddenly fell backward, only to catch hold of the trapeze by her ankles at the last possible moment. The perfectly timed move not only gave the much-relieved audience a thrill, but also provided the momentum that she now used to guide the trapeze through an increasingly wider arc.

"It looks like her style, but," Kurt said in a soft undertone, "it can't be."

"Did you say something?" asked Kitty, trying to hear over the music.

As the trapeze reached the apex of its arc, the aerialist suddenly released her feet from the trapeze bar. She soared upward, tumbling over and over until she fell to meet the trapeze on its return. The audience burst into cheers as she effortlessly grabbed onto the bar with both hands, then swung her legs up over it as well.

"It is!" Kurt shouted with glee. Before Kitty could react, her teammate disappeared with a *BAMF!* She recoiled from the cloud of sulfurous smoke that always followed in Nightcrawler's wake when he teleported.

Before the cloud had the chance to clear, there was a second *BAMF!* as a demonic, blue figure in a red-and-white costume suddenly appeared above the ring. The audience oohed and ahhed, assuming it was part of the show. But as Kitty coughed the smoke out of her lungs and wiped the tears from her eyes, all she could manage to say was, "Oh, no . . ."

Nightcrawler grabbed one of the guy wires that held up the poles supporting the tent. He spun around the wire and hurtled through space toward his unsuspecting partner in the makeshift aerial act.

To say that she was startled would be an understatement. With only split seconds to react, she gaped at the grinning figure that soared headlong toward her. In shock, she mouthed a single word:

"Kurt . . . ?"

"Fancy meeting you here, *liebchen*," he replied with a grin as he grabbed her outstretched hands.

Johanna recovered quickly. She swung Kurt up toward the trapeze, which he grabbed tightly with his tail. With liquid grace, Johanna released her legs and allowed the two of them to swing free, supported only by the grip of the mutant's tail.

Kitty started paging madly through her program in search of the aerialist's bio, hoping it might give a clue as to Kurt's strange behavior. *Or at least her next of kin, so I can call when Kurt kills them both*, she added to herself.

Slowly, though, Kitty noticed the silence that enveloped her. She looked up from the program to find the crowd transfixed. Even the music had stopped.

When she turned her attention upward, she understood why. Kurt and Johanna had found their rhythm now, and the result was unlike anything she had ever seen. It was less an act than an aerial ballet, unfolding dozens of feet above the ground. The pair glided and leaped, tumbled and twirled in perfect harmony. The enthralled audience sat motionless and stared.

After what seemed like forever, the performers touched gracefully down on the ground. For a long moment, the silence continued. Then, all at once, it was replaced by a clamor of cheers and applause as the audience leaped to its feet. The triumphant duo bowed once, then a second time and a third before exiting hand-in-hand from the tent.

The audience continued the ovation long after Kurt and Johanna had left—all but one member of the audience, that is. When she saw Kurt leaving the tent without her, Kitty set her jaw determinedly. "Oh, no you don't," she said under her breath.

Kitty glanced around to make sure no one was watching her. No one was; in fact, everyone was cheering so hard that she could have set off a bomb without being noticed. The teenage mutant phased her body to intangibility and sank down through the grandstand. Walking through the network of metal supports, she made her way toward the performers' exit, slipped through the fabric of the tent wall, and found herself outdoors in the backstage area, surrounded by colorful tents and trailers. She squinted into the darkness for signs of Kurt and Johanna, and let out an exasperated breath.

"*Now* where did they go . . . ?" she mused.

* * *

"I'm bored," said the bigger man as he and his partner sat on the ground, hidden by a large trailer.

"Patience, Fred," his partner replied. He looked up past the circus lights at the starry sky above them. "It's nice out. Besides, the show can't last more than another half hour or so. Why don't you go get something to eat?"

"Around *here*? Ya can't even get a decent box of popcorn at this two-bit dump."

"What, you're not in the mood for a nice cappuccino?"

"Funny guy." With a grunt, the bigger man raised his massive bulk from the ground, stood up, and stretched. "Listen, you can play in the dirt if you want. Me, I'm tired o' waitin'. I'm hittin' that box office now."

"But the plan . . ."

"Forget the plan. Who cares if the rubes are here? I mean, look at us! Who's gonna stop us?"

His partner frowned. But he didn't argue.

The bigger man cracked his knuckles loudly. "I'm doin' it. You with me?"

His partner sighed and shook his head resignedly.

"Sure," he said with a shrug.

Johanna's trailer was small, but nice by the standards of the Cirque. She sat on the bed with legs crossed, leaning forward with an eager smile. Kurt sat—or more precisely, perched—in the chair opposite her. He sat in a comfortable crouch, his feet resting on the seat of the chair, as the two of them caught up.

"Ja, ja, und wie geht's mit Jemaine und Stefan?"

"Du weisst Jemaine—wie immer. Sie wohnt jetzt in New York. Aber Stefan, ach—"

Before Kurt could finish the thought, the door burst open. "You!" shouted a slender young man in a stylish, tailored suit and high-collared shirt.

Kurt started to straighten in his chair. *"Mein herr,* I must apologize—" he began.

It was already too late, however. "Claude, no!" shouted Johanna.

Claude lunged at Nightcrawler, but the young man was no match for the mutant. With lightning-fast reflexes honed by long hours of practice, Nightcrawler simply flipped up and out of the way, allowing Claude to crash headlong into the chair. Kurt's feet adhered to the ceiling, even as Claude landed in a heap on the floor.

"Diable!" Claude hissed through clenched teeth. He jerked to his feet, ready for a second try. Johanna jumped in front of him and pointed a finger sternly.

"What do you think you are doing?" she demanded.

"Me?!" he shouted incredulously. *"No one* disrupts my show—my art!"

"Will you stop acting like a child, and start thinking like a creative director?" she replied. "Did you see the audience? They *loved* Kurt's performance!"

"But he—"

"You are behaving irrationally. Do you even realize what you are doing? You are trying to fight a man who is standing on the ceiling!"

"The . . . ceiling?" Claude's eyes cleared as he began to cool down. For the first time, he took a good look at his quarry. Nightcrawler remained in his upside-down crouch, making no move to attack, but with his tail swaying back and forth cautiously as he watched his opponent.

"Yeah, the ceiling," came a new voice. "And he'll stay there if he knows what's good for him." In all the confusion, no one had noticed the teenager who stood at the door of the trailer. Yet, there she was. If her icy tone wasn't enough, the hands on her hips and daggers in her eyes showed beyond a doubt that this young woman was not happy. "What's the big idea of ditching me?"

"Kitty!" Kurt exclaimed, as he flipped over to land on the floor. He looked back and forth between Kitty and Claude. "I am afraid that I owe both of you an apology. I was so excited when I saw Johanna that I fear I could not contain myself . . ."

Kitty eyed Kurt skeptically, but Claude looked thoughtful as he ran a hand through his carefully moussed hair. "The audience did react well, didn't they?" he mused. "Still, a few lighting cues could have enhanced the sense of drama . . ."

Suddenly, Claude looked as though he'd been struck by a thunderbolt. "The audience!" he exclaimed. "I must get back to the show!" He quickly straightened his clothes and hurried past Kitty to the door.

Almost as an afterthought, he turned back toward Kurt before making his exit. "Perhaps later, you and I can speak about a more permanent position." Then he was gone.

Johanna threw her arms around Kurt in an excited hug. "Kurt! Did you hear? 'A more permanent position!' "

"*Shyeah*, right," Kitty snorted with a smirk. "Like you'd really give up . . . um, everything to join up with a circus again. Right, Kurt?"

It took a minute for Kitty to realize that he hadn't answered. Her expression softened and she looked less confident. "Uh, Kurt . . . ?" she ventured.

The blue-furred hero looked away.

Paolo sat in the small, red trailer, a look of intense concentration on his face. The child of industrious immigrant parents, Paolo had come to the United States when he was six years old. His *mamí* and *papi* had worked long hours to make sure that he was the first member of his family to finish high school and go to college. When he graduated with a degree in accounting, he thought they would burst with pride.

Of course, his folks were so wrapped up in their own dreams that they hadn't ever stopped to consider his own. Two months at a major accounting firm in New York merely confirmed what he had always known: the button-down world of accounting wasn't for him. When he came home one night and announced that he was quitting the firm to join the circus, Paolo's family didn't know whether to faint or burst out laughing. After all, Paolo was small, bookish, and slight of build—not exactly the type they could picture taming lions or defying death night after night.

What Paolo's parents hadn't considered, though, was the fact that circuses need accountants, too. As chief bookkeeper for the Cirque, Paolo was the one who made sure that everyone got paid on time and the show stayed in the black. Even better, as manager of the box office, his face was the first one that customers saw as they arrived. The job didn't pay as well as the one he'd left behind, but all in all, he was a whole lot happier.

Paolo was in the midst of reconciling the evening's receipts when he was startled by a pounding on the box office door. It figured. No matter how many times he made it clear that he was not to be disturbed when he was working, there was invariably some performer or roustabout who'd blown a paycheck on booze or cards and wanted "just one little advance" on the next one. Didn't they realize that every night's receipts represented literally thousands of dollars? He was doing important work. With an annoyed grunt, Paolo ignored the door and went back to work.

Still, Paolo's visitor was not so easily discouraged. The pounding started again, louder this time. "No advances! Go away!" Paolo snapped.

That should be the end of it, he thought.

But he was wrong.

Paolo jumped at the sound of screeching metal and crunching fiberglass as the heavy box office door was suddenly ripped off its hinges. Through the doorway, he caught a glimpse of the largest man he had ever seen in his life. The man staggered backwards, then regained his balance, as though he had torn off the reinforced door simply by pulling on it with all his weight. As the huge man casually tossed the door away, the one thought that flashed through Paolo's panicked mind was that, at least, the man looked too large to fit through the entrance.

That was when his partner entered instead.

Dressed in red tights and orange trunks and boots, the partner was smaller than the man outside. Still, "smaller" was only a relative term. More than six feet tall, the ruggedly handsome man entered the trailer with a knowing smile. "Sorry, we can't just go away," he said. "Not without the money."

Frantically, Paolo groped beneath the ticket counter and pulled out the shotgun that the tellers kept there for protection. Fumbling, he managed to cock the gun and pointed it at the intruder with trembling hands.

The thief seemed undisturbed by the weapon. "That would be a mistake," he said.

Paolo would never be sure whether he had meant to shoot. Either way, the trailer filled with sound as the gun went off—aimed point-blank at the intruder's chest.

To Paolo's surprise, however, the intruder was not even fazed by the blast. And to his even greater surprise, Paolo was knocked off his feet in a burst of searing pain . . . as some of the buckshot ricocheted and burrowed deep into his own shoulder!

"Toldja," the man said with a wicked smirk.

As Paolo writhed on the floor, he watched the tall man gather up the money and pass it to the bigger man outside before heading out himself. The last thing Paolo heard before he passed out was the words of the bigger man as the pair walked away:

"Now for the fun part."

"You're . . . you're really thinking about this, aren't you?" The corners of Kitty's mouth turned down, and she looked sadly over at her friend. Kurt hadn't said much as they wandered alongside the river through the darkened backlot. Then again, Kitty hadn't asked too many questions, either. But she had a good reason: She was afraid to hear the answer.

Kurt looked down at his cloven feet and breathed heavily. "I do not know," he said softly.

"Who is this Johanna, anyway? Old girlfriend?"

Kurt stopped in midstep. He turned toward Kitty and nearly smiled despite himself as he shook his head. "Girlfriend? No, no, no. Johanna and I were a team, but only professionally. Remember, even in my years with *der Jahrmakt*, I was still very much in love with Amanda—or Jemaine, as she called herself back then."

His yellowish eyes grew wistful with memory. "Johanna was always wonderfully gifted," he continued. "She came from the city, from a very proper Bavarian family"—he puffed himself up to illustrate his point—"one that would never even consider tolerating the shame of a child in the circus. So one day, Johanna ran away. She joined our little show, and suddenly, my solo act became a duo. We were—and I say this with no fear of modesty—quite wonderful."

"How long were you together?" Kitty asked.

"A year, perhaps two," Kurt replied. "One night, a man in an expensive suit came to one of our performances. He offered Johanna a featured slot in the big circus in Munich."

"Just her? Not you, too?"

Kurt smiled bitterly. "It wasn't a freak show."

"Oh."

The two grew silent at that, and they slowly resumed their stroll. It was a nice night, clear and warm. The stars overhead competed for dominance with the brighter lights from across the river.

Kitty gazed across at the distant riverbank and considered Kurt's words. Sometimes, it was hard for Kitty to remember that, much as her mutant powers set her apart from most people, she was still relatively lucky. Her powers did not come with the price of any physical abnormalities. She did not have to hide herself behind ruby quartz glasses or an image inducer. Kurt liked to put up a charming front, but Kitty couldn't even imagine the loneliness that lurked beneath it.

She didn't want to ask the question, but she had to. "You'd leave the X-Men?"

Kurt looked at her with a troubled expression. "I do not know," he said again. "The X-Men do such important work, and you all have become so important to me. You are more than my friends. You are my family."

He stooped down to pick up a stone and skipped it across the river. It bounced once, twice, three times, then sank into the dark water. "Yet, I had another family before the X-Men. Equally colorful, equally . . . strange," Kurt continued. "This is my chance to rejoin that family. How often does such an opportunity arise? How do I choose between my families?"

Kitty said nothing. She stared at the flowing water and thought about the sight of her friend soaring high above the crowds. She'd witnessed his prowess dozens of times in training and in the heat of battle, but it had never been like this. There was something transcendent in his style tonight, something glorious. Something—public.

Maybe that was it. For someone like Kurt, forced to hide for so much of his life, the joy of taking center stage must be beyond words. In the circus, Kurt could show off his God-given talents without fear, because the audience would simply assume he was wearing a costume.

As long as the world feared mutants, though, the X-Men would always be forced to stage their own "performances" in secret. The bulk of their work took place away from eyes of the public. Even when the X-Men saved the world, the world rarely saw them do it. And no one was applauding.

Kitty recalled the rapture on Kurt's face as he had sat beside her and watched the show. She remembered his sheer delight as he joined the show himself.

Finally, she took his hand and looked into his eyes.

"Fuzzy-elf," she said quietly, "I think you should do it."

Kurt looked back at her, a little surprised. He opened his mouth to reply.

But before the words could come, the silence was shattered by the sounds of crashing and panicked shouts. Kurt and Kitty spun toward the sound and identified it as coming from the main tent.

"Let's go!" Kurt said.

They broke into a run.

By the time Kurt and Kitty reached the tent, the panicked audience was pouring out of every available exit. There was no way to tell what was going on inside. *Whatever it is, it's bad,* Kitty thought.

Just then, Kitty spotted a little girl who'd been knocked to the ground in the mad rush to escape. The girl screamed and raised her arms to her face in a vain attempt to avoid being trampled by the unthinking mob.

Instantly, Kitty leaped into the thick of the crowd, phasing her body into intangibility as she went. She fell through the bodies of the maddened crowd, turning solid only when she reached the little girl. Kitty shielded the girl with her own body, grimacing with pain as she took a heavy foot in the base of her spine.

Wish we could phase out of here together, she thought. But while it was theoretically possible for Kitty to turn other people intangible, neither she nor Professor X had figured out how to make it happen yet. No, Kitty was going to have to do this the hard way.

Ignoring the pain, Kitty fought to her feet. She cradled the girl in her arms and rode the crushing push of the crowd until the two of them reached safety. Setting the girl down on her feet in a clearing, Kitty made sure she was unharmed before ducking into the shadows to change into her uniform.

Kitty knew that she wasn't supposed to be placing herself in potential combat situations. Her training had really only begun, and she still had a lot to learn. Professor Xavier would have a fit if he knew.

Okay, but who says this is a combat situation? Kitty thought. *It's probably just an escaped tiger or something. The Professor never said anything about tigers.*

And besides, she added silently as she took one more look at the fleeing crowd, *this is an emergency.*

Even as Kitty began to peel off her outer clothes, Nightcrawler was already inside the tent. He hadn't been able to teleport his way in—

there was too much confusion to be certain that he wouldn't materialize inside one of the scrambling bystanders—but his superhuman agility allowed him to leap, tumble, and sail over the heads of the crowd until he was through the entrance and in the clear.

At once, Nightcrawler saw the source of the panic. He hadn't been sure what to expect, but it certainly wasn't the familiar figure in trunks at the center of the ring.

"The Blob," Nightcrawler said.

The Blob was one of the X-Men's oldest foes. Nightcrawler had faced him once before, in Washington. Nightcrawler had been with the rest of the X-Men, and the Blob was with the latest incarnation of the Brotherhood of Evil Mutants. Tipping the scales at over five hundred pounds, the Blob was a solid mass of flesh—flesh that was impervious to harm. Bullets, cannonballs, even torpedoes would simply embed themselves in his ample layers of fat, only to shoot out again with a flex of his mutant muscles. What's more, once the Blob had rooted himself to a spot, it was all but impossible to move him.

Not that the roustabouts from the Cirque weren't trying. A dozen burly men swarmed over the evil mutant, yanking, pulling, and beating him to no effect. Or maybe there was some effect. The Blob seemed amused, if nothing else. "Show's closed, rubes!" he mocked. "Ya think you can stop the Blob? Go get another couple hundred guys. *Then* maybe we'll talk!"

It was obvious that the all-too-human circus crew was powerless against the Blob. Yet, the Blob didn't bother retaliating. He was too busy with another task: bringing down the center pole.

The Blob used his tremendous weight to rock the fifty-foot titanium pole back and forth, loosening it from the ground. Already, the pole had begun to sway perilously in either direction. And since the center pole provided the main support for the tent, if the pole went, the entire big top would follow.

Meanwhile, the Blob's longtime partner and best friend, Unus the Untouchable, was busy in his own way. Nightcrawler had never met Unus, but he had read the file Professor Xavier had assembled on him. Unus was moving quickly among the stands, using an axe to smash concession cases, seats, and anything else that got in his way. Unus was smaller than the Blob, but the circus folk were having no better luck against him than against his partner. Unus's impenetrable force field saw to that.

Nightcrawler had seen enough. The odds that he could do any serious damage to the Blob were slim, but they'd be better with momentum on his side. Leapfrogging over a pair of Chinese acrobats, Nightcrawler soared upwards, grabbing hold of the guy wires and using them to boost his momentum as he headed for the roof of the tent. It was a risky operation that demanded expert timing; with the center pole swaying the way it was, the guy wires were constantly moving. If one of them went slack in midswing, Nightcrawler would head straight for the ground. Acting more out of instinct than conscious thought, Nightcrawler navigated his course until he was directly over the Blob.

And then Nightcrawler let go.

Nightcrawler plummeted feet-first down the fifty-foot drop toward the Blob. He was counting on the Blob's mutant power to absorb the shock of the fall and save his life. *I suppose I have done more foolish things in my life,* he thought. But somehow, he couldn't think of any.

Glancing upward, the Blob caught sight of something speeding toward him. "Huh?" was all he could say in the moment before Nightcrawler hit him full force.

And then Nightcrawler bounced off.

Nightcrawler rocketed toward the bleachers as though propelled by a jet-powered trampoline. Even dazed, he twisted his body in midflight to try to soften his landing, but there was only so much he could do. He hit hard, crashing through the seats. When the dust settled, all was silent in the bleachers.

The Blob eyed the distant seats and chuckled. He was about to go back to work on the center pole when a furious figure ran screaming toward him.

"No one ruins my show!" Claude howled as he charged the Blob.

The Blob's eyes narrowed and grew dark with anger. "Oh, so this is *your* show, huh?"

Kitty noticed that Unus was basically ignoring the performers' attempts to stop him. Not that Kitty could blame him, given how ineffectual those attempts were. But as she got closer, her uniform obviously caught his attention.

"Aw, cripes," he muttered. "The X-Men." Then he took another look at her. "What is this, kiddie night?" he said, sneering.

Kitty struck her best heroic pose. "The name's Sprite, big man," she said, defiantly. "You're busted!"

" 'Sprite'? *Sprite?* Oooh, there's a name that strikes fear into my heart," he replied with a guffaw. "Just go home, little girl, before you get hurt."

The *little girl* crack was more than Sprite could stand. Unus was still laughing when she phased through his force field, drew back her foot, and drove it straight into his solar plexus in a thundering kick. Just the way Wolverine had taught her.

Unus flew backwards to the ground, gasping for breath with the wind knocked out of him. He was considerably bigger than Sprite, but he obviously wasn't used to fighting defensively; usually, he simply relied on his force field. Before Unus could recover, Sprite was on him, pummeling the villain left and right.

Despite her spirit, though, there was only so much that Sprite could do against her stronger opponent. Much as Sprite tried to phase her way through Unus' blows, he eventually connected and knocked her away.

Regaining his feet, Unus picked up the axe and reared back. "Sorry, kid," he said, "but you're a little too dangerous."

Just as the axe swung down, Sprite phased and let the weapon pass harmlessly through her. Then, with Unus off balance, she turned solid, grabbed the axe handle, and smashed it across the bridge of his nose.

Unus went down like a ton of invulnerable mutant bricks.

Slowly, painfully, Nightcrawler pulled himself out of the twisted mass of ruined seats. *Perhaps that was not the best approach I could have taken,* he thought dryly as he shook his head to clear it.

Looking around to get his bearings, Kurt had to smile at the sight of Sprite standing over Unus's unconscious form. Kitty didn't have much experience yet, but there was no denying that the young mutant had what it takes to be an X-Man.

Kurt's smile dropped, however, when he turned his gaze back to the center ring. The Blob was holding a terrified Claude over his head. And the Blob was angry.

". . . ain't no circus!" the Blob was shouting at the helpless Claude.

"My buddy an' me, we worked the carny circuit half our lives! Elephants, candy corn, a four-armed geek or two—*that's* a circus! This two-bit pansy act ain't nothin' but a joke! A joke on everyone who ever put an honest day's sweat into a *real* show! Well, the joke's over now!"

Claude screamed as the Blob hoisted him as high as he could and prepared to drive the Frenchman headfirst into the ground. But just then . . .

BAMF!

The air in front of the Blob filled with smoke as Nightcrawler suddenly appeared from nowhere. Swiftly, the teleporter scooped up a handful of sawdust from the ground and hurled it into the Blob's face. The Blob staggered back, coughing and choking, his eyes stinging from the combination of dust and smoke.

Taking advantage of the momentary distraction, Nightcrawler somersaulted over the Blob, snatching Claude from his hands and depositing him safely on the ground. Claude seized the opportunity and ran. Nightcrawler watched the Blob warily as he remained in a crouch, ready to move at a moment's notice. "Tsk, tsk. You mustn't kill the creative director, *Herr* Blob," Nightcrawler said with a pleasant smile. "Haven't you ever heard that the show must go on?"

Despite his flip façade, Nightcrawler was worried. He'd been running rapidly through his options in his head. The bottom line was that he could think of only one way to defeat the Blob. And it might just kill them both . . . if it worked at all.

The Blob cleared his lungs and wiped the tears from his eyes. He pointed a hammy finger at the mutant. "Bad move, freako. Ya shoulda stayed out of it."

"With all due respect," Nightcrawler replied coolly, "you have no business calling anyone 'freako.' "

"And now ya hadda go an' make it personal, huh, X-Man? Yer little trip to the cheap seats ain't nothin' compared to what I'm gonna do to ya now!"

"You are welcome to try."

"Ain't you learned yet? Nothin' can stop the Blob!"

Kurt's lips tightened. "I can," he said.

Nightcrawler leaped on top of the Blob, throwing his body across the massive mutant's shoulder and head. With a *BAMF!*, the two were obscured by a cloud of brimstone. An instant later, they were gone.

The only evidence that they had been there at all was the echo of their screams.

The unlikely pair was still screaming in agony when they reappeared in midair two hundred yards away. Too weak to move, they fell limply into the cool waters of the Hudson River.

By the time he broke the surface of the water, the Blob was already out cold from the excruciating strain of the trip. The Blob's immense size worked in his favor, though, making him buoyant enough to stay afloat even as the unconscious villain drifted aimlessly downriver.

Nightcrawler wasn't so lucky. It was always painful for Nightcrawler to carry someone along when he teleported. But he had never attempted to transport someone with the sheer mass of the Blob. Nightcrawler felt as though every cell in his body had been torn apart and reassembled . . . backward.

Can't . . . black out, he thought with gritted teeth as he struggled feebly to keep his head above the surface. Kurt knew that he wouldn't float like the Blob. If he allowed himself to succumb to weakness and pain, he'd be done for.

Yet, the sight of the shore filled him with nothing more than despair. Dry land wasn't more than ten or twelve yards away, but it might as well have been a mile.

So I . . . suppose I'd better . . . get started. Despite the aches that wracked his limbs, Kurt forced himself to raise his leaden arm. He tried one feeble stroke, then a second, and began the unremitting process of inching his way to shore.

Suddenly, Kurt felt a hand cup his chin and hold his head above water. A strong, slender arm wrapped itself around his chest.

"Kitty . . . ?" he murmured.

"Beruhige dich," Johanna said, soothingly. *"Ich bring dich rüber."*

With powerful, graceful strokes, Johanna began to tow her old friend to safety.

Some time later, Kurt sat on the ground near the river, far from the flashing red lights of the special police van that would soon transport Unus to a waiting cell. The Blob had vanished, which seemed almost comical in light of his size. But the current was strong enough to carry him a fair distance away, and there were simply too many places where he could have come ashore.

Kurt sat with a large towel draped about his shoulders, his hair still damp from his plunge into the river. Now and again, he sipped at a steaming cup of cappuccino from one of the concessions that hadn't been destroyed. Johanna sat to his left, rubbing her own hair vigorously with a second towel to dry it in the night air. Kitty had long since changed back into her street clothes, and sprawled comfortably across the ground to Kurt's right.

Kurt turned to Kitty over his coffee. "*Kätzchen?*" he said, smiling.

"Hmmm?" she replied without opening her eyes.

"Thank you. This is the most memorable birthday present I have received in a very long time."

The three of them laughed at the thought.

The laughter died away as Kurt looked up to see Claude striding purposefully toward them. "I am sorry for the delay," Claude said as he approached. "The repairs will be extensive, but they are under way. In addition, the police had many questions."

Kitty raised herself up on her elbows. "You kept us out of it, right?" she asked.

He nodded in reply. "As the two of you requested. It is the least we could do. Which brings us to the next order of business." Claude turned to face Kurt. "After all that you have done," he said, "you may have a place here for as long as you choose. May we count you as one of us?"

Kitty bit her lip bravely as Kurt rose slowly to his feet. Johanna stopped drying her hair and looked on in anxious anticipation.

Kurt reached back to rub the scruff of his neck as he searched for the proper words. "It is a most generous offer, *mein herr*," he said, "and I would be a fool to refuse. Nevertheless, I am afraid that is exactly what I must do."

Kitty's face lit up in happy surprise. Johanna jumped up from her position on the ground. "You are turning it down?" she asked, incredulous.

"I have to," Kurt replied, placing his hands on his old partner's shoulders. "This circus is filled with wonderful performers who are perfectly capable of delighting an audience without my own meager contribution. Yet, how many of them could have stopped Unus or the Blob tonight? How many could have saved all of those lives?"

Kurt's gaze turned to Kitty, who smiled proudly in silent approval. "I have a gift that is all too rare," Kurt continued. "It is my duty to use it—my duty to the world, and my duty to myself."

For a long moment, Johanna stared into Kurt's eyes. Then, she shrugged. "I understand," she said with a sigh. "But will you at least come to visit sometime?"

Kurt smiled warmly. "Now that I know where to find you? Of course." He gathered her in a gentle hug. *"Auf wiedersehen, liebchen."*

"Auf wiedersehen, mein freund," she replied.

Kurt released Johanna gently and extended a hand to Kitty, helping her to her feet. "Come, kitten," he said. "It is getting late. It's time to go home."

A Fine Line

Dori Koogler

"COME ON, TIN MAN, is that the best you can do?"

Callisto, the de facto leader of the Morlocks, shoved at Colossus's arm, making him lose his focus, and he dropped the dumbbell he was holding.

"Comrade Callisto," he said calmly, "how am I supposed to work if you keep distracting me?"

"If you were working, I wouldn't have to distract you." Even seated on the weight bench, he was taller than she, but that didn't appear to faze her at all. She glowered at him with her one good eye and prodded the dumbbell with her toe. It didn't move. "Come on, pick it up. You'll never get back into shape if you just sit there."

He leaned down, sighing. Yesterday she'd managed to make him drop the weight eight times in the first half hour of their session. Today they were almost finished, and he'd only dropped it half that many times. This could be deemed an improvement.

Callisto, assigned the job of physical therapist, had taken up the task with her customary singlemindedness, setting up a corner of the infirmary with weights and bars and driving her patients as mercilessly as she drove herself. Most of them complained, but they knew better than to quit on her, and they got better.

Colossus lifted the weight, looking at her out of the corner of his eye. She jerked her chin at the dumbbell. "Ten more," she said curtly; he sighed again and began curling the weight upward.

When he got to eight, she joggled his shoulder. He hissed in a breath, and the weight wobbled to the side, but he kept hold of it, closing his fingers with such force that the handhold compressed and the end of the dumbbell tilted downward.

"Bozhe moi!"

Callisto, surprised, gave a short bark of laughter. "Well," she said, "I see your strength is coming back."

Looking down at her with a smile, Colossus said, "So it would seem. I have not done that to the equipment in a very long time."

"Used to do that often, eh?" she said, one corner of her mouth twitching. "But Xavier could afford it."

Colossus's mouth quirked ruefully. "Actually, he made me replace every weight I damaged, out of my student stipend. At one point, I owed him money for three months. It was an unsettling experience, so soon after I left Russia. I did not realize how expensive the equipment was."

"Well," she said, shrugging, "we might as well stop, unless you want to keep working with that thing the way it is."

"No, thank you, Comrade Callisto," he said quickly, and set the ruined dumbbell on the bench. "It would pull to the side too much."

That was a lie, and he knew Callisto knew it, but she let it pass. "All right, then," she said. "Now you get to try the change again."

Colossus grimaced. He hated this part of the session, when he tried to change from his armored form to human. The first time they'd tried it, he'd collapsed, unconscious, and Moira had given Callisto the sharp side of her tongue. Callisto kept pushing him, though; there was no other way to get the neural pathways working again.

"Very well," he said, and closed his eyes. After a moment the cords in his neck stood out and his hands, doubled into fists, began to tremble. A ripple passed over the organic steel of his skin, a sort of bow wave of pink as his body tried to turn to flesh again. His back arched and his head fell back, eyes wide and staring, mouth open in a silent scream as pain spread along his limbs. The ripple widened and gained speed, so that his body almost seemed to flash from silver to pink and back; for a moment he thought he was going to manage it, but he fell to his knees with a strangled cry. He braced himself against the floor with one hand.

"Sorry . . . Comrade Callisto . . . I cannot . . ."

"You nearly made it this time, Tin Man," she said, in what, for her, was a gentle tone. "It's getting easier."

The giant Russian gave a humorless laugh as he pushed himself upright. "Easier is a relative term," he said.

At that moment, an alarm klaxon sounded, a braying blare of noise.

Moira MacTaggart and the medical team burst through the infirmary door, hustling a gurney toward the isolation unit. Callisto shifted as the gurney passed her, and swore violently under her breath when she saw the patient's face.

It was Jessie, one of the two Morlock children who had made it to

Muir Island. Callisto started forward, but Colossus laid his massive hand on her shoulder and held her in place.

"No, Comrade Callisto," he said, his voice pitched low. "Let Dr. MacTaggart take care of her."

Callisto twisted out from under his fingers and turned to glare up at him. "I don't know how you X-Men do things, but we Morlocks take care of each other," she snarled, and jerked past him, following Moira and the gurney.

Colossus shook his head and went after her. It seemed that life had become a series of medical emergencies ever since the Marauders attacked the Morlock tunnels beneath the island of Manhattan. Very few Morlocks were left alive after that, and the X-Men had suffered casualties as well: Colossus and Nightcrawler were both left comatose, and Shadowcat had been trapped in an ethereal state, unable to turn off her phasing power.

Things had been looking up, however. Shadowcat was on the mend, thanks to the intervention of Reed Richards of the Fantastic Four, though she still could not achieve a solid form, and Colossus was on the road to recovery. Nightcrawler, though, was still in a coma.

The Morlocks, however, weren't all that lucky. Colossus prayed that Jessie would not be the next member of that outcast group of mutants to die.

When they got to the isolation unit, the emergency team was transferring Jessie to a hospital bed.

Moira looked up and opened her mouth to order them out, saw Callisto's scowl, and went about her work without a word. Callisto stood quietly while the medical team worked over Jessie, but as soon as they seemed to be finished, she stepped over to Moira.

MacTaggart held up her hand before Callisto could speak, and waved the medical team out of the room. When they'd gone she spoke. "She was out playin', and Jamie Madrox heard her scream. When he got to her, she was lying on the strand in convulsions, and boulders were explodin' all around her. Her mutant power was out of control. It took him five minutes to get to her, for having to dodge the buggers." She pushed her glasses up with her knuckles. "Now," she went on, "before the . . . Before you brought her here, had her power started to manifest?"

Callisto nodded. "There had been three or four incidences."

"And she'd sustained a blow to the head in the fighting?"

"Yes," Callisto replied shortly. "She was unconscious for days."

"Ach," Moira said softly, "I remember. A nasty concussion she had, poor bairn. But she seemed fine once she woke." Her brow furrowed. "But now that I come to think," she said, "I don't remember her powers manifesting while she's been here. Is that right?"

Callisto thought for a moment, then nodded. "She was supposed to report to a grown-up if it did."

"Bloody hell," Moira swore. "Having the powers shut off like that is a bad sign." She sighed heavily. "Well, we have a new problem now. She's in a coma. There's naught to be done, save keep her comfortable, until her power settles down."

"Keep her comfortable? That's all?" Callisto took a step toward Moira, thrusting her face to within an inch of the other woman's, snarling.

Moira was unfazed by the threat. "I will do what's best for my patient," she said in a deceptively even tone, "and when you have your own medical degree, I'll listen to your suggestions. Now clear out and let me help the child as much as I can."

"Comrade Callisto, Dr. MacTaggart is right," Colossus said from the door. "There is nothing we can do here, and your anger will not help Jessie."

Callisto rounded on the Russian, ready to light into him next, when the cardiac monitor began to beep faster. Jessie moaned, and Callisto was by the bedside in an instant. "Jess?" she said, "Jess, are you awake?"

The child's eyes opened and the monitor began to beep erratically. She stared, not seeing anything in the room; then her back arched and her mouth opened as though to scream, and the blanket folded at the end of the hospital bed flew into the air and burst into flames.

Callisto swore and snatched at the burning cloth, but Colossus was there before her and batted it out of the air. It landed in a heap on the floor and he stomped the flames out with his massive foot.

Moira hurried to the drug cabinet and began preparing a syringe. The mirror over the sink exploded, sending deadly shards flying, and

Moira cried out as one sliced through her lab coat and scored her ribs, but never stopped what she was doing.

Colossus had the presence of mind to bend over Jessie, protecting her from the flying glass, which merely bounced off his armored skin.

"Move!" Moira shouted, and Colossus straightened, throwing up an arm to fend off a flying roll of burning bandages, which Callisto stomped out. Moira fumbled one-handed for the injection port as small items flew off the shelves of the drug cabinet and burst into flames or exploded, and injected the contents of the needle into the IV line. Within seconds, Jessie's back relaxed and the flying objects fell to the floor. The heart monitor settled into a slow, uneven rhythm. Colossus found the fire extinguisher and began putting out the fires.

Moira blew out a breath and dropped the syringe into the disposal bin. "Well," she said, "I see we'll have to amend the dosage."

"What?" Callisto hissed. "What do you mean, amend the dosage?"

Moira sighed and pushed her glasses up with her knuckles again. "The sedative we gave her before wore off too quickly." She pulled a stethoscope out of her pocket and bent over Jessie, listening to her lungs.

"But I thought you said she was in a coma," Callisto said, narrowing her eye. "Why does she need sedatives?"

"Because if she begins to regain consciousness, her power goes berserk," Moira replied tiredly as she straightened up. "We *can't* wake her up, not unless we can figure out how to get her power under control. You saw what happened just now. Do you think she could stand that kind of thing for long?" She moved to the cardiac monitor and began checking the printout for the last few minutes. "Ach!" she said, pulling the paper through her fingers, "It's worse than I thought. That last siezure put enormous strain on her heart. If there's another episode, it'll kill her." She looked up at Callisto, grim-faced.

"And if she wakes up, it'll happen again," Callisto said tonelessly.

Moira nodded, one short jerk of her chin. "I'm afraid we're goin' to lose her, no matter what we do."

Callisto's jaw tensed. "Then you'd better come up with something," she said through her teeth, "because I'm not willing to give up on her. If Jessie dies I'll cut you up into pieces too small to use for bait." She turned on her heel and stalked out of the small room.

* * *

The next morning when Colossus came for his physical therapy session, Callisto was not there. Colossus smiled to himself; she was always caustic if he was so much as a minute behind time. But when she still had not arrived after fifteen minutes, he began to worry and went to look for her.

She was in the isolation unit with Jessie. Once he saw her there, he realized that he wasn't completely surprised. What did surprise him, however, was the fact that she was reading to the child. He stepped back from the large window that looked into the room, moving so that the curtain to one side of the glass would hide most of him if she looked up.

But she never did. She bent over the book, absorbed in the story. She looked odd, almost wrong, somehow, and Colossus realized that for the first time in their acquaintance, she didn't look strung taut, waiting to launch herself at the next problem. Her voice, though he could not understand the words through the glass, had a gentleness in it, even in the midst of what were obviously rousing action scenes, that held him fascinated until she paused to reach for a glass of water on the table next to the bed.

It seemed a shame to interrupt her, but she'd have his head on a plate if he skipped the session. He took a deep breath and tapped gently on the glass with his finger.

Callisto started when she heard the noise, and in an instant she went into what, even seated, was a defensive posture. She turned, scanning for trouble, and scowled when she saw Colossus. She closed the book and laid it on the table, pausing for a moment to smooth Jessie's hair from her forehead before she strode to the door.

"What?" she demanded once she was outside. She'd forgotten their session completely. Colossus knew better than to grin.

"I believe it it time for our therapy session," he said gravely, and she swore under her breath.

"Right," she said. "Okay, then, why are we wasting time here? Let's go."

That day's session was the roughest one she'd put him through yet. He was happy to find that his coordination was returning along with his strength, and that both were nearly back to normal. When she finally asked him to try the transformation again he didn't complain, because he knew that she'd let him rest afterward. He fared a little better than he had the day before, but still could not complete the change.

Callisto gave a satisfied nod. "You're doing better, and you really don't need these sessions anymore. Consider yourself declared fit for duty." She turned and walked away without waiting for a reply.

Even though Callisto had ended the therapy sessions, Colossus continued to go to the infirmary at the usual hour. It was a good time to visit Nightcrawler. He hated to see his friend so still; in all the time he had known Kurt Wagner, Colossus had rarely seen him motionless, and it was disturbing. But Moira said that somewhere in there, Kurt might be aware of what was going on around him, so Colossus followed Kitty's example, and talked to him.

"Friend Kurt," he said when he arrived on the third morning, "I see you have company." Jessie had been moved from the isolation unit to a bed at the near end of the main ward. He was glad to see it; perhaps it meant she was getting better.

"When you are both well," he went on, "the two of you will get along famously. She loves to play hide-and-seek." For a moment he sat, watching Kurt, thinking of all the times the furry blue teleporter had popped in on him with no warning, and a smile tugged at the corners of his mouth. It had sometimes been annoying, but Jessie would have loved it.

Another voice drew his attention, and he looked up to find Callisto sitting next to Jessie's bed. She was reading again, and Colossus shook his head.

"I do not think I would have believed it if I had not seen it with my own eyes," he said softly. "Comrade Callisto did not seem the type to read aloud." He looked at Kurt, imagining his response to the sight of Callisto with a book.

For a time he kept silent, listening to the rise and fall of Callisto's voice. As before, Colossus could not make out the words, but the sound of her voice was comforting. He waited for a pause in the narrative, then, with a whispered good-bye, left Kurt's bedside.

He had to pass Jessie's bed on the way out, and as he got nearer, he began to make out the words Callisto was reading.

He stopped, fearing his footsteps would disturb her, and watched in amazement as she continued to read. She looked so different, not at all like the bitter, cynical woman who had cracked the whip during his therapy. Her face, without its customary scowl and curled lip, looked much younger, and even the black eyepatch she wore seemed somehow less fierce and intimidating. For the first time he noticed that she was starting to lose the gaunt, emaciated look she'd had when they came to Muir Island.

She seemed to sense that he was behind her, and her posture did that queer shift he had seen before. She closed the book and stood up. By the time she was out of the chair, the scowl had come back to her face.

"What?" she snapped, and her scowl deepened, but Colossus thought that he caught a faint undertone of embarrassment in her voice.

"I am sorry, Comrade Callisto," he said, looking down at his silver toes. "I did not mean to disturb you. I was . . . I could not help listening." He looked up again, curiosity in his face. "What is that story? I have not heard it, I am sure, but it sounds familiar."

"*The Wizard of Oz*," she said, and Colossus nodded. Kitty had made him watch the movie with her once.

"Ah," he said, and then could think of nothing else. For a moment they stood, staring at each other. "Well," Colossus said after an uncomfortable moment, "please do not let me keep you from your reading." He gave a small nod and walked past her. If his armored skin had been capable of it, he would have been blushing.

Over the next several days he watched for Callisto when he visited Kurt, hoping to hear more of the story. Oddly, after that first day, she read a little louder and he could make out most of her words. After a few days, her voice began to sound strained, and one morning she closed her book with a snap.

"Look," she said sharply, "if you want to hear this, come on over here and listen. My throat's getting sore."

Colossus, caught, did not reply.

"Well, come on, Tin Man," she said irritably when he didn't move. "I don't have all day, here."

After that, Colossus made a point to be in the infirmary when she was reading—he found out her schedule from Moira. Several times, when she'd finished reading and they were both leaving the infirmary, they began talking about the passage she'd just read, discussing it all the way to the dining hall. During those talks he was amazed to find that Callisto could hold up her end of a conversation when she wanted to. He told no one of his discovery—no one would have believed him. To everyone else in the island complex, she presented exactly the same taciturn, scowling face that she always had, snarling at people if they tried to make friendly overtures. But there was definitely a chink in the emotional armor she'd layered around her to keep people from getting too close, and Colossus was glad. The woman behind that armor was lonely, and needed a friend, and he meant to be that friend.

Kitty, of course, was the fist one to notice that Callisto behaved differently to Colossus.

They were in the Battle Room. She was perched in the air, watching him go through a simple practice routine. She took no notice when the solid holographic opponents and their weapons passed through her phased form, though she did him the courtesy of moving out of his way when he would have passed through her as well.

"Much better," she said when he had finished. "You knocked five seconds off your best time." She twisted around in the air so that she appeared to be lying on her stomach. "So," she said nonchalantly, after a pause, and Colossus groaned inwardly. "What's up with you and Callisto?"

Colossus lifted an eyebrow at her. "Nothing."

Kitty sat up again. "Oh, come on, Peter, I don't believe that for one minute. She's . . . different when you're around. Haven't you noticed?"

Truthfully, he had. He'd hoped it was because they were becoming friends, but Kitty seemed to think there was another reason. Best to disabuse her of that idea, and quickly.

"We have been discussing a book she is reading to Jessie," he said, and Kitty gave an unladylike snort.

"Right. Discussing a book. Look, Peter . . ."

"Kitty," Colossus interrupted sternly. "Callisto is worried about Jessie, and needs a friend."

"Callisto doesn't need anybody." She stood up and came over to him, putting a phantom hand on his arm. "Look, you need to be careful, okay? Callisto isn't someone you want to be too friendly toward. She's not used to it, and she could take it wrong. She'll turn on you, Peter, if you push her too far."

Colossus sighed. Kitty had seen the Morlock at her worst, more than once. But that was blinding her to the changes in Callisto, he was sure of it. And there had been changes for the better, since they'd come to Muir Island.

"Do not worry," he said. "Callisto has lost much, and that loss has changed her. She is not entirely the same woman you remember."

Kitty frowned. "That's for sure. The woman I remember wouldn't have been snooping around about your personal life."

"What?"

"Yeah, she was asking me all kinds of questions yesterday about . . . about us." Kitty bit her lip and turned away from him, her fingers trailing through his arm. "Don't worry, I didn't tell her anything. I figured it was for you to tell." There was the slightest tremor in her voice, and Colossus winced. She acted so normally to him most of the time that it was easy to pretend that nothing had ever been wrong between them, that their friendship was the same as it had always been.

Friendsip, hah! a voice in his head scoffed, *Piotr Nikolaievich, you are a fool.* But he ignored it, as he usually did.

"Kitty, I am sorry," he said. He reached out to put a hand on her shoulder, but remembered that he could not, and drew it back. It would not have comforted her anyway. "I will speak to Callisto, and she will not ask you any more questions." He turned to leave, but stopped when Kitty passed through him and hovered in the air directly in front of him.

"Peter."

She looked worried and solemn, and he sighed. "Don't worry, Katya, I will be careful," he said. She nodded and stepped aside, and he left the room without looking back at her.

It was not Callisto's usual time to read to Jessie, but Colossus checked the infirmary anyway. She wasn't on the ward, but neither was Jessie. A cold dread settled around his heart.

"Peter!" Moira called to him from Kurt's bedside, and Peter hurried over to her.

"What happened? Where is Jessie?"

"Easy, lad, easy," Moira replied. "We've taken her back to the isolation unit. Poor bairn, she started to wake up, and then things began to fly around the room. That was about an hour ago. Callisto is with her now."

"Thank you, Doctor," Colossus said. "I was just looking for Callisto."

Moira, seeing his grim expression, clucked her tongue at him. "Here, now, boyo, don't go storming in there after her. You'll upset her, and that might upset Jessie. Mind you be gentle wi' her, she needs that right now."

Colossus's jaw tightened, but he had to admit she was right. He gave a grave nod. "Do not worry, Dr. MacTaggart. I will remain calm."

Moira lifted an eyebrow and gave him a hard look. "See that you do," she said, and turned back to her patient. It was obviously a dismissal, and Colossus turned away and headed for the isolation unit.

Callisto was sitting next to the bed, leaning with her elbows on the mattress, holding Jessie's hand in both of hers. She looked emotionally wrung out, as though she were weary of clinging to hope. She sat up when she heard Colossus come into the room.

"Comrade Callisto," he said, "What happened? Is Jessie all right?"

Callisto closed the book on her lap. "Her body adjusted to the sedative, and they had to change the dosage. Jessie's a scrapper, though, she'll get through this." But Colossus heard in her voice that, for the first time, she didn't believe it.

"So, what brings you here, Tin Man?" Callisto asked. "If you came to listen to me read, you're too late."

"Actually, no," he replied. "Kitty said that you were asking questions about me. She would not have told you this, but what you were asking was . . . painful for her. I would prefer that you ask such questions of me."

"Well, well," Callisto said, one corner of her mouth lifting in a humorless half smile. "You're her knight in shining armor, are you?"

"I simply prefer that you ask me directly if you have questions about me," Colossus said gravely.

She stared at him for a moment, studying him, then seemed to come to some decision. "All right, if that's the way you want to play it. What's up with you and the kid?"

"If you mean Kitty, nothing is 'up' with us."

Callisto gave a short, low laugh. "Right. That's the reason she looks at you like you hung the moon."

"My relationship with Kitty is . . . complicated," Colossus said. He looked away, focusing on the medicine cabinet. "Kitty is older than her years in many ways. She believed that she loved me, and I felt . . . I believed . . . I thought she was too young to understand those feelings truly, and I was determined to wait until she was older to tell her how I felt. But then an entity called the Beyonder transported many of Earth's heroes to another world to study us, and I met Szaji." He stopped, remembering,.

"You fell in love with her," Callisto said. "What happened?"

"She died."

For a moment neither of them spoke. The cardiac monitor's steady *beep-beep-beep* filled the silence between them, and Colossus focused on it, letting the grief swirl around him and drain slowly away.

"Kitty took it badly, I suppose?"

"She took it better than I expected."

They fell silent again. The monitor continued its beeping.

"Look, Tin Man," Callisto began, but before she could continue the heart monitor burst into a frenzy of beeps, a wild, irregular pattern. An alarm klaxon began to blare.

Callisto leaped for the IV line and punched a button on the sedative delivery mechanism. Several CCs of the medicine poured into the IV. Jessie, just beginning to convulse, relaxed, and Colossus gave a sigh of relief. But the next instant the child's back arched so fiercely that she touched the bed only with her head and heels, and the monitor went berserk again. The chair Callisto had been sitting in began to vibrate, the medicines in the cabinet rattled on their shelves, and the bedside table began to rock back and forth.

Colossus grabbed Callisto and, lifting her bodily off the floor, carried her out the door. She struggled to get free, and cursing him, shrieked for him to let her go back to Jessie, but he ignored her.

At that moment, Moira MacTaggart arrived at a dead run. She

barely spared a glance at them on her way to the isolation unit. Colossus set Callisto down and followed her

Colossus reached the door first, and caught the cardiac monitor as it came flying through. Moira ducked underneath his arm and went to Jessie's side, reaching for the sedative delivery. Colossus dropped the monitor as it burst into flames and went to stand beside Moira, shielding her with his bulk and batting away as many airborne items as he could.

The sedative had no effect. Moira was about to deliver another dose when Callisto barrelled into the room and grabbed her arm.

"No!" she shouted. "She can't take three doses that fast, it could kill her!"

Moira shook Callisto's hand from her arm. "Spending her power like that will definitely kill her," she said fiercely. "The sedative is her only chance." They stared at each other as the EEG machine began to rattle on its table. Colossus picked it up and hurled it through the door. It exploded in the air.

"All right," Callisto said at last, "do it." Her face was bleak, and she turned away as Moira pushed the button again.

For a second Jessie relaxed, but only for a second. Her mouth opened and she gave a high, wailing scream. Every loose object in the room rose into the air, burning or exploding, and the window wall began to tremble. Colossus grabbed Moira and Callisto and pushed them to the floor, covering as much of them as he could with his body as the entire window wall exploded. Jessie's scream broke off, and she slumped to lie flat again.

Everything fell to the floor, rattling and thumping and crashing, and then the crackle of flames was the only sound besides the klaxon.

Colossus stood, then helped the women to their feet. They all looked down at Jessie, lying unnaturally still. Moira reached out and put her fingers on the child's throat, but it was merely a formality. They'd all seen death too many times not to recognize it.

Callisto picked up Jessie's limp hand, cradling it in both of hers. "Poor kid," she said. "You didn't deserve this." She reached up to close the child's eyes. When she turned to face the others, her expression was cold and hard; it was the old Callisto, the Morlock leader whom no emotion but anger touched.

"I should never have let you give her that last dose," she growled at Moira. "I should never have brought her here." She stalked off, knocking aside the medical team who got in her way.

Moira sighed. "She shouldna blame herself. There was nought she could have done." She laid a hand on Colossus's arm. "Go after her. See that she doesna break anything of importance, will you, lad? I'll take care of things here."

Colossus nodded and went after Callisto.

He found her in the Battle Room, running a training scenario. He stood in the observation bay that looked down on the room and watched her as she fought. She wasn't graceful, precisely, but she had an economy of movement that held its own beauty. She spun from opponent to opponent, dodging blows and landing her own, never stopping any of them, but slowing them down considerably. She held her own until one huge lout—who looked, Colossus was dismayed to note, somewhat like him—grabbed her from behind in a choke hold. She used her elbows and feet and even her teeth against him, but he was holding her off the floor and she had no leverage. After a few moments her struggles slowed, then ceased as the oxygen to her brain was cut off, and she slumped in the fellow's grasp.

At that point the simulation should have shut itself off and the solid holograms should have vanished, but neither of those things happened.

"*Bozhe moi*! The safeties are off!" Colossus bolted out of the observation room and down the stairs. The door was locked, and he slapped his hand over the palm plate. Several agonizing seconds later the door slid open and Colossus ran inside. The big hologram was still holding Callisto, and Colossus shouted, hoping to distract it. The hologram turned, and Colossus hauled back and hit it as hard as he could. The hologram's eyes rolled up in its head and it dropped Callisto. Colossus caught her.

"End simulation!" he shouted as the rest of the holographic goons started toward him. They flickered out and he sat down, cradling Callisto in his lap.

After a few seconds she began to cough, and sat up.

"What the hell are you doing here?" she rasped, pushing herself off his lap.

"You turned off the safeties. One of the holograms was killing you."

"So you charged in here to rescue me," she said acidly. "How sweet. But what made you think I wanted rescuing?"

Colossus made no reply, and she shrieked and flew at him, aiming a kick at his chest. He turned so that her foot brushed him and slid off.

"Comrade Callisto . . ."

"Why can't you just mind . . . your . . . own . . . business!" Every word was punctuated by a blow, and Colossus shifted so that none of them landed squarely; if they had, she'd have shattered bones. His easy avoidance of her fists and feet seemed to enrage her further, and she dealt him blow after blow. He continued to avoid them, leading her around the room in what almost seemed like a dance.

When the rain of blows finally started to slow down, and she began to miss completely, he stopped his evasion and scooped her up in his arms like a child.

"That is enough," he said gently, and held her still when she struggled. "You need to rest now."

Ignoring her protests, he carried her out of the Battle Room.

By the time they reached Callisto's quarters, she'd stopped struggling and lapsed into a sullen silence. She refused to open the door, so he took her wrist gently and set her hand over the palm plate. The door opened, and he carried her inside and set her down on the bed.

Without looking at him, she lay down, cradling the wrist he had held to her chest. He could see red marks where his fingers had rested, even though he'd been as careful as possible not to hurt her. He sighed and pulled the blanket over her. She turned away from him to face the wall.

He sighed. "Comrade Callisto," he said softly, "Do you not think we have suffered enough losses already?"

Her reply was to pull the blanket tighter about her.

Colossus sat down on the floor next to the bed. She had just suffered the last in a series of devastating losses, and whether she acknowledged it or not, she needed human comfort. He looked at his hand, the organic steel gleaming in the light. It was, he knew, warm enough to the touch, but it was hard, and hardly comforting. And he had barely learned to master his strength again in this form. Even if he could convince her to let him offer comfort, he was liable to hurt her.

Closing his eyes, he tried again to change from armored to human form. The pain was as intense as ever, but this time he was able to keep it from overwhelming him. He gave a mental push and the transformation was complete

He sat up, and found Callisto leaning on her elbow, looking at him. "I knew you'd figure it out sooner or later, Tin Man," she said. Then her eyebrow lifted and she looked him up and down. "Aren't you cold?"

Peter felt the heat rising in his cheeks. "Er, well, yes," he stammered, suddenly conscious of just how little he was wearing. "Perhaps I should go and, er, get dressed."

"Spoilsport," she said, and the flush spread down Peter's neck. She laughed and made a shooing motion. "Go on, before you freeze. Or die of embarrassment," she said. Peter went, gratefully.

He paused at the door and turned back to her. "Would you mind," he said gravely, embarrassment forgotten, "if I came back once I am dressed? I would like the company."

"I think I would like that, Piotr Nikolaievich," she said.

It was only after he got to his quarters that it occurred to him to wonder how she had learned his real name.

An hour and a half later, after a trip to the dining hall and then back to his quarters to collect his sketchbook and pencils, Peter arrived back at Callisto's door. It was open, so he stepped inside.

Callisto was asleep. Rather than wake her, he settled down in the chair to wait until she woke. She looked so different in sleep, so peaceful, that he pulled his sketch pad onto his lap and began to draw.

Hours later, when his hand began to cramp and the picture to blur on the page, Peter put down his pencil. Though she had stirred several times, Callisto had not waked, and he was ready to fall over from exhaustion himself. He stretched his hand and rubbed his eyes, and looked at the drawing.

He had drawn her sleeping, one hand curled under her cheek like a child. The hard planes of her face had filled out with regular and sufficient meals, and her mouth, usually drawn tight, was fuller.

All in all, it was a good likeness, even though it scarcely resembled the waking woman. The woman in the picture, though, was the one who had read to Jessie, the woman he thought of as his friend. Yes. A good likeness.

Peter pulled the drawing from the sketch pad and left it on the dresser. He'd told Callisto he'd be back, and he wanted her to know that he'd kept his word. Quietly he left the room and headed for his own quarters, and bed.

He was in the dining hall eating breakfast—a huge breakfast—the next morning when Callisto stormed in, the drawing he'd done of her clenched in her hand.

"What the hell is this?" she demanded, brandishing the paper at him. Heads turned in their direction.

He blinked, a forkful of eggs halfway to his mouth. "A drawing, Comrade Callisto," he said. When she didn't say anything, he added, "Of you."

"This is not me," she said through her teeth, and ripped the paper in two. "I look nothing like this." She emphasized each word by ripping the pieces again.

Suddenly Kitty's head and shoulders appeared in the middle of the table.

"Sit down!" she hissed at Callisto. "People are staring."

"Kitty," Peter said sharply, "I can deal with this on my own."

"Yeah," Callisto added, "Butt out."

"Well, excuse *me* for trying to help," Kitty said huffily, and walked through first Peter's plate and then Peter himself, her chin high in the air.

Peter winced. "I hate it when she does that."

"Poor baby." Callisto did not sound very sympathetic.

He sighed. "Please, Comrade Callisto, sit down." He looked at her, waiting, and after a moment she sat, reluctantly. "Thank you."

"Why did you draw me like this?" she said in a low, fierce voice, and shook the ragged quarter sheets at him. "I am nothing like that woman. Nothing!"

"I drew you that way because I saw a woman capable of compassion, of gentleness," he said. "Forgive me if I made an error." He tried to keep the anger out of his voice, but was not entirely successful. He'd left the drawing for her, after all, and she was entitled to tear it up if she chose. But he didn't understand how she had so misconstrued his intent.

"Compassion and gentleness are for people who don't have to scramble just to feed the ones who depend on them. People who live in the human world. Where I live, compassion and gentleness will get you killed."

"Is that really how you see yourself?"

"Yes. And if you had any brains, you would too. Don't try to glamorize me, Tin Man. I'm not all sweet and pretty like Kitty. I'm a Morlock, and I always will be." She pushed away from the table and stalked out of the dining hall.

Peter was just pushing his own chair back from the table when Kitty stopped him.

"Wait, Peter," she said. "She doesn't want company right now."

He leaned back in his chair. "The last time she stormed off like that, I found her in the Battle Room with the safeties off. I am not so sure that lettting her go off alone when she is this angry is a good idea."

"That was right after . . . after Jessie died, right?"

Peter nodded.

Kitty laid her hand over his arm. He couldn't feel it, of course, but it was comforting all the same. "She wasn't thinking straight then, from the grief. This is different. Right now, she's just mad."

"Still . . ." Peter frowned. "I do not like it, Kitty."

She jerked her hand back. "Why are you so worried about her?" she said sharply. "This is Callisto we're talking about, here. She led the Morlocks for years. Why do you suddenly have this urge to protect her?"

Peter opened his mouth to deny it, but found that he could not. He did feel that Callisto should be protected. Which, on the face of it, was ridiculous. He'd seen her take on opponents who were bigger and stronger than she, and leave them lying in the dust. But opponents she could hit with her fists were not what she was fighting now. She was fighting her own emotions, and that was a battle for which she was ill-prepared.

Kitty, watching his face, made a small, surprised sound. "Peter," she said tightly, "I told you before, you need to be careful of Callisto. She's not used to kindness." She turned and walked away, her back eloquently stiff.

Peter sat back in his chair. *Wonderful*, he thought in disgust. *Now I have made them both angry.* He looked at the shreds of paper on the table. *And I don't even know why.*

He puzzled over it on and off most of the day, and went to bed no nearer to an answer than he had been at breakfast.

He fell asleep quickly, and that night, for the first time in many weeks, he dreamt of Szaji and her death. As always, he tried to prevent it, and as always, he failed. He held her in his arms and watched the light go out of her eyes, and the grief burned through his limbs like a fuse, and when it reached his heart it burst outward, sweeping fire before it. He struggled to cry out, but the fire consumed his breath and he could make no sound. After some indeterminable time, the pain stopped, leaving only the echo of itself along his nerves.

He sat up and put his hand to his head—and touched organic steel.

"That looked like a right bitch."

It was Callisto's voice, and he squinted to see her in the dark.

He heard a click, and the bedside light flared on. He threw a hand up to shield his eyes, and when they had adjusted, he saw that Callisto was sitting in the chair beside the bed.

"I heard you yell," she said, "and came to see what was wrong."

"It was a bad dream," he said, still not quite believing she was there.

"What kind of bad dream?" She sounded idly curious, but there was something in her expression that told him she seriously wanted to know. "It's all right," she said softly when he hesitated. "You don't have to tell me. Might make you feel better, though."

"I . . . dreamt of Szaji. Of her death. She died to save me, and I . . . I could not prevent it." He put his head in his hands. "I loved her, and I could not save her."

He heard her move, felt her fingers on his shoulder, a tentative, brief touch, and then she moved away. "You can't always save them," she said in a low, bitter voice. "No matter how hard you try."

He looked up. She was standing with her back to him, her shoulders hunched and her arms wrapped around herself. He had never heard her admit defeat before, and it sent a chill down his spine. He went to her and laid a hand on her shoulder.

"And yet you do not stop trying. We do not stop trying."

"Yeah, we keep tilting at those windmills. What kind of fools does that make us?"

"Hopeful ones."

She gave a short bark of a laugh. "Didn't anyone ever tell you that hope will sink its teeth and claws into you and leave your guts all over the floor?"

He turned her around to face him. "If you had no hope, then why did you keep reading to Jessie?"

Her face contorted and she took a deep, hitching breath. "Screw you, Tin Man," she whispered, turning away. "And screw the Marauders. If I ever find them, I will make them pay for every Morlock who suffered at their hands. Especially the children." She wrapped her arms around her middle again. "God, the children . . . I should have . . ."

"Hush." Colossus curled an arm around her, pulling her back to rest against his chest. "Sometimes you cannot save them, no matter how hard you try."

"That sucks."

"I know."

They stood there for a long time, and since Callisto, the bitter and cynical Morlock leader, would never cry, Colossus ignored the tears that occasionally fell on his arm.

Eventually Callisto shook herself, and Colossus stepped back.

"I should go," she said. "You need your sleep." Keeping her back to him, she started toward the door.

"Wait," he said, and she paused. "I would rather talk than sleep, if you would not mind keeping me company. I would like to know about the Morlocks. To remember them, if it would not be too hard to speak of them."

Callisto turned around. "No," she said, "It would be good to remember them." She came back and sat down. "Thank you."

She talked into the wee hours, more than Colossus had ever imagined she would, more than he'd ever heard her say in all the time he'd known her put together, and finally fell asleep in the chair. He picked her up and tucked her into his bed, then looked ruefully at the chair. It was far too small for him. He sighed and stretched out on the floor.

Loud voices outside his door woke him. Callisto was gone, but she must have just left, because hers was one of the voices. The other was Kitty's. Colossus groaned. The two of them treated each other with a cordial civility most of the time, but their conversation now sounded neither cordial nor civil. He reached for a robe and pulled it on as he opened the door.

"Oh, really?" Kitty was saying hotly. "I sure know what it looks like."

"Looks can be deceiving, kid," Callisto retorted.

"You'd better be careful, Callisto," Kitty said, "because if you hurt him, you'll regret it."

Peter, recognizing that Kitty was making a serious threat, stepped through the door to stand between them. "I believe I can take care of myself, Kitty," he said mildly. Kitty flushed and began to stammer an apology.

"Oh, don't worry, kid," Callisto said, and shocked Peter by insinuating herself under his arm and laying her hand on his chest. "I have no intention of hurting him. Unless he wants me to." She slid her fingers underneath the lapel of the robe and looked up at him.

Peter stared down at her, unable to say anything in his amazement. She was smiling. Callisto, whose idea of a smile was a wolfish, too-many-teeth-to-be-friendly grin, was smiling at him. Flirting with him. And the way her fingers were moving underneath the robe gave the definite impression that she wasn't doing it entirely for Kitty's benefit. That thought scalded him out of his stupor. Carefully, so as not to bruise her wrist again, he lifted her hand from his chest, shifting as he did it so that she was no longer pressed against his side.

"Comrade Callisto," he said, "I am quite flattered, but . . ."

There was the briefest flicker of hurt in her eye, but then she laughed and pulled her hand from his. "Don't worry, Tin Man," she said, "I wasn't serious. You're too young for me." She reached up and gave his cheek a mocking pat. "I like my men a little more . . . seasoned. Now, if you don't mind, I believe there are bluebery pancakes for breakfast." She winked at Kitty and walked away, her back straight and her chin up, whistling.

Peter turned to Kitty. "All right," he said, crossing his arms over his chest, "What was that all about?"

Kitty rolled her eyes. "Oh, come on, Peter, I know you tend not to notice these things, but even you can't be that clueless." When he didn't reply, she made a frustrated sound. "Peter. She's starting to fall for you, you dope."

"Katya, you are mistaken." The denial was instant, and Kitty snorted.

"Ha. Right, women who just want to be friends put their hands all over you like Callisto just did."

"She was doing that to make you jealous."

Kitty looked away, tucking a strand of hair behind her ear in a nervous gesture. "Yeah, well, it worked," she muttered.

There was nothing he could say that wouldn't hurt her, so he ignored the comment. "Kitty, truly, I think you are imagining things. Callisto has no feelings for me beyond friendship, I am certain."

Kitty flung her hands up in the air. "Okay, I give up. You *are* that clueless. Just remember I tried to warn you." She turned and walked away, muttering under her breath and shaking her head.

Colossus stared after her. She was wrong, of course. But a creeping doubt lingered, like the memory of Callisto's fingers moving on his skin.

And it occurred to him in a blinding flash that the trouble wasn't that Callisto might be developing a romantic interest in him. The problem was that he could not return them if she was.

After a futile hour spent trying to distract himself from that realization by changing back and forth from armored form to human, Peter dragged himself back to his quarters. Though his mind was still in turmoil, he was pleased to find that his ability to transform had become easier with repetition, and he could now convert to human form with no pain, and to organic steel with only minor twinges. He dressed warmly, packed up his sketchbook and pencils, and went out for a walk on the beach, hoping the wind and the sound of the ocean would help him think.

He sat on a rock a little above the high tide mark and opened his sketchbook, but after half an hour, he had drawn nothing.

He set his pencil down on the rock next to the gum eraser. *This is pointless*, he thought, but didn't get up to leave. He had loved Szaji, and she died because of him, because he was an X-Man and mortal peril was a regular occurrence in his life. He had loved Kitty, and broken her heart trying to ease his own conscience, and keep her from Szaji's fate. The truth was, love hurt too much when it ended. He didn't think he could handle that again. Twice was more than enough.

He sighed and picked up his pencil again. He would go away. If Callisto were beginning to have feelings for him, they would soon wither in his absence; Callisto was not one to pine for something she couldn't have. He would talk to Moira, arrange a trip to London or

Edinburgh, or, if she thought he was strong enough, perhaps he could rejoin the rest of the X-Men in . . . wherever they were. It had been several days since they'd had word, and the X-Men tended to move fast.

He ignored the voice in his head that said he was running away.

Two days later he was standing on the dock, his bags packed, waiting for the ferry to take him to the mainland. Moira had not felt that he was quite ready to rejoin the X-Men, so he was bound for Edinburgh by train.

Moira MacTaggart, wrapped to the ears against the wind, had come with Kitty to tell him good-bye.

"Safe journey, safe home," she said, pulling Peter into a hug.

"Take care, Peter," Kitty said. "I'll . . . I'll miss you."

"Yeah, Tin Man, take care." Callisto's voice came from behind them.

Kitty gave Moira a speaking look. "Come on, Doc, didn't you have an appointment about now?"

"Yes," Moira said, lifting an eyebrow. "I believe I did. Come then, you can walk me back. This wind is wicked."

Kitty stepped up on the air and kissed Peter's cheek "Good luck," she whispered in his ear.

There was a moment of awkward silence, and then Callisto said, "So, where you headed?"

"Edinburgh," Peter replied. He ought at least to have told her he was leaving, he supposed, but he had found that Kitty's suspicions had made him uncomfortable around her.

"Look, Tin Man," she said, "about the other day . . ." She glanced away. "You're not leaving because of that, are you? Because it wasn't serious." But she didn't look at him as she said it.

He was saved from having to reply by the arrival of the ferry. Peter gave a silent sigh of relief and dug his sketchbook out of his duffle. He pulled out the last drawing he had done. "Here," he said, holding it out to Callisto.

It was a sketch of Jessie, skipping along the beach and laughing. Callisto took it and gently, so as not to smudge the lines, ran a fingertip over Jessie's hair, flying in the wind.

"Thank you," she said, the words sounding strange, for she seldom used them. "You got her perfectly."

The ferryman leaned over to tie up his boat. "Hurry up, laddie," he said gruffly, "I've no time for dawdlin' good-byes." He began loading Peter's baggage.

Callisto stuck out her hand. "Good-bye, Tin Man."

Peter took her hand and shook it. "Good-bye, Comrade Callisto," he said. And then, prompted by what devil he didn't know, he added, "Perhaps, when I return, you will let me draw you again." He let go of her hand and stepped aboard the boat. The ferryman cast off the line and gunned the motor once, then pulled away from the dock.

"Hey! Tin Man! Think fast!" Callisto called, and Peter turned, putting his hands up to catch the object she'd thrown at him. It was a book, *The Wizard of Oz.*

"Finish it," she shouted across the widening distance. "When you get back, we can talk about it."

"Thank you," he called back. "I will."

But the Fates had other plans.

It was hours after the midnight broadcast from Dallas, hours after Kitty had broken the dreadful news to Kurt—finally awakened from his coma—and Moira that the X-Men were dead, that she remembered Callisto. She sat straight up in her bed, drying her face with her hands.

Callisto must be told. She had cared about Peter, after all, and, in a strange way, for Ororo and the other X-Men, though they had often been at daggers drawn, and no matter how much Kitty hated the thought of having to offer comfort to someone who had caused her so much pain, she owed it to Peter to do it.

She sighed and rubbed the last traces of tears from her face, blew her nose, and set out for Callisto's quarters.

At first there was no answer to her knock. She knocked again, louder, and was rewarded with a snarled, "Go away." *Well, at least she's home*, Kitty thought, and knocked again, still louder.

Something crashed against the door—glass, by the sound of it— accompanied by violent swearing. "Can't you hear?" Callisto shouted, "I told you to bloody go away."

Kitty stuck her head through the door. "I heard you," she said calmly, "but there's something I need to . . ." She stopped.

Callisto already knew. She sat slumped in a chair by the desk, a bottle of Moira's best single-malt Scotch at her elbow. It was two-thirds empty. There was no glass; that must have been what she threw at the door.

"Well," she said, her mouth curved in a bitter, mocking smile, "come to bring me bad news? Too late, I already heard." She turned away from Kitty and reached for the whiskey. When she couldn't find the glass, she shrugged and took a swig straight from the bottle.

Since Callisto, like Wolverine, had an accelerated healing factor, it took a deliberate and concerted effort for her to achieve inebriation. Kitty phased the rest of the way through the door, worried. Callisto was dangerous cold sober; a drunken Callisto didn't bear thinking about.

"Is this really a good idea?" Kitty said. She wasn't quite able to keep the anxiety out of her voice.

Callisto took another pull from the bottle. "Oh, don't worry, kid," she said. "It was half-empty when I swiped it." She set the bottle on the desk and turned to Kitty. Her eye was clear, her voice unslurred. "I'm just having a toast to absent . . . friends." A haunted look came over her face. "There are so many of them now . . ."

A knot rose in Kitty's throat as she thought of Ororo and Wolverine and Rogue and Madeline, of all the Morlocks slain in the Massacre. She tried hard, but failed, not to think of Peter. "Yeah," she said roughly, "there are."

For a moment there was silence, and then Callisto pushed out of the chair and took three restless steps across the room.

"How the hell did he get to Dallas?" she said, thumping her fist on her thigh. "How did he know where they were?"

"I don't know," Kitty said, her voice pained. "Moira tried to call New York, but nobody answered. And the hotel in Edinburgh said he'd paid through the end of the week."

Callisto turned and paced back to the desk, where she toyed with the bottle for a moment. But she didn't pick it up. Instead, she looked at Kitty. "You think it's my fault," she said. It was, for Callisto, a statement surprisingly devoid of hostility.

Kitty hesitated. If Peter hadn't been running from how he thought Callisto had started to feel about him, he wouldn't have been in Edinburgh, and so might not have wound up in Dallas. She suspected Callisto knew that, and also blamed herself. But she also knew that Peter wouldn't have blamed the older woman, so she said nothing.

"It's all right," Callisto said, her hands curled into rigid fists at her sides. "It is my fault. I shouldn't have pushed him the way I did that morning outside his room. I knew he didn't want anything like that, not after . . ." She trailed off, her glance flickering away from Kitty for a second. She was, Kitty realized with some astonishment, trying to be tactful.

"No," Kitty said softly, "you shouldn't have. But whatever took Peter to Dallas might just as well have turned up here. And if he knew the X-Men were in trouble, he'd have gone anyway."

Callisto raked a hand through her hair. "I know that. Any of us would have." Her fingers were tight on the back of the chair, the knuckles white and strained, and Kitty wondered if she realized that, for the first time, she had included herself with the X-Men. Perhaps Peter had been right about her, after all.

The sudden crash of the chair on the floor made Kitty jump.

"Dammit!" Callisto swore. "Haven't we lost enough?" Her mouth was pulled into a tight line and she held her fists in front of her, ready to pummel something.

"We've lost too much," Kitty replied. If it had been anyone else standing in front of her, she'd have offered a comforting touch, but Callisto would only reject it, so she stayed still. "And we'll lose more before we're done. It goes with the job."

"Well, then, the job sucks."

Kitty couldn't argue with that, so she changed the subject.

"Callisto," she said, "Peter . . . He cared about you." It was hard to say, it brought a burning pain underneath her breastbone, but Peter would have wanted Callisto to know it.

Callisto's hands tightened on the chair back, and the wood groaned. "He wanted to be my friend," she said, the words sounding as though they were pushed through too narrow a space. "I'd forgotten that it was even possible for someone like me to have friends. But he . . ." She reached forward and opened the desk drawer, took out a paper.

It was the picture he had drawn of her, the sections painstakingly taped back together. She laid it on the desk. "This is how he saw me. God knows why."

Gently Kitty stretched out a finger and smoothed it over the bottom corner of the drawing, leaving a faint smudge in the line. "Because," she said, "that's the kind of man he w . . . was." Her voice shook over the word, and the picture suddenly blurred. "He saw a woman worth befriending, a woman who could still care about people. And if he saw it, it must have really been there. Don't make him into a liar by getting rid of that woman." She walked to the door. "He deserves better than that."

Callisto picked up the drawing. "Yeah," she said, looking at it with an odd expression, "he does."

Though she didn't move, she seemed somehow to draw in on herself, and Kitty knew that the conversation was over. She phased and stepped through the door, leaving Callisto to grieve in private.

Steel Dogs and Englishmen

Thomas Deja

SEAN CASSIDY WAS USED TO BEING WATCHED. He had worn so many hats in his life—Interpol agent, New York City cop, super-villian, X-Man—that people tended to watch him furtively out of either arrogance or fear.

And at this moment, in a nondescript pub in London, he felt himself being watched very closely indeed by everyone in the place.

He made his way to the bar, raking his eyes across the place. Like dominoes, the gazes of the patrons fell away. There was a uniformity to their collected number, a mix of rumpled suits and white shirts and ultra-straight postures that screamed out *intelligence agency*. Sean knew the specifics varied. Some would be MI5, some MI6, a few from the paranormal investigative agency W.H.O. But all were agents, looking-glass warriors who somehow didn't match the public's concept of the spy. In Sean's life, he'd met a couple of larger-than-life types—Nick Fury, head of S.H.I.E.L.D., came to mind—but no one as handsome, ruthless, and icily assured as Sean Connery or Roger Moore.

One particular man, with skin the color of bittersweet chocolate and a twitch in his left eye, met Sean's gaze. He sneered and mouthed an invective questioning Sean's ruggedness and parentage. Sean considered saying something. He heard the scrape of chairs as he stopped and contemplated the man.

Before a showdown was inevitable, a scotch-and soda voice, smooth and rough at the same time, called out, "Oi, Cassidy—over here!"

When the voice called out, the fight went out of Sean's opponent.

Turning, Cassidy saw a dark-haired man, handsome, with sharp features and a decided intensity. Like the others, the man was dressed in a black suit, white shirt, and Oxford tie, the shirt's collar unbuttoned. But there was something about the way this man wore them, a comfortable disdain suffusing the man that set him apart from his brethren. The man motioned to Cassidy with a long-fingered hand, said hand barely holding onto a cigarette with a too-long ash dangling on its tip. The man glanced around the bar and said, his voice dripping benign contempt, "It's okay, people—the screw's with me."

Sean walked over to the man's table. "Peter Wisdom?"

The slithering snakepit of gossip had fallen silent.

The man dug into his jacket pocket and flipped open a leather case. Inside was a familiar ID. "Yeah . . . Weird Happenings Organization. Fancy a pint?"

"No thanks," Sean responded, eyeing Wisdom carefully. "I make it a point not to drink in front of spies."

Wisdom's face curled into what possibly, after some debate, could be considered the thought of a smile. "Huh. I make it a point to always drink in front of spies." He motioned to the barman.

"So, Mr. Wisdom," Sean asked as he slid into his booth, "What's so blessed important that you had me come down to London?" Sean's hand instinctively reached into his pocket and slid his house keys in between his fingers. After losing his mutant sonic abilities, Cassidy had learned to rely on his street fighting knowledge. Which meant improvising.

Wisdom took a long drag off his silk cut. "The same thing we need every time we call on one of Xavier's people."

"It's been some time since—"

"I am aware of that, Cassidy. It's why I thought of you and not those Excalibur burkes." The barman placed a pint of bitters in front of the agent, causing that not-quite-smile to surface on Wisdom's face again. "Ta. You're a man who's been around Cassidy. You ever heard of Justin Hammer?"

"Industrialist, isn't he?"

"I'd have used the phrase 'rat-faced git,' but tastes vary. Interesting one, he is. His company was going under, so he plundered some Stark International technology and sold it to various sorry super-types across the world. Well, Iron Man put a right stop to that, and Hammer's decided to run back to Europe and set up shop here."

Sean studied the man across from him. There was something off about Peter Wisdom, besides his atrocious mode of dress. The way he talked, the way he carried himself, seemed designed to keep a lot of space—physical and emotional—between him and those around him. Sean tightened the grip on his keys.

"That's quite nice and all," he told the agent, "but why come to me?"

Peter met Sean's gaze and smirked. He produced a manila envelope and slid it Sean's way. "Take a look at this and ask me the same question."

Sean undid the clasp on the envelope. Inside were photos, grainy but recognizable for what they were: schematics, electronics diagrams, and blueprints. As Sean took in the distinctive purple color scheme, Wisdom added, "These were forwarded to us by MI6. The photographer, who was a decent sort, even if he did have a lousy taste in Scotch, was found drowned in the middle of a field. We figure one of Hammer's clients put him down as a make-good."

The plans Cassidy studied were for Sentinels—towering, mutant-hunting robots created years ago by an anthropologist named Bolivar Trask. They'd been re-created several times since by a variety of lunatics who wanted to wipe out mutantkind—the U.S. government being among that number. A wave of bad memories washed over Cassidy, and he muttered quietly, "Jesus wept."

"According to reports, Hammer sees us as the next big market for paranormal armaments. You've had firsthand experience with these things, Cassidy; just knowing their reputation, we want them to stay away from our shores. If we arranged a properly enormous payment for you and your ladyfriend's institute, could you help us shut the blighter down?"

"Has the Master Mold been built?"

"Intelligence indicates it has."

"Then it's deep, Mr. Wisdom. Master Molds have a way of getting away from their creators."

"Then help me, Mr. Cassidy."

Sean looked at the photos again. "May I keep these? I wish to consult with a friend of mine."

Wisdom waved them away and stubbed out his silk cut. "If your friend will help us wreck this one, go ahead."

Sean took another look at Peter Wisdom. The man was already reaching into his jacket for another cigarette. "I just don't understand why you didn't go to Excalibur with this, Mr. Wisdom. There are people on that team with more experience than me."

With a slight, satisfied curl of the lip, Wisdom uncovered a small silver lighter. "May be true, Cassidy, but they don't have your knowledge of covert intelligence. Besides . . ."

Wisdom leaned in closer, his voice dropping to a soft whisper. "I'll tell you a secret, shall I? W.H.O.'s on its last legs. They're being restructured, and there's been a lot of confusion as to what situations get looked at. Some files are falling through the cracks—"

"This isn't sanctioned, is it?" Cassidy said, meeting Wisdom's furtive glance.

There was a pause. Something flickered in the younger man's eyes—an odd darkness that made Cassidy pull back. Wisdom's face softened. His arrogant and obnoxious air seemed to evaporate in the dim lights of the pub. Still speaking in a conspirator's whisper, Wisdom simply stated, "It needs doing, don't it?"

The W.H.O. operative pulled back almost immediately. He took a long, deep drag of his silk cut and blew a plume of smoke. "Hammer isn't a fool. He's expecting Excalibur, not a retired leprechaun and a chain-smoking salary man. Can I count on you?"

Cassidy sat in the plane and wondered why he said yes. The plane, dark and sleek and vaguely manta-like in form, was waiting for him at an airstrip in Cardiff. Sean had dug an old S.H.I.E.L.D. uniform out of his closet, a relic from a long-ago training program. It still fit, even with the alarming snugness around his shoulders. Wisdom seemed to be wearing the same outfit as the day before, only more rumpled. He also seemed to have the same unpleasant attitude.

Cassidy and Wisdom sat opposite each other as a balding man in shirtsleeves rolled up beyond his elbows handed the agent a blue diskette. The man, whose name was Cully, was responsible for the relative lack of luxury they were sitting in. The dankness of the place, with its exposed struts and the constant thrumming of the baffled engines, made Cully's skin seem pale and ghost-like.

"Right," Cully said before wiping his nose with the back of his hand. "This virus should effectively slag any electronics run from Hammer's computer systems—including the Master Mold. Hammer's floating villa is anchored outside the five-mile limits, and our satellite is picking up cellular transmissions; he's making appointments with England's worst and ugliest—Slaymaster, the Crazy Gang, Jackdaw, the Hellfire Club . . . the whole lot."

Wisdom looked at Sean. "You've had experience with criminal

masterminds; how can they think they're traveling secretly when they're in a floating villa?"

Cassidy ignored the question. "When's the first client showing up?" he asked Cully.

"Late this afternoon. Tennis is apparently involved," Cully said between sniffles. "Time is of the essence, gentlemen. You will need to introduce that virus quickly, as well as destroy any hard copies in evidence."

"Fair enough. How d'we do it?" Cassidy adjusted the collar on his uniform; it was biting into his neck. *Faith, I'm gettin' too old for this*, he thought.

"Plan is," Wisdom said, "you and me drop down under radar cover and do a seek-and-destroy. We got W.H.O. helicopters waiting to close in for cleanup. You can support the two of us with that sonic scream, can't you, Cassidy?"

Cassidy leaned back and chuckled. "I would if I still had powers."

"Pardon?"

"My vocal chords were wrecked a while back—I overextended myself trying to save the world from another industrialist, name of Moses Magnum. Wasn't that mentioned in my file?"

Wisdom threw a nasty glance at Cully. "You would think that, wouldn't you?"

"I—I'll get the parachutes," Cully stammered.

As Cassidy took a secret pleasure from his discomfort Wisdom muttered, "I hate bollocky paratrooping insertions. Ruins all my silks."

"Half a bleedin' pack, lost!" Wisdom complained to Cassidy as the two men climbed out of their paratrooper overalls.

Cassidy wasn't paying attention. He was too busy being overwhelmed by the scale of Justin Hammer's efforts.

Back on the plane, when references were made to Hammer's villa, Sean thought it was some sort of euphemism. But, as they approached their target, just before he and Wisdom parachuted out of the stealth fighter, Cassidy realized he meant it literally.

Justin Hammer had brought his home along with him, carrying it on his back like a turtle.

The barge was a quarter of a mile long, a low, heavy thing of steel with a discreet wheelhouse at one end. Piled on top of the barge was an actual Victorian villa, riding on a gently sloping artificial hill that afforded the occupant marvelous sight lines. Surrounding this architectural anomoly was a landscaped topiary—hedges and trees and quaint dirt paths, all beautifully kept up. It was as if Hammer had taken a piece of the New England countryside whole and set it down on top of a ship.

Cassidy stashed his parachute in the nearby brush, all the while looking about. "This is madness."

"It is that," Wisdom said as he came up behind Sean. "And it works to our advantage, leprechaun. Nice thing about Hammer's taste for greenery is it provides wonderful cover."

"D'ye mind not calling me leprechaun?" Cassidy said after a pause.

Wisdom clapped him on the back. "Right, according to surveillance, the patrol's on the other side of the ship around this time—it's fairly minimal as it is. So let's see if Hammer wants some Girl Guide cookies."

Cassidy drew his pistol. "I'll go first."

Before Wisdom could respond, Cassidy took his first tentative steps into the brush. He wondered almost immediately if Wisdom should have been leading him; the man was a full-blown secret agent, and as such was still in touch with the latest techniques. But that jangling sense of distrust still occupied Sean's mind. Whoever Peter Wisdom was, he was only interested in his own counsel. And Cassidy wasn't willing to put his total trust in a man who seem to trust no one save himself.

They moved through the well-sculpted landscape quickly. Cassidy was awash in a sea of greenery lacking one thorn, one dead branch. Behind him, the W.H.O. agent kept pace. The man was good; if Cassidy wasn't aware of his presence going in, he would not have known Wisdom was there.

Their progress seemed to take a tension-filled eternity. As he made his way closer, Cassidy caught glimpses of the mansion. Cassidy went through possible Master Mold hiding places in his mind, wondering what access would be available. He wanted to get as much of the thought done in his head before the time came to destroy the thing.

It was during Cassidy's musings about the Master Mold that the guard got the drop on him.

Cassidy had just emerged from a thicket of trees onto a tamped down dirt trail. The hoofprints of shod horses ruined the perfect symmetry of the raked ground. Judging from the sounds of Wisdom's footfalls, he was a few feet behind.

"Hold it right there!" a voice barked at Cassidy's right. The accent was American, Brooklyn. . . . there was indication that the man's throat had been rubbed raw by too much alcohol and too many smokes.

Cassidy turned slowly, calculating his options. He held his pistol lightly, making sure his finger was nowhere near the trigger, and raised his hand. The man wore a battlesuit of green and teal (*teal*?) that obscured his features; even his eyes were concealed by opaque ruby goggles. He held a submachine gun tightly in his hands, keeping it trained at chest level.

The guard took in Cassidy's appearance and let loose with a particularly vile curse. "You're S.H.I.E.L.D.! What are you doing here?"

"Looking for a fourth for bridge, lad." Inwardly, Cassidy winced. *Did I actually say that?* His eyes scanned the area for something, anything he could use to his advantage. "It is 'lad,' isn't it? You don't sound verra old."

For a moment Cassidy swore he saw the guard take his attention off him. Then there was a crackling whistle to his right. A wave of warmth raked itself over Cassidy's rib cage. Streaks of bright orange flame resembling Day-Glo stained glass whipped past Cassidy and through the guard. Wisps of smoke rose from the thin burn marks, accompanied by a charred meat smell. The guard convulsed, his gun clattering to the ground before he collapsed.

"Might want to trade up," Wisdom suggested. Cassidy turned and saw the agent standing behind him, the fingers on his left hand slowing a deep, bright red.

"That explains the 'it needs doin' garbage," Cassidy mumbled as he went to examine his attacker. It was a formality. Cassidy had seen many dead bodies, some displaying wounds even more bizarre than the guard's. A series of very thin scorch marks, still painfully hot to the touch, riddled the man's chest. Judging from the damage and the smell, the boy was roasted from the inside.

Wisdom walked up behind him. "Take his submachine. It has to be better than what you're carrying. And see if he's got any cigs, eh?"

Cassidy faced the agent. Wisdom was casually rolling up his shirtsleeves. A chill climbed up the Irishman's spine by millimeters.

"D'ye mind? You killed the lad."

"I killed a threat to our mission."

"You didn't have to kill him, you idiot."

Wisdom met Cassidy's gaze. That softness Sean had seen at the pub had found its way to the surface again. "You were in trouble, leprechaun. I don't have pinpoint control over my powers. He would have killed you."

"You call me leprechaun again and I'll rip out your heart," Cassidy said quietly. "And saying that boy could've killed me is not the point."

"It is everything *and* the point, Cassidy," Wisdom said, closing distance. "You've been the prisoner of the Sentinels, what, twice now?"

Cassidy nodded.

"Well, I'm thinking *at this moment* that this burke is one of the burkes that are close to releasing that sort of pain on me and mine, Cassidy—and all in the name, not of some misguided vision, but of commerce! If I have to kill some guard who's just doing his job to keep the Sentinels from marching on Trafalgar Square, I'm going to bloody well kill him, age be damned." In spite of the vehemence of his words, Wisdom's voice was level, controlled, quiet.

"You're a cold monster, you are."

"Call me what you like. This needed doing."

There was movement in the brush, stealthy, careful movement. Sean Cassidy, former police detective, former Interpol agent, former subversive, a man who spent most of his life living under fire, registered it in the back of his head. It stayed in the back of his head, the anger boiling up inside him because of the man he was working with.

"I don't think you know what that means," he spat out. An expression of dismay flickered across Wisdom's face.

Tree branches rustled. There was the whispering *shurr* of dust being kicked up.

Wisdom brought up an accusing finger. "You don't know me. Remember that."

And then it was too late. Something padded into view behind Wisdom. It loped onto the path on thick, canine paws, an ill-formed skull resembling a pit bull's riding low on his thick neck. A massive barrel chest tapered into a slim abdomen. The two red glowing slits in place of eyes were the sort of thing every mutant brought with him to his nightmares, the misbegotten sons of Bolivar Trask come hunting. . . .

Cassidy pushed Wisdom down and reached for the dead man's submachine gun. Sean ignored the agent's curses as the canine Sentinel unit focused upon its prey, taking off at a run, small hatches opening up above its shoulders. Acting on instinct, Cassidy brought the gun up and let loose with a burst, the bullets spanging across the monster's snout and pushing it back. Cassidy fell to the floor, still squeezing the trigger, and saw a flash as a buttlet hit the exposed hatchway. Whatever was inside detonated, shredding metal and propelling its head forward as its body was blown back.

The skull skidded to a stop beside Cassidy, red eyes dimmed. The telltale sizzle of Wisdom's mutant powers hummed in the air. "What in the—" he exclaimed with bald-faced shock. Cassidy looked over his shoulder to see another purple-and-pink horror keel over as Wisdom's energy projections cut through armor plate and friend circuitry.

"Aim for the ribs!" Cassidy shouted as he refocused his attention—another was coming up the path, two of Hammer's goons taking up the rear. Cassidy rolled to the side of the path and squeezed off another round.

Sparks flew off the metallic hide of the approaching creature. Bullets richoceted, prompting the guard shepherding it to dive for cover. There was another wave of sizzling air above Cassidy's head, and another volley of Wisdom's heat platelets sped toward the Sentinel. The energy blades neatly sliced a portion of the creature's ear and shoulder like so much cold cuts. The creature stopped for a moment, then resumed its running gait.

"What the hell do you mean, 'aim for the ribs'?" Wisdom barked breathlessly.

"Mind your flank!" Cassidy took the creature's moment of hesitation to steady his aim. This time the stream of bullets peppered the Sentinel's underside. He heard a satisfying crack, pulling away quickly as one of the gunmen strafed a line of fire right in front of him. The canine Sentinel stopped in its tracks, its red eyes dimmed. Cassidy was elated. He swung his gun into position to focus on the guard to his left—

—and saw the brush was thick with teal-dressed guards. The report of weapons being primed was deafening.

Cassidy slowly turned around. The two of them were surrounded.

"All right, secret agent man," Cassidy said sarcasticly as he raised his arms over his head. "What do we do now?"

Wisdom shrugged. "Fall back on standards." With a sardonic grin, Wisdom called out to no one in particular, "Take us to your leader."

One thing Cassidy learned about his partner: The agent was not too fond of tennis whites.

"Can you believe this outfit?" he asked Sean for the seventh time.

"Sit down," Cassidy shot back. He concentrated on studying their prison. It wasn't too terrible, as far as cells went. In fact, it was an elegantly appointed guest room. The carpets were plush, the fixtures crystal and chrome, the furniture hand-tooled by the best European designers. Sean focused himself past Wisdom's grumbles. He concentrated instead on the results of a meeting he had the night before.

"This is wonderful," Wisdom hissed as he grabbed a cigarette from the teak presentation case by the armoire. "At least I can feed my habit."

"This isn't gonna help," Cassidy said softly as diagrams and charts went through his head.

The sound of the locks being undone quieted the men. Two of the guards entered, followed by a tall, elegantly dressed man in his early sixties. He strode into the room with an air of assurance to him, bordering on regalness. He looked from Cassidy to Wisdom and back with clear, intelligent blue eyes.

"You gentlemen," Justin Hammer said casually as he adjusted the lapels of his suit, "are seriously depleting my stock—which is not good, considering I have a demonstration to give tonight."

Wisdom shrugged. "Awful of us, eh?"

Hammer settled into the armchair opposite Cassidy. He stroked his chin thoughtfully. "Of course, the question is, what are you two doing here?"

Cassidy looked at the agent. "I thought we were looking for the squash court."

"Why do I need squash courts when I have a stable and a tennis court? Stick to the classics." Hammer fixed his gaze on Cassidy. "You—you are interesting. We found you wearing a S.H.I.E.L.D. uniform, yet my files show you've never been one of Fury's men. You were with Interpol, and later an X-Man, yes?"

"I was, yeah."

"Mmm. Lost your abilities stopping Moses Magnum, didn't you? Boorish sort. Horrible taste in champagne. Anyone for brandy?"

Cassidy shook his head. "No thanks, I'll pass."

"I've got my death of choice right here," Wisdom added, displaying the cigarette. Hammer focused his attention on the agent.

"And you—you're new, aren't you? Obviously, you're a mutant, but you don't show up in anyone's records: MI5, MI6, W.H.O.—"

Cassidy looked up. *Pardon?*

"—yet someone must be paying for your operation. Care to enlighten?"

Wisdom took a deep drag of his cigarette. "Nicotine Council. Don't like prats like you smoking. Gives us a bad image."

Hammer laughed. A third guard entered the room, a decanter of brandy and three balloon snifters balanced on a silver tray in his hands. "Ah, bravado. I would never have guessed." The industrialist poured a portion of the amber liquid into a glass and looked up. "Last chance, gentlemen."

"No thank you. I've learned my lesson about drinking with madmen," Cassidy said politely, his gaze flickering to Wisdom. The agent leaned against the armoire with his cigarette. "Tell me, Hammer—has the Master Mold been constructed?"

"Certainly it has, Mr. Cassidy. I need to start mass production at a moment's notice." The industrialist swirled the brandy in his glass, an expression of satisfied glee on his face.

"Then ye know the Master Mold has a history of turning on their creators."

"I do, Mr. Cassidy," Hammer replied between sips. "That is why I've taken precautions. Certainly, you and your unknown friend took notice of the radical redesign I did. The AI has been reworked to be much more manageable, disabling its intuitive process, which was a problem with previous models. I've altered the protocols in their programming, turning the burning desire to hunt mutants into a dull ache. On the other hand, I have retained much of the mutant recognition software—considering how prevalent mutant vigilantes are these days, I figured it would be a nice selling point."

"But you've built the Master Mold, you ponce," sneered Wisdom. "With the big dog in place, the AI is already expanding itself. You're going to learn quickly just how badly it's going to bite the hand that feeds it."

Hammer chuckled. "That is where you're wrong my friend. I have turned the scourge of the atom into humanity's lapdog. And I've turned a handy profit as well."

Handing his snifter back to his underling, Hammer rose. "You'd be surprised at the applications for this technology. The cybernetic implications alone will give us a tidy surplus." He once again studied both of his prisoners. "Still won't tell us what you're doing here?"

"Trying to figure out how big an idiot you are?" Wisdom suggested.

"Very well." Hammer turned to the attendant. "Contact Scarlotti. Have him flown in. We may have a nice, messy interrogation for him." Turning to Cassidy, he added, "I will return. I'd advise you to cooperate. It's so difficult getting blood out of white carpeting."

Cassidy watched Hammer lead his entourage out. The second the doors locked, he smiled and maneuvered the lock pick out of the space in his cheek. He knelt by the door and asked the agent. "What's your mutation, lad?"

Wisdom rolled his eyes. "Why don't you just wear a black turtleneck and watch cap while you're at it?"

"Your mutation, Wisdom!" Sean worked the tool around in the lock, shaking his head all the time at the idea of a man using an ordinary guest room for a jail cell. Of course, there would be a guard outside, armed. . . .

"I'm able to produce these 'hot knives,' thin platelets of superheated plasma."

Sean nodded. "Right, as I thought. Now listen to me. I took those photos to a friend of mine named Forge. There isn't anything this man doesn't know about machinery. Considering how primitive these plans were, chances are Hammer has Bolivar Trask models—the earliest Sentinels built. Trask needed enormous amounts of space for the weapons and mutant recognition software. That explains that rather broad chest construction. However, Hammer's designs are smaller; he already told us he modified the programming, and I'm positive he cleared out more space for better weaponry."

"Hooray for science," Wisdom sneered. He stood at the door, watching Cassidy with a distinct lack of interest.

"You might not be so doubting, Wisdom. Trask's models placed their sensor arrays in a nodule at the top of the rib cage. Judging from the response we got earlier, the sensors are still there. I suspect that's why the wee beasties have such a large chestplate. If Hammer sends any more after us, use your knives to smash the nodule and it'll be effectively blind. It'll shut itself down until repairs are made."

"And there's always those delightful weapon hatches," Wisdom offered dryly.

Sean heard the click of the lock pin being retracted. He rose and grabbed a lamp. Yanking the lamp free of the socket, he asked. "Can you use those 'hot knives' to disarm instead of kill?"

"It has been done."

Sean tied the lamp cord to the doorknob. "Then do."

With a silent pause to ready himself, Sean pulled the cord. The door opened soundlessly. Wisdom and Cassidy stood at either side of the doorjamb. Light from the corridor outside, harsh and artificial, streamed into the room. Cassidy counted the seconds. The reasons he originally agreed to play superspy with a loudmouthed chain-smoker in a foul mood drifted through his mind. As the seconds crawled, he looked at his decision from all angles, like a pragmatist, and came up with the same answer.

I'd still do this daft thing, Cassidy realized, *because it needs doing.*

A shadow crossed the long, thin rectangle of light. Another teal-and-forest–garbed employee of Hammer walked in tenatively, a wavering, "What the?" on his lips.

Wisdom didn't bother with a crack. He brought his fist down hard on the man's head, then pushed him down hard onto the carpeted floor.

Cassidy slammed the door and watched his partner kick the man's gun out of his hand. The hapless operative's weapon bounced on the carpet as Wisdom fell hard on the man, his knees landing squarely on his opponent's chest. Two shots to the head drove the guard deeper into unconscious.

Cassidy picked up the gun. "I said disarm!"

"He's disarmed, in'he?"

The guard stirred groggily, and got an elbow to the head for his troubles.

Wisdom got up and tore down the curtains. "Right, our time is limited before sleeping beauty is missed." He kicked the unconscious operative over and bound his hands and feet.

"Fine. Start shooting those knives of yours off the second we enter the corridor."

Wisdom checked his handiwork. "Right—confuse the infrareds."

Cassidy smiled. "You know the location."

Wisdom pointed to his skull, his hands glowing a dull orange. "Right here, mate."

"Then let's."

The corridors of the complex continued the hunting lodge motif of the building. There was something surreal about the wood paneling and soft lighting hiding a high-tech arms operation. Behind Cassidy, Wisdom muttered, "Now where is it. . . ." before slapping him on the back and pointing to the left. "This way."

Wisdom was off at a run, the hot knives shooting from his fingers at random directions. Cassidy allowed himself to drop behind the agent, looking over his shoulder frequently. An alarm sounded, as high and shrill as a child's scream.

For a long moment, the only sound in Cassidy's ears were the claxons and the sizzle of hot knives. Wisdom appeared to be mumbling under his breath, carrying on a conversation with himself.

More complaints about his cigarettes, more like, he thought to himself before gunfire rent the air above him. Spinning he saw two of Hammer's operatives, coming up fast. Cassidy's heart slammed against his rib cage as he aimed low and squeezed the trigger. A spray of bullets pinged directly in front of his pursuers, one ricocheting and embedding itself into a guard's thighs.

The afflicted guard fell to the ground in pain, while his partner let loose with another spray. Cassidy ran beside Wisdom now. There was a sudden, sharp, nasty pain in his arm. A line of blood slowly spread out to stain his tennis shorts. Sean returned fire and cursed.

"What?" Wisdom barked as another pair turned the corner in front of him. The agent let loose a volley of hot knives, cutting them down.

Turning, he did the same for the remaining gunmen.

"Nothing!" Cassidy hissed. "How much farther?"

"Around the bend and fifty feet!"

"Then let's!"

The warmth of Cassidy's blood trickled down his arm as the two men turned the corner. *Just a flesh wound*, Sean chanted silently as his partner blazed the trail. His mind was focused on the sound of footsteps, the discordant siren's shriek, the beating of his heart—anything but the sting of the divot taken out of his flesh.

Coming up quickly was a double doorway guarded by two of Hammer's men.

Instinctively, Wisdom shot a volley of hot knives through the one on the right, who was larger, taller, and better built than his compatriot. Closing distance quickly, the agent placed one hand, burning like an ember, in front of the surviving thug's face.

Wisdom's expression made his intent clear.

"Little pig, little pig, let me in," the agent snarled.

A new noise disrupted Cassidy's concentration as the terrified guard unlocked the doors. It was a heavy, insistant thunder, and all too familiar. Cassidy spun around to see a Sentinel dog coming up quickly.

"Faith, Wisdom, they've released the hounds," Cassidy gasped as he fell to the floor and started shooting. The bullets climbed up the monstrosity's leg in a shower of sparks. The dog continued moving in, its long, silvery tail curling upward. A corona of energy was forming around the tip.

The double doors opened. Wisdom pushed the guard inside and grabbed his gun. Cassidy shot again, this time sending bullets ricocheting off the dog's shoulder. The corona of energy gained a blinding intensity before a beam of pure white light seared across the distance. Cassidy rolled to the left, just in time for the beam to scorch an oval hole in the carpet where he was a second earlier.

"Inside, leprechaun!" Wisdom shouted as he fired off another set of hot knives, pushing the canine Sentinel back and shredding its head. The creature hesitated, then continued its loping stride.

"Stop callin' me that!" Cassidy shouted as he pulled back, heart pounding. The headless dog ate up the distance between it and its prey quickly. Raising his gun, Cassidy fired just as the technological hound leapt. There was the satisfying crack as a bullet smashed the plastic nodule. The Sentinel, now effectively blind, fell backwards into inactivity.

Cassidy swore and slammed the door. The place was cavernous, its ceilings soaring and filled with computer banks, testing equipment and various monitors. On one monitor, labeled B3, Cassidy saw an installation of steel girders and glass. The centerpiece of this facility was a canine Sentinel writ large, secured in place by wires and gantries. This was the Master Mold for this version, the macromodel that produced the normal-scale Sentinel units.

Wisdom stood in front of one terminal. "So this thing is the super-user mainframe," he muttered to himself before shouting, "Cassidy—have our prisoner put everything that's not bolted down in front of the doors."

"The Master Mold is here!" Cassidy shouted back. "I'm going to find the programming terminal and disable it." He grabbed the gun from the guard's hand and motioned toward the doors. "Ye heard the man," he growled. The nick he received from the bullet throbbed dully.

Wisdom stood before the main console muttering to himself. Cassidy inspected each terminal, trying to determine which one led to the Master Mold. He kept his gun trained on its former owner.

A small console in the back bore the B3 appellation. The password prompt flashed. Cassidy experimentally punch in a few guesses while Wisdom continued working. "Faith, man, I'm not a roboticist. I can't even get into the terminal!"

"Poxy instructions," Wisdom hissed under his breath before shouting, "Try 'Napoleon'—and look for the coolie vent. Should look like a large conduit surrounded by baffles."

"Napoleon?"

"Considering how obsessed this pillock is with his brandy, it's worth a shot."

Cassidy started plugging in phrases associated with liquor—then added tennis terms. Wisdom slid the virus disk into the superuser terminal and began typing furiously, muttering, "Slow down," at uneven intervals.

Cassidy switched his attention from the password prompt to the room. To his right, he saw a large metal cylinder taking up the length of the wall, thin metal panels surround it. "Found it!"

"Good, because whether we beat down the puppy or not, we're finishing up with Plan B. . . ."

Running out of tennis turns, Cassidy recalled the evidence of horses on the grounds of the villa. He started punching in horse riding terms furiously. "Plan B?"

Wisdom pressed a button on the superuser console.

Cassidy typed in the word LIPEZANER.

HELLO, MR. HAMMER, the terminal responded.

Wisdom smiled. "Plan B. B for 'blow everything up.' "

Thump!

The noise from the double doors caused both men to look up with alarm. Cassidy had the venting protocols called up on the screen. Wisdom returned to the superuser terminal, a string of invectives issuing from his mouth longer than a Welsh name. "Why won't this thing load? You have to keep them occupied, Cassidy!"

"Me? I'm about to shut down the Master Mold!"

At that point, several things happened. There was another thump, this one buckling the doors. Cassidy's attention went from the terminal to the doors just as the guard held prisoner screamed and launched himself at the Irishman. Cassidy went down hard, a throbbing pain in the back of his skull suddenly blossoming to keep the dull ache in his arm company. The guard punched Cassidy in the mouth, screaming unintelligibly. And all the while, Wisdom stood before the superuser console and swore at it.

Cassidy, feeling his jaw swell, brought his knee up hard into the thug's groin. The screaming stopped, and Cassidy could swear he saw surprise behind the man's red-tinted goggles. With a frustration and ferocity borne of the situation, Cassidy brought the gun butt hard into the side of the man's head.

For just a moment, as the lackey fell unconscious, Cassidy thought the loud report that accompanied his blows was just his anger contributing to the force of the swing. But once he pushed the man off him, Cassidy saw the real source of the cacophony—two more of the canine Sentinels, buzzing electronically in a way that sounded like they were growling.

"Yes!" Wisdom yelled, oblivious to the monstrosities behind him.

Cassidy got into a kneeling position and squeezed the trigger, sending a stream of bullets across the Sentinels' legs and snouts. The two moved back as one in response to the attack. One of the canine nightmares hunched down, allowing a panel to open up on its back.

"Wisdom! They're here!" Cassidy yelled. He spayed bullets at the armed Sentinel. Hot lead flew across the creatures' backs, some of the stray bullets spanging into the hatch. The overheating of the interior mechanisms caused the Sentinel to break in two under the force of the resulting explosion. Wisdom looked up, then back. He swore in a tone loud enough to echo off the walls. Spreading his arms wide, aiming one finger at the cooling vent, the other at the Sentinel, Wisdom let fly, sending hot knives into both objects.

Cassidy dived down as the platelets of superheated plasma jetted in his direction. He heard the satisfying crackling pop of the remaining Sentinel's sensor dome bursting, followed by a deafing hiss of steam directly behind him. Looking up, Sean saw the front half of the Sentinel scrabbling along on its two forepaws, obviously still locked in on his mutant signature. Cassidy ran backwards, aware of the damp heat of the punctured cooling vent, and shot again, chipping away at the robot's armor.

"On your feet, Cassidy!" Wisdom shouted over the noise. He had moved to the B3 teminal and punched in some commands. Spinning, he sent a set of hot knives hurtling into the Sentinel's head, slicing it to ribbons. Moving toward Cassidy, he put his hands together, grinned and shot a full complement of plasma into the now broken vent.

The whump of the energy striking home rang in Cassidy's ears. Wisdom grabbed Cassidy's hand and pulled him up. There was a series of smaller noises the Irishman found disturbing, followed by a changing of the steam into smoke. "Let's find us a support wall," his partner suggested.

The two ran out of the room. Cassidy felt his pain dull as another adreneline surge hit him. In the hallway, Hammer's lackeys were running around, leaderless and uncomprehending in the face of chaos. Cassidy let fly with another short burst to push them back just as an explosion under their feet shook the whole mansion. "Every man for himself!" he advised the hapless Hammer employees.

Wisdom scanned the area for an exit. The quiet country-club–like atmosphere of Hammer's hideaway was being pushed aside for the ambiance of a war zone—shattered glass, falling masonry, flames, and thundering noise. Cassidy was surprised to find himself calm in the middle of all this. He was intimate with this sort of catastrophe; a similar act of destruction took his wife away from him. That he was the cause of this glimpse into hell occurred to him, but Sean continued telling himself the cause was just—as was the cause that cost him his powers.

"Window!" Wisdom shouted over the thunder. Smoke obscured their vision. As they rushed to the glass gateway to safety, Cassidy tried desperately to figure out what floor they were on.

"Faith!" Cassidy exclaimed as they came up fast on the window. He threw up his hands as they hit the barrier. "I'm gettin' too old for this!"

He felt the glass shatter and give way, some of it slashing through the cloth of his outfit. Cassidy felt for one blissful moment that sense of weightlessness he used to experience when he flew on waves of sonic energy. But then the ground came up to meet him and he landed hard, tumbling end over end out onto the perfectly manicured lawn.

Sean sat there for a moment, feeling the adrenaline high slowly leech out of him, restoring the varied aches and pains he was able to focus beyond moments before. He looked back at Hammer's home; thick smoke billowed from the openings, and an ominous groaning rumble was increasing in volume.

"Eight-point-eight by fifty-one! Prepare Cape Clear landing port! Situation Red!" Wisdom shouted, apparently to thin air, before turning to Cassidy and saying, "No time for woolgathering, man, we have to run!"

Cassidy got to his feet and took off after the retreating agent. Wisdom repeated his curious statement, and headed for the tennis courts.

"What the hell are you doing?" Cassidy shouted as the red clay of the playing field came into view.

"Subdermal transmitter," Wisdom shouted back. "Kept us in contact with Cully. Have to get the damn thing out once we're safe; it's like having a poxy beesting on your jaw that won't go away!"

A small flight of stairs led to the courts. Off in the distance, a helicopter was speeding to their position. Cassidy looked at his partner, feeling every single one of the cuts and bruises and bumps he had earned doing what needed doing. "And that time in the main computer room—you were consulting with Cully?"

Wisdom raised an eyebrow. "You think I was talking to myself?" he asked, taking a moment to catch his breath. "You are a right toerag sometimes."

Another explosion could be heard in the distance, this one powerful enough to cause the trees to shake. The two looked back and saw a column of oily, black smoke where the mansion once stood. Cassidy couldn't help but smile, even as he calculated the number of hours his present lover, Dr. Moira MacTaggart, was going to spend berating him for his wounds. The aircraft moved closer, and Cassidy could hear the thrum of its rotors over the flickering of the flames.

But there was another noise—hoofbeats, heralding the arrival of a horse, upon which sat Hammer. To Cassidy's amazement, even though the man was covered in dirt and grime, he still managed to appear elegant.

"This is not good," Cassidy said.

Following Hammer out of the woods was a cadre of a half-dozen torn, tattered, and aching gunmen. With their soiled, ripped uniforms and unsteady gaits, they did not look happy to be in their boss's employ at this moment. Hammer brought his mount to the tennis court's edge.

"You had to go and muck things up," spat out Justin Hammer.

"Of course, you poncy tosser," Wisdom spat back. "That's our job."

Before the gunmen could advance, the agent laid down a spray of hot knives at their feet. The helicopter was on top of them now, and a rope ladder was being thrown down.

"I will make certain you pay for interfering in this operation, sir," Hammer said.

"How? You and your ragamuffin brigade aren't a threat anymore—just a toerag sitting on a pile of broken masonry. And you can't believe those lager louts are going to impede our flight into the sunset."

The industrialist's face reddened. "You ruined my home!"

Cassidy smiled as he grabbed hold of the ladder. Shouting over the sound of the rotors, he said, "And what evidence d'ye have, boyo? I'm willing to bet all your security tapes are up in smoke."

Sean began climbing the ladder to freedom. Wisdom laid down another blanket of hot knives, singing the lawn at the edges of the tennis court. As he grabbed onto the lowest rung, the agent laughed and said, "Go on back to America, you git. Your homeland doesn't want you."

And then the rumpled looking Brit followed Cassidy up the ladder.

This time, Cassidy agreed to have a pint with the agent. Wisdom was dressed as he was when first they met, the degree of disorder inherent in his dress unchanged. There was a lot less tension in the air this time, as if the other intelligence agents realized that Wisdom had accepted Cassidy as one of them. They clinked glasses before drinking. The toast was silent. Cassidy's involved a wish that he never did anything that foolish again.

"Reports indicate that Hammer has turned his operations around. He's America's problem once again," Wisdom remarked.

"Do ye think the Master Mold is gone?"

"Rather. We overheated that place's power plant. Anything needing temperature regulation is useless now."

"If you say," Cassidy remarked. "I just don't want to think about those things again."

"Wish I had the luxury, Cassidy." Wisdom checked his watch. "I have a meeting with Stuart in fifteen."

"The W.H.O. head?"

Wisdom nodded. "Wants a debrief. Ask me, he's going to just burden me with paperwork. I'll find some way to get out of it, though."

Wisdom walked into the main meeting room of the Spire, the obsidian building that housed the offices of Black Air. Very few outside the building had heard of the organization, and then only in whispers; there were even some government officials unaware of the purpose of the irregularly shaped office tower that threw its shadow over North London. Wisdom's heels clicked on the floor as he approached three men with predatory eyes sitting on a raised dais.

Wisdom produced the diskette from his jacket and placed it on the dais. He averted his eyes from the gaze of his superiors. "There you are—all the schemata and information Hammer had on Sentinel technology."

The middle official, tall and spider-thin, retrieved the diskette with insectile fingers. "vErY gOoD, WiSdOm. We ArE pLeAsEd."

The man on the left raised one bushy eyebrow. "Your cover to the Cassidy man is intact?"

"Had no reason to think otherwise," offered Wisdom in a voice as brittle as old leaves.

"Proceed to Omega branch, Agent Wisdom," added the man on the right in a phlegmy voice. "There have been developments in the Cyttorak situation."

Wisdom pulled out a cigarette and lit it. "Right. Top man, that's me."

He headed out, thinking all the while, *I'm getting too moral for this.*

The Stranger Inside

Jennifer Heddle

"It is hard to fight an enemy
who has outposts in your head."

—Sally Kempton

May ~~12 13~~

Tuesday

For crying out loud, I don't even know what the date is today. I bet Storm or Alex would know, but I'm not about to make a fool out of myself by asking. It doesn't matter what day of the month it is, anyway, or even what month it is in the first place. Everything's always the same here, day in and day out. It's enough to make a girl crazy.

Heck, maybe I *am* crazy, to even be thinking about writing in here. I'm still not sure why I'm doing it. Professor Xavier told me a long time ago that keeping a diary might help me deal with all the stuff going on in my head, but I laughed at him back then, thought he was the crazy one for suggesting I write anything more complicated than a grocery list. Now though, things are different. The Professor's gone, and, well, maybe this is the least I can do for him since I wasn't real great to him when he was here. Better than nothing, right?

Who am I kidding? The truth is, Inferno really did a number on me, what with members of the team turning against each other, that horrible evil I felt when I kissed Warren Worthington, my showdown with that demon, Nasty—and I guess it can't hurt to try using a diary to help me sort things out. Besides, it's not like the rest of the X-Men are falling all over themselves to take my mind off things or help me feel better.

I found this notebook in an abandoned room in the ghost town where we're living right now, me and the rest of the X-Men. The Reavers left it a shambles when they cleared out but there's lotsa buried treasure to be found if you look hard enough. There were a bunch of recipes scribbled on the first few pages but it was all for food I'd rather die than eat so I just ripped them out and threw them away where no one'd find them because I didn't want Psylocke getting her hands on them and making us alligator stew for dinner. Yuck! Times like this I really get homesick for Mississippi. No one in the whole Outback can

183

make fried chicken worth anything and sometimes I think I'd beg, borrow, or steal for a real sweet potato pie.

Geez. Is this what I'm supposed to be writing about? Food? The Professor's not here to tell me what's right and I don't know what I'm doing. Maybe I should just give up now before I do something really stupid.

Friday

Well I'm back. I don't like to think of myself as a quitter so I'm not going to give up on this even if I'm the only one who knows about it.

The Professor told me way back when that I should try writing down my feelings about Carol Danvers being trapped inside my head, but the problem is I don't *understand* what I'm feeling half the time. Right now all I know is that I'm sick of her being in my head and taking over my life. I don't want her here, I didn't ask for it. But I don't see that there's anything either one of us can do about it any time soon.

Storm's yelling for a team meeting, so I gotta go. At least she still considers me part of the team. I guess that's something.

May 16

What a wonderful surprise!

This journal I discovered in Rogue's possession brings back long-forgotten memories of my childhood. I used to hide up in my room on rainy afternoons, recording my hopes and dreams in the diary I'd bought with my allowance money. I remember that it was small, hardbound, and white, with pink roses etched around the border, and of course a shiny gold lock with a key to keep my secrets safe from the rest of the family. It made me feel so important, to have a lock and key of my very own.

I have to laugh now at the thought of what I used to write in those pages. I can remember with surprising clarity my girlish plans for an ideal future: marry a doctor or a lawyer or a military man like my father, have a brood of children, and live in an elegant colonial home on the outskirts of Boston or Washington, where I would host tea parties and be the chair of the local PTA. Such "normal" ambitions! They seem more like fanciful pipe dreams, now. And I have not had room in my life for pipe dreams for a very long time.

Not that I ever could have predicted how the cards of my life would be dealt—Kree powers, a stint with the Avengers, giving birth to Marcus, and now this: trapped in the body of a mutant. My life—my very being—has been forcibly taken from me and I fear I will never be whole again. Instead I lurk in the recesses of Rogue's mind, waiting for the occasional opportunity to take control, to try to construct some semblance of a life. Not that it's much of a life in any case, since I can't even touch anyone skin to skin—Rogue's bizarre mutant power sees to that.

Where are those white picket fences and car pools now? Sometimes I think I'd trade my soul for a station wagon. Even one of those horrible wood-paneled ones.

Monday

GET OUT OF HERE! Why do you have to be *everywhere*? Can't I have something, anything for myself? *Anything?*

Tuesday

I can't believe the nerve Carol has, writing in here. I'm not sure how much more of this I can take. I'm not even alone in my own body and I never know when Carol is going to take over and banish me to the back corners of my mind and I'm starting to feel like I really could split in two, into two different people, not just two minds but two bodies and even then I'd *still* have her in my head all the time. I keep having nightmares about it. I was hoping they'd stop coming so much when I started writing stuff down in here, but it hasn't helped yet. Maybe the Professor really was wrong about this.

May 20

Well, it seems that Rogue has not taken kindly to my "intrusion." I suppose I should once again remind her that it is her fault I'm trapped in here, and that if we can share a body—no matter how difficult that may be—we should somehow be able to figure out how to share the pages of a black marble notebook.

I was foolish to forget that Rogue couldn't care less what I think, or how I feel.

I am an invader in her life and nothing more. Still, I wish she'd keep in mind how I wound up here in the first place.

On a lighter note, it could have been worse—at least she didn't, in the midst of her rage, hurl this notebook out her window like some sort of projectile weapon and hurt somebody. Not everyone on the team is as impervious as Colossus, and Rogue's strength (stolen from me, I might add), already gets her into enough trouble as it is.

You stole my life, Rogue; now I'm stealing some pages of your notebook. It seems like an uneven trade to me, with you still holding on to the advantage.

Thursday

Fine. So Carol thinks she can take over this diary just like she takes over everything else in my life. Leech. I'll just ignore her, is all. She can write whatever she wants but I don't have to read it. This is *my* notebook. I found it first.

Little Miss Perfect. I bet she doesn't even mind being stuck out here in the middle of nowhere, as long as she's got the other X-Men around. I get so jealous when they bring Carol up—I know they like her better than they like me. I just wish they weren't so darn obvious about it. I put my life on the line just as much as anybody else, but I'll never be able to live down my past.

I'm not throwing myself a pity party. Most of the time things are fine, really, but sometimes . . . well, sometimes I miss my foster mother, Mystique. At least I knew that she cared about me, even if she did have kind of a funny way of showing it.

May 26

Rogue threw a little tantrum today, so I took over for a while to give her a chance to cool off. It seems that she got into a heated argument with Alison Blaire and it almost escalated into physical violence. Dazzler is one of the more formidable X-Men, but I'm not sure that even her impressive powers would win out over Rogue's (my) brute force in a one-on-one match. I don't know why Rogue does this; not only does she regret it later, but it doesn't win her any points with the others, either. For someone who worries so much about fitting in, and I *know* she does, she doesn't make much of an effort to play nice.

As for me, I am more and more grateful for the companionship of my friends: Storm, Elisabeth, Logan, and the rest. Storm in particular helps me to get through each day. She is so . . . serene, in an almost otherworldly fashion, and that serenity has a way of rubbing off onto those around her. I've seen her calm Wolverine down from one of his rages with only a few words, and there are few people who can claim a talent for taming that beast. Rogue would do well to be more open with Storm, more trusting. Storm is used to being an outsider, and if approached the right way, just might take Rogue under her wing, given time. But ever since the events of Inferno (and believe me, I am thankful I didn't have to bear the brunt of that trauma), Rogue has been so raw, so wounded . . . I can only hope she starts the healing process soon, before someone gets hurt.

Monday

Well I blew it, again. Got into a tangle with Dazzler and everyone took *her* side, of course. It started out innocent enough—I told Longshot I was keeping a diary and he'd never even heard the word before, can you believe that? So I was having a grand old time explaining it to him when Alison showed up and gave me a hard time. Things went from bad to worse real fast after that. Can't she leave him alone for one minute? You'd think I was bouncing on his lap the way she got her back up like a polecat in heat. Like I *could* seduce him even if I wanted to.

(Hell, maybe I do want to. But nobody has to know that but me. And I guess Carol will know if she reads this but so what. I'll put down my secrets and she'll put down hers and we'll both be just as unhappy as when we started. Together but alone, as usual.)

I wonder how long it'll be before Storm kicks me off the team and makes me fend for myself. Heck, I wonder why I don't just beat her to the punch and have Gateway send me somewhere far away from here.

But where would I go? Mutants aren't safe anywhere, especially when they're on their own. Besides, I bet as soon as Carol took control of my body again she'd come right back to Australia.

I'm just so tired of them hating me.

Thursday

I can't believe that cold-blooded snake in the grass. She went shopping with Dazzler and Betsy yesterday and brought back some of the ugliest clothes I've ever seen—pleated skirts, boring blouses, frilly dresses . . . I can't stand the thought of my body in those rags! Ugh! I'm tempted to burn them.

Guess I'll have to accidentally on purpose forget to do the dishes this week. I know how that makes her nuts.

June 3

I am continually appalled at the slovenly mess of Rogue's (our) living quarters. I cleaned the place from top to bottom today, although I almost gave up when I discovered that she'd torn up my new clothes and threw them in the garbage. But I do live here, too, and I just couldn't deal with the filth anymore. This is supposed to be a home, not a zoo.

One good thing about being able to fly—you can even wipe the cobwebs out of the corners of the ceiling! Now if I can just get Alison to take me shopping again—not that I think *that* will be a problem. Alison Blaire? Shopping?

It feels so good to laugh . . .

Tuesday

The place is so clean I don't even recognize it. Does she expect me to thank her? She's gonna have a long wait.

Thursday

Longshot and me went for a walk today. Somehow I managed to get him by his lonesome and we wandered around the outskirts of town for a while. I tried to talk him into taking his motorcycle for a spin but he didn't want to, guess he needs things to be quiet sometimes. I can understand that better than anyone. He was in one of his moods, where he's thinking about something serious and nobody can figure out what's the matter and he won't tell nobody what's wrong. So I thought maybe he'd talk to me if we got away from the others. Heck, I got through to Gateway, once. Longshot should be a snap compared to that old aborigine, right?

Even though I tried my best to draw Longshot out he didn't say much, but it was nice keeping company with him anyway. The conversation went something like this:

Me: Are you feeling okay, sugar?

Him: Fine. Thanks.

Me: Sure there isn't anything you want to talk about?

Him: I'm sure. Thanks.

Me: The sky sure is a great color green today, isn't it?

Him: Yeah. Thanks.

Oh well, can't blame me for trying. On our way back to town we found some pretty wildflowers that he put in my hair for me, careful not to touch my skin of course. The reds and blues and purples stood out real nice against my brown and white mop. Longshot must've thought so too because he kept staring at me. I was in a real good mood about it until we got back and I saw Alison scowling at us. Kept the smile on my face though and didn't say anything nasty. Waited until I could come back here and write about it instead.

She can touch him. I can't. So why is she jealous? It's not like she would want to trade places with little ol' me, is it? Hah. That's almost funny. Almost.

June 10

Poor Rogue. I know that she has a crush on Longshot, but she must realize by now that crushes are fruitless for someone with her (our) cursed power. Besides, it is obvious to anyone who takes the time to look that Longshot and Dazzler are desperately in love, even if they aren't yet aware of it themselves.

I wonder if Rogue will ever find someone who will look past her skin and love the woman on the inside. And if I'll still be trapped in here when she does.

To be honest, I don't know how she's lived this way for so long. *I want to be touched.* Is that horribly selfish of me, to have these moments of weakness, when I block out the constant danger around us and daydream instead, dream of a strong hand touching me in the dark, of warm, soft lips touching mine, of hot fingertips caressing my bare skin? Am I a horrible person just because whenever I do see Dazzler and Longshot together I envy them so much that my vision turns red?

I need, I want . . . I want to feel hardened chest muscles beneath my fingers. I want to touch the firm planes of a man's abdomen, the soft down of his hair. I want to smell that indefinable . . . *maleness*, that musky yet sweet scent that drives me just a little mad. I want to breathe it in and out and feel it course through me. I want to feel the heat between our bodies when a man hovers over me, his forearms guarding my chest, his legs framing mine.

In a way I pity Rogue, who has never known the touch of a man, who has never surrendered to the oblivion that love can bring. But in another way I think she has it easy, since she doesn't know what she's missing. I find myself getting lost in remembrance sometimes, and it's all I can do to keep from screaming in frustration. Is it truly better, to have these memories, knowing that I won't be able to experience those feelings ever again? Perhaps Rogue has the better end of the deal on this one.

Friday

I haven't been reading what Carol writes in here for a while because I don't really care, but today I peeked and I wish I hadn't. Going on and on about love, like that's all she can think about. She doesn't know the half of it. The only time I ever kissed a boy because I wanted to he went into a coma, and she thinks she has problems? Spare me the "poor little Carol" act.

At least she knows how it feels, to have someone touch you like that. I've seen movies and read books and stuff but I can only imagine what it's really like to . . . to . . . I can't even write it down! It's too embarrassing, since I'll never be doing it.

Sunday

You know what? I'm used to being alone. I've been doing it for so long that I don't even think about it anymore, it's like breathing or not touching people, it's just second nature to me. People try to talk to me or be nice and I snap at them or bite their heads off or tell them to get lost. And then I sit here wondering what I did to get them all hot and bothered. What the hell is the matter with me? Am I that afraid of someone getting too close to me that I push everyone in the opposite direction? Is it my own fault that I can't really call any of the X-Men my friends? Carol always seems so confident when she talks about her friends, or her old lovers. I wonder what it's like, to be so sure of who you are and where you came from and who will be in your corner when things get tight. I don't have Mystique anymore, I don't even have the Professor. How does she lean on people so easily? Who do I have to lean on?

June 19

Rogue is apparently jealous of my confidence—I wish I could tell her face to face that there's no reason for her to feel this way. She holds all the cards, and has ever since that day on the bridge in San Francisco when she stole everything from me. Self-confidence? Please. I'm not even sure of who I am anymore.

Perhaps I should explain. I've been feeling, well, *incomplete* lately, even when I am the one in full control of this body. The other day I tried to remember the last time I saw my brother Steven, and came up empty. I remember him, and our relationship, and the fact that he died in Vietnam, but that final meeting with him is no longer within my grasp. What does it mean? Did Rogue perhaps take some of my memories into herself, never to return them? Does she even now have a mental catalogue of the significant events of my life that are lost to me forever? Or is this some personal failing on my part, an inability to keep close all the memories that I hold so dear? Or maybe, just maybe, it is the beginning of the end—the first step down a road toward becoming completely submerged in the depths of Rogue's psyche, never to resurface.

It's a riddle I am loath to answer. I don't know if it's a result of the psychic transference I experienced when Rogue absorbed my essence into herself, or if maybe I have had a hole inside of me all along, a hole that needed to be filled, and now never will be.

Maybe a trip to New York would help clear my head. I'll see if Storm could spare me for a day or so in the near future.

June 22

God, I'm so depressed today. Sad and lost. I'm not sure why, but it's smothering me.

Well, Raven, you have finally gotten your revenge on me, haven't you? It was your own foster daughter who trapped me in this hell. Congratulations; the victory is yours.

I hope you choke on it.

Sunday

I had a talk with Storm today. I'm not sure what brought it on. Maybe it's because I saw what Carol wrote a couple weeks ago about how I should try giving Storm a chance. Maybe it's because I've been feeling even more down than usual lately, and I know that Carol has too. I don't know. But Storm and I talked, and no one's more surprised than me, but it went well. Storm said something really smart, and let me make sure I get this right:

You can't love other people until you love yourself.

I've heard it before, of course, but somehow when Storm says it there's more wisdom in the words. Must be a holdover from that weather goddess racket she had going on in Africa.

I thought about what she said for a while, and then I went and sat with Gateway for a couple of hours. The quiet company was just what I needed. When he started playing his flute I imagined that the music was making all my problems go away.

The problems are still there, of course. But for those precious moments, they didn't exist. I'll take what I can get.

July 3

I guess Rogue isn't the only one willing to take advice these days. I went to visit Gateway myself, this evening. I sat there with him on his plateau and watched as the sun sank below the horizon, flooding the sky with purples and pinks and harsh streaks of orange. The sunsets out here are unlike anything I have seen—wild and untamed, just like the terrain they shadow. They are awe-inspiring and humbling all at once.

Gateway, of course, took it all in with impassivity. He has seen similar sunsets hundreds of times and will most likely see hundreds more. I wonder if he truly has become accustomed to the sight or if his placid countenance masks a continuing reverence. I suspect and hope it's the latter.

There's nothing quite like a sunset to put yourself and your problems into perspective. Even after we have all come and gone the sun will continue to rise and set. The thought didn't make me sad, as it once might have, but instead infused me with an unaccustomed sort of peace. There is comfort in the eternal, I suppose.

Monday

Something funny happened today.

I took my body back from Carol during dinner a few hours ago. I was tired of being shut out and so with one giant *push*, bam! I was back in control. The only thing is, Carol was in the middle of eating pea soup, and I *hate* pea soup, and I spit it all over the place and almost choked on it and wound up covering poor Petey with green goop.

I guess it doesn't sound funny when I just write it down like that, but the thing was that everyone started laughing, even Petey. Not laughing at me, but along with me, and then I was laughing too, and suddenly I felt like maybe I did belong there after all.

Wednesday

I wonder if it would make Carol feel better if she knew that I would give all of her memories and her life back to her if I could. I hate her being in my head all the time, don't get me wrong, but even so I'm not the same person who attacked her in San Francisco. If I had to do it all over again I wouldn't make the same choices. I've changed. I hope she realizes that.

July 8

You know what, Rogue? I do know that you've changed. And I understand that you're suffering, too.

But I'm not letting you off the hook, and I never will. Your regrets don't change the fact that this situation is your fault. It just means that we've all made mistakes, and this one was a doozy.

I can't promise to like you, but I can try to hate you a little less. And I hope that's an arrangement we can finally both live with.

Thursday

I don't think I really need to write in here as much anymore. Things are better with the X-Men, the memories of all that went down with Inferno are finally starting to fade, and as for me and Carol . . . well, I don't think we'll ever truly get along, but we'll get by. For now, anyway.

I think the Professor would be proud, if he knew. Maybe, wherever he is, he does know. I hope so.

Once a Thief

Ashley McConnell

THE SUNLIGHT WAS WARM and golden in the little patio of the hôtel. A lattice of wooden strips striped uncertain shade across the half-dozen round tables scattered over the red cobblestones. At this hour, the patio was half empty. Even the bees were considering a midmorning nap.

Remy LeBeau leaned back in his wrought-iron chair and surveyed the other occupants of the little courtyard through half-closed eyes. His fingers, long and limber, tore restlessly at a croissant, flicking crumbs at small, fat birds who chirped at his feet, complaining when the shower of largesse slowed.

He glanced down as the chirping became even more demanding, and found the croissant had been reduced to its component flakes.

The last time he had stayed here he'd been much more satisfied with his world. That was why he'd returned, after all—this place, a nameless little hôtel in the little town of St. Chinien in the south of France, was one he associated with a feeling of solid satisfaction and well-being.

It was a feeling he couldn't quite nail down this time.

"More coffee, *m'sieu?*"

The birds had flown away, indignant.

Part of that feeling of well-being, of course, was associated with the pert, blue-eyed Madelaine, who smiled down at him with the coffee and anything else he might desire or offer.

Madelaine was only sixteen, and he responded to her as he always did, with a lazy flirtatious grin and a knowing wink. Madelaine giggled and blushed and poured another cup of strong coffee. At least that hadn't changed. The coffee was always strong, and Madelaine always flirted. He smiled as she turned back to the kitchen, her skirts swishing violently back and forth.

Those blue eyes—looked like Xavier's. Bright, sharp, intelligent eyes.

Honest eyes.

Xavier.

LeBeau stretched uncomfortably.

"How d'you manage it?"

LeBeau didn't bother to look up at the man who cast the solid shadow across his table. Every ointment had its fly, and this was the fly in the St. Chinien ointment. Even this fly wasn't all bad—the last time he'd been here he had taken great pleasure in swatting it.

Every time he came here he indulged himself, come to think of it.

Heaving a sigh, he took a cigarette from a pack on the table, lighted it in a leisurely fashion, and exhaled a long stream of blue smoke before looking up. "Manage what, *mon ami?*"

The other man moved around the table, letting the sunlight fall across LeBeau's eyes, and scraped a chair over the cobbles to sit across from him.

"You'd think they'd look deep in your bloody eyes and run like all the devils in hell were after them. Instead they melt in your arms. Or is that another one of your mutie talents? Seduction?"

LeBeau smiled and exhaled again, deliberately directing the smoke into the other man's face. "One cannot account for what attracts de ladies, *mon ami*. Other dan deir good taste, of course. I note you are unaccompanied, still?"

The other man grimaced and changed the subject. "So what are you celebrating this time, Gambit? Let's see, the last time it was the Heilston jewels, wasn't it?"

LeBeau merely lifted an eyebrow.

"Little Madelaine lost the earrings you gave her, you know. Careless little girl. Had no idea what they were worth, of course. Probably dropped them in the hay somewhere."

LeBeau shrugged.

"Time before that it was the last will and testament of the Vicountess Liverakos, wasn't it? The heirs paid a very pretty penny to have that one back."

A line of ash drifted to the ground. LeBeau's face remained impassive.

"But those things were quite some time ago, weren't they?"

The other man was well dressed, his clothing of best quality. Gambit's eyes ticked over him, noting one by one the signs of affluence: the gold Patek Phillipe watch, the bespoke tailoring, the handlasted shoes, the perfectly trimmed mustache.

But there were dark lines beneath Richard Reynaud's fingernails, and that mustache failed to hide the flash of a gold cap on one of Reynaud's upper front teeth as he grinned unpleasantly at the impassive LeBeau.

"Mutie," the other man whispered, enjoying the sound of the word. "I always said that was the only reason you got anywhere."

"Oh, p'rhaps a little knack for picking d'locks has somet'ing to do wit' it, *non*?" LeBeau said, deliberately slurring his words with a thicker-than-usual overlay of his native Cajun accent.

Predictably, the mangling of his beloved mother tongue outraged Reynaud even more than LeBeau's bland façade.

"Merde," he said at last. "Why have you come here, mutie? I know you. I know every job you've done—and *haven't* done—in the past three years. And lately you haven't done anything at all, have you?"

While the other man, of course, had made at least seven major scores in the past three years. Remy LeBeau, the mutant called Gambit, silently recounted them to himself. Old Master paintings, gold, jewels, *objets d'art*. Yes, Richard Reynaud had done quite well for himself.

While he, Gambit, had been rather distracted of late. Never even finished his last job; there had been a little matter of saving a white-haired child from the Shadow King. And since then . . .

"Retired, have you?" Reynaud said.

Behind him, Gambit saw Madelaine peek out of the restaurant doorway, catch sight of Reynaud, hesitate and withdraw. A young couple, newlyweds, based on their billing and cooing, came into the patio and took a table at the far end, nuzzling and giggling together.

"That's why you've come, isn't it? To finally admit which of us is the better man?"

Gambit's eyebrow climbed very high indeed. "De better *man, mon ami*? Dere is no question, I t'ink!"

Reynaud's face turned bright red as he leaned across the table. "You come here time after time to celebrate your successes, *mon ami*, to throw them in my face, but this time you have *nothing* to celebrate. I have said for years that you are a freak, a mistake, a blight on our profession. Your ridiculous Guild, your joke of a family—"

LeBeau raised a warning hand, and the other man sat back.

"You know better dan to bring de Guild into dis," he said, very mildly. Not to mention—so he did not—his family.

Reynaud snorted. "This is my territory, and you know it, LeBeau. You've been coming here for years to gloat. But you're a mutie and a disgrace. You couldn't even—" he spluttered, searching for a sufficiently degrading action, and looked wildly around, finally focusing on the couple across the courtyard. "You couldn't even steal that woman's wedding ring!"

Despite himself, Gambit found himself glancing in the woman's direction. She was flaunting a very nice set of rings indeed, with diamonds that caught and broke the light into rainbows. He noticed her shoes and dress, its hem a bit frayed.

"Dey've put all *leur argent* into dose rings," he observed softly. "Every penny."

Reynaud snorted. "Let me guess. You think it's not *galant*? They're little fools with jewels too good for them. And you're a fool as well. Look at you, the famous LeBeau, the famous Gambit. *Mutant.* You can't do it." He got to his feet, the chair sliding back across the cobbles with a shriek of abused iron. "I still say you came to acknowledge your master."

"Je vous verrai dans l'enfer d'abord," Gambit responded pleasantly. *I'll see you in hell first.* He could speak good French, Parisian even, when he chose.

Reynaud snorted and stalked away.

"C . . . coffee, *m'sieu*?" Madelaine was not at all certain of her reception.

"Merci."

But he wasn't really seeing her. He wasn't even really seeing the couple across the courtyard, who finally noticed the red-eyed man staring blankly at them and decided to take their affection indoors.

He was seeing Xavier's blue eyes. Storm's. The fiery, passionate Rogue. The short, massive bundle of outrage that was Wolverine, the annoyingly righteous Scott Summers.

They were mutants, all of them. No one there had found anything remarkable about his red and black eyes, his ability to channel biokinetic energy. They all had mutant abilities of their own, and he was one of them. He was welcome to be one of them. One of Xavier's X-Men.

Except he wasn't, of course. He was Gambit—thief, scion of the Thieves' Guild of New Orleans, acknowledged among them as one of the very best.

Of course, behind his back they called him *mutie*, but never to his face.

The X-Men were devoted to the principle that mutants and nonmutants could live together in peace, that justice could be accorded to all. As a thief, he found that *très amuser,* and not, perhaps, the most desirable of situations.

But it was an oddly appealing idea, all the same: a world in which it would never occur to Reynaud to raise the issue, in which Remy would never have to talk smooth and convincing to the girls like Madelaine to persuade them to overlook his bloodred eyes.

He spent the day walking in the hills, climbing up and down among the vines of Languedoc, touching the new green leaves with the tips of sensitive fingers, kicking at pebbles. From the ridgeline he could see the rooftops of St. Chinien, red against white, blue against gray, and spangled with all the colors of flowers.

Up above the town, a grand and too-modern château distorted the skyline. Reynaud's, of course. He was slime, but he was successful slime. And Reynaud, the fox, was right—one of Remy's pleasures in coming to St. Chinien was to annoy the fool. He had overlooked that this time.

He didn't have to spend the rest of his life dueling for price of place with such as that. He sat on the rocks overlooking the vineyards, feeling the caress of soft summer wind ruffling his long hair, running coins back and forth across his knuckles, and thought about his life.

They didn't know all about him, those X-Men. They might not be so welcoming if they knew. He was a thief, after all. A master thief. *The* master thief.

Of course, he didn't know all about them, either. Fair enough. He was used to keeping secrets, and used to dealing with others who kept theirs.

And this quixotic tilting at bigotry, well, he'd always been suspiciously fond of lost causes and helpless—hopeless—battles. It appealed to his sense of honor, or at least his sense of humor. He could give it a try.

He doubted Xavier would countenance his other life.

He could change.

He *could* change. He didn't have to remain the man who—who had done some of the things he had done. And this was a chance. *N'donnez j'mais sur un occasion,* his foster father would say, in his soft Cajun mother tongue. *Never overlook an opportunity.* In their business it would be a sin.

Remy LeBeau occasionally liked to sin, but even he drew the line sometimes.

A ten-franc piece went spinning across the sky, to explode in a joyous eruption of biokinetic sparks.

"Vous devrez enregistrer cette matière à la police!"

Despite knowing perfectly well that he was completely innocent—this time, at least—Gambit flinched at the words that greeted his entrance to the little hôtel. Report *what* matter to the police?

The tiny lobby of the hôtel was cramped at the best of times, with barely enough room for the registration desk, the cubbyholes for keys and messages behind it, Madelaine's father acting as registrar and concierge. The area in front of the desk was decorated with a worn rug and one single overstuffed chair. Now, with the hysterical newlyweds alternately clinging to each other and pounding on the desk, there was no room at all.

"Please, sir, madame, you must call the police."

"No!" the woman cried. She was not one of those made beautiful by her tears, Gambit noticed. "No, it was the girl, it had to be the girl, bring her here, ask her! I saw her looking—"

She was flailing her left hand against the desk, slapping it hard, then spinning around to grab her new husband, collapsing into a mascara-streaked soggy mess and his arms.

"I'm sorry," her husband apologized. "It's just that the rings—they were all we had—"

"Madame, we will bring the police. My daughter has nothing to do with this." *Le père* was being very firm and remarkably self-possessed, Gambit thought.

Le père looked over the heads of the newlyweds, and his gaze met Gambit's. For an instant he looked angry, and perhaps even disappointed.

The man knew what he was, Gambit realized. The look of disgust wasn't for Gambit the mutant, it was for Remy LeBeau the thief.

He had never, never stolen anything in St. Chinien. It was his safe place, his refuge. He did not foul his own nest.

But there was someone who would. His lips tightened, and he

returned the look straight on, nodded once, and stepped back out into the world.

The saying goes that there is honor among thieves. Gambit had never been quite sure what that was supposed to mean. Within his own Guild, of course, one took it for granted that one treated the Brothers, like, well, brothers.

But for Richard Reynaud, who would rob a bride of her wedding ring, well, honor was not a concept that quite applied.

And if Reynaud thought it was a concept that would protect him from a thoroughly irritated Remy LeBeau, he was wrong.

The entrance to the Villa Reynaud was marked by a pair of columns topped by foxes. They weren't carved out of marble; Gambit could see the fur ruffling in the wind.

He could also see the marks of birds splattered across the russet and white hair. The foxes were stuffed, maybe even freeze-dried. Once, when originally put in place, they might have been startlingly lifelike. Now they looked ragged and just as well pleased to be dead.

The front gate stood ajar, unusual in this part of the world. Gambit studied the inviting opening for a moment or two, then looked up to the moth-eaten foxes. Glass eyes stared back down at him. He was reasonably sure that behind those eyes were camera lenses, in which case he was already on film. Not that the prospect bothered him; he'd already starred in several such films. The trick was to find out whether he already had an audience.

"What the hell," he muttered to himself, and pushed the gate open wide enough to let himself in

The front garden showed the same impeccable taste as the front columns. A pile of black plastic bags, presumably filled with trash, came nearly to the top of the wall. Several rakes and shovels were leaning crazily against the house wall or scattered on the ground. A gardener stared down at some weeds growing between slabs of pavement, as if seriously considering doing something about them, someday. He glanced up at Gambit and then shook his head, as if the whole idea of weeding was entirely unreasonable.

Gambit nodded pleasantly and walked around toward the back of the house, as if he knew precisely where he was going. He'd never been to Reynaud's home before, but that made no difference at all.

He passed seven large double windows along the side of the house before coming to a discreet white door. The back garden, he was glad to see, was in somewhat better condition.

The door was locked, at least for a moment or two. He let himself in and found he was alone in the laundry room. It smelled of soap and bleach and mildew.

Most robberies took place during the daylight hours, for the very good reason that there were usually fewer people around during the day than at night. Gambit could reasonably expect that Reynaud would be elsewhere during the day as well—he wasn't the type to spend a lovely day indoors.

His only real concern, in fact, was that Reynaud might not have dropped off the rings before taking off for the day.

He swept through the house, room by room, tossing each one with the ease of long practice. Twice he interrupted housemaids at their work, at least once restoring an armful of clean linens that the flustered grandmother had dropped at the sight of the stranger in the inner sanctum. She was smiling at him, confused but obscurely flattered, as he bowed his way out of her sight and into the next room.

Time. Even in the daytime, Reynaud would have alarms set. Each time he opened a door he ran the risk of setting them off, or worse. Surely one of the maids, or the gardener, or someone, had already called the police. He moved faster.

Hallway. Stairs. Bedroom, not in use. Library, with row upon row of perfectly color-coordinated books. A rather grand bath. Water closet. More bedrooms—all sterile, all empty. Evidently *M'sieu le Fox* had no Madame and no kits with whom to share his den—a pity, that.

He moved soundlessly through the house, checking briefly before entering each room, an unconscious smile dancing around his lips as he breathed deeply, waiting for discovery. His search was rapid, sure, and as each room was throughly inspected his smile widened.

And then one last bedroom, this one freshly made up. A pair of handlasted shoes were aligned neatly at the edge of a silk rug. The top of the armoire showed scratches under the gleam. This bedroom, unlike the others, had a regular occupant. And at the far end of the room was yet another closed door.

He reached for the handle, and paused. The knob was brass, worn, had evidently seen years, perhaps centuries of use. All the other fittings in the house were less than twenty years old.

Even if someone had been watching the video cameras at that moment, he would have missed the gesture that caused the playing card to appear between Gambit's fingers. Holding it between the first two fingers of one hand, he tapped the edge against his thumb, contemplating. Then, with a flick of his wrist, he tossed the card against the door.

Nothing happened. The card, lacking any biokinetic charge, rapped edgewise against the brass doorknob and slid, slightly dented, to the floor.

A shout from the garden announced that his time was running out. He reached for the knob—and yanked his hand back with a gutteral Cajun curse as it sparked just before vulnerable flesh came in contact with lethal metal.

He could hear more sounds now from outside the room. There wasn't any time for finesse; he kicked out, *à la savate*, and shattered the wood of the door—pressboard it was, instead of the solid heart oak that beautiful doorknob deserved, and just as well, too, for the sake of his foot.

Alarms, silent and audible, went off at last. Someone—surely not the grandmother?—screamed. Gambit spared the bedroom door one glance and reached through the hole, opening the mysterious door from the inside.

That evening, Remy LeBeau chose to eat inside the restaurant, the better to admire the newlyweds exclaiming between every bite at the jewels glistening on the young woman's hand.

"She is very pretty, *m'sieu*," Madelaine remarked as she took away the soup plate and replaced it with a very nice brace of ortolans.

"Every new bride is beautiful, *ma cherie*." He smiled at her. His smile widened as Reynaud loomed up behind her. Madelaine squeaked and scurried away.

"You pig," Reynaud snarled, staring past him at the newlyweds. "I should have you arrested."

"Ah, I t'ink not. *Les gendarmes* would be so very interested in all I have to say, after all." Gambit shook out a fresh napkin and placed it delicately in his lap. "Would you care to join me? De food is superb."

"Thief."

The incongruity of it caught even Gambit by surprise, and he laughed out loud. "I? Ah, it's not stealing to recover de goods, *mon ami!*"

"Then *worse*," Reynaud spluttered, "you're *not* a thief, and so I shall tell your Guild!" Baffled at Gambit's laughter, rich and loud in the tiny dining room, he spun on his heel and walked out.

"Ah, no," Gambit murmured to himself. "X-Man or not, I t'ink I never give up dis game, *mon ami.* 'S too much fun." He turned to look at the newlyweds, and winked long at the bride, raising his wineglass in a toast. The groom glanced back and forth between Gambit and his new wife, a light of suspicion dawning, and Gambit laughed again as she distracted him with more gushing over the glistening ring.

Some things don't ever change, he thought, still smiling, thinking of the ransom for the jewels that adorned her slender hand. *Once a thief, always a thief. Even when the only thing I steal today is a kiss.*

Ice Prince

K.A. Kindya

JUBILATION LEE HAD NO IDEA how much trouble it would cause when she made the simple decision to go roller-blading.

Things had been quiet for the X-Men for a change. No mutant super-villains had reared their heads recently. Some of the residents of Professor Xavier's mansion had gone on much-needed vacations. Wolverine had slunk off in the night on one of his unannounced spiritual quests. Jubilee, meanwhile, chose a warm autumn day to skate around the mansion property and enjoy the golden sunlight and colorful leaves.

Clad in her typical shorts and T-shirt, and clutching her skates, she sauntered into the living room. She found Jean Grey and Rogue, dressed in slouchy sweats, sprawled on the couch. They were staring at the television.

"Hey, guys," Jubilee called, walking over. "What's with *you* two glued to the boob tube? You're always getting on *my* case about how much TV I watch."

Jean, without taking her eyes off the screen, said, "This is a special tape. We've been waiting for a spare moment to watch it."

The teenaged Asian peered at the screen. "Ack! What is this?"

"Wide World of Sports," Rogue said. "It's a report on the first major figure skatin' compctitition of the season. It's coming up in about a week."

Jubilee rolled her eyes. "Figure skating?" She sniffed derisively. "How can you two watch something so wussy? It's a bunch of girly-girls in pink tutus, wearing too much makeup, making pretty-pretty poses for the judges . . ."

"That's not what it's like at all," Jean said.

"Yeah," Rogue put in. "It's hard work, and tough exercise."

"And it's not a beauty pageant," Jean said. "Skaters train for years to do those jumps. They lift weights to build their muscles. It takes incredible strength. I've been watching skating since I was a kid, and it always impresses me."

Rogue added, with a mischievous smile, "And it's not just for girls." She nodded as words appeared on the TV screen: MEN'S COMPETITION.

"Oh," Jubilee remarked acidly, "I can just imagine what kind of guys. . . ." Her voice trailed off as a vision of male gorgeousness suddenly appeared.

He was young, Asian, and she could see the tight cords of muscle beneath his loose, yet clingy skating costume. He wore his glossy black hair in a spiky short cut. His eyes were liquid pools that reflected the harsh ice-rink lights. His skin shone with a golden cast, set off by the black satin of his low-cut jumpsuit.

"Who . . . is . . . that?" Jubilee gasped.

Rogue's smile turned to one of trumph. "That," she announced, "is Christopher Kim. He's new."

Jean nodded. "He's about your age, Jubes. He's just starting out, but everyone is amazed at how advanced he is. He was just another Junior National finalist last year—this season he has a shot at the Olympics."

Jubilee could say nothing. Her eyes were glazed and she couldn't quite catch her breath.

The two older X-Women exchanged knowing glances and turned up the sound on the set. It was showing one of those "up close and personal" profiles, with the requisite interviews and shots of the skater training. If he made it this season, he could be the youngest man to ever win an Olympic gold medal. First, though, he had to run a gauntlet of preliminary competitions. The first of these would be in Connecticut, not far from the Xavier Mansion in Salem Center, New York.

As the report ended, Jubilee sighed audibly.

"Well," said Rogue to Jean, "our work here is done."

"Yeah," the redhead replied. "I don't have to be a telepath to tell that *someone's* in love."

Jubilee shook her head as if waking from a dream. Then, she noticed the amused looks on the others' faces. She smiled sheepishly. "Well, gotta go!" she said quickly. "I'm gonna go out and get that exercise!" Then she hustled out of the room.

Outside, Jubilee strapped on her skates and protective gear and stroked off furiously on an asphalt paths. "Let 'em laugh," she muttered to herself. "I think Chris Kim and I have a lot in common." After all, they were both young, with unusual talents. They were both precocious. They were both thrust into an adult world, and trained really hard for their goals. They were a perfect match.

She sped past the red, yellow, and orange trees, relishing a cool breeze against her face under the perfect blue sky. She had to admit, the men's skating competition did look cool. It wasn't all like that boring ballet stuff she had thought figure skating involved. Chris Kim used music with a beat, and he moved around the rink with fluid power, like Wolverine on the prowl. When Chris jumped, you could see the spring of his muscles. Then he'd fly through the air, landing effortlessly. It was a performance worthy of any of super hero.

Jubilee loved being with the X-Men. She traveled to exotic locales: Australia, Madripoor, Africa. She helped save the world. She was a hero. But even a hero, like everyone else, fantasized about what it was like to live another life. Ever since her mall-rat days, she would sometimes gaze longingly at the expensive designer dresses and makeup kits displayed in the stores. A part of her wondered what it would be like to be glamorous, an admired and beloved celebrity—instead of a semi-outlaw, publicly reviled mutant.

She imagined herself on an ice rink, in one of those little skating dresses. (They weren't that bad, if you avoided pink.) She pictured it decorated with gold sequins and dangling sparkly beads. Now, Chris Kim was skating beside her, lithe in his black satin, moving like a panther. They held hands; they spun together. He lifted her up above the ice and then he threw her; she flew across the rink, then landed feather-light. Jubilee spread her arms out and tried to lift her leg behind her like the skaters did.

"Aagh!" she yelled as she hit a bump, lost her balance, and sprawled onto the pavement; only her knee pads saved her from some nasty scrapes. She picked herself up painfully and decided to head back home for a more sedate pursuit. Maybe she could go on the computer and find out more about Christopher Kim . . .

The weather was a little colder and gloomier a couple of days later as Jubilee sat on the living room couch, staring at the television. She rewound the tape she was watching and played it frame by frame. "Hmm," she murmured, "is that a Triple Axel or a Triple Lutz?"

So intent was she that she didn't hear anyone coming until, suddenly, right behind her: "So you're the one who's been rooting around in our skating tapes!"

"Aaah!" the teenager spun around to see Jean Grey and Rogue standing over her, hands on their hips. "I'm sorry!"

Jean smiled. "It's okay."

Jubilee sighed and slumped her shoulders. "You got me . . . I've gotten into skating. I found some footage of Chris Kim from last year's Junior Nationals, and that tape you were watching the other day."

Rogue placed a comradely hand on her shoulder. "It's all right to have a crush," she said, then came around to sit next to Jubilee. "Hey, I don't watch skatin' just for the skatin,' if you know what I mean." She winked. "I've got a thing for Philippe Candeloro."

Jean joined Jubilee on the other side. "Oh, you mean that handsome, French-speaking, devil-may-care Olympic medalist? I can't imagine you'd go for someone like that."

Rogue pouted as Jubilee and Jean giggled together.

"So," Jean said, turning to Jubilee. "Are you enjoying the tapes?"

"Yeah, it's kind of interesting. I admit, it isn't as wussy as I thought. I'm trying to tell apart the different jumps. It's not easy, though. Like, this one—what is this?" She replayed the tape.

"Ah," Jean replied sagely. "That's a Triple Axel."

There followed for several minutes an earnest discussion of figure skating basics, and the upcoming prospects for the season. The women sounded like a group of armchair quarterbacks discussing football or some such sport.

The conversation turned to the present performance of Chris Kim as they examined his latest routine.

"So," Jubilee said, "they say he can do a Quadruple Axel, which is, like, the hardest jump in the whole world. But I don't get it. He could barely do Triple Axels last year."

Jean nodded. "Yeah, all the older, more experienced and stronger skaters can't do it at all. Some say it's even physically impossible." She played the jump in slow motion. "With all my years of physical training, even I can't really see how Chris is getting enough height to do four-and-a-half rotations. He's muscular, but he's not nearly as pumped-up as Stojko or the other power-jumpers. And look at his face—he's showing no physical effort. Usually to do an Axel, they grimace like gargoyles . . ."

Rogue scratched her chin. "Yeah. You're right. And the way he's jumping—he doesn't take off with the force that other skaters do. It's weird."

"Well," Jubilee said, "They're going to show that competition next week on the sports network. Maybe they'll have more about it then."

Jean suddenly caught sight of her watch. "Oh, Rogue, we'd better get to the store before all the good shoes go. You want to come, Jubilee?"

Jubilee shook her head. "No. I think I'm starting to be able to tell the Flip from the Toe Loop."

"Wow. You must really be getting into this," Rogue said with mock amazement. "You're turning down shopping!"

As they got up and turned to go, Jubilee told them, "Thanks for talking to me for a while. We never really get a chance to just hang out together, you know?"

Jean smiled at her. "Yeah. This was nice." She and Rogue exchanged a knowing glance, then left the room.

"Robert, mon ami, you are insane." Gambit was mopping his brow as he, Iceman, and Jubilee emerged from the Danger Room the next day.

"I thought it was cool," Jubilee crowed. "We've never fought velociraptors in the Savage Land!"

"Do dey even have velociraptors in de Savage Land?" Remy LeBeau asked wearily, throwing his towel over one shoulder and taking a swig from a water bottle he carried in the other hand.

Bobby Drake, de-icing into his human form, shrugged. "I've never seen one, but they're probably there. No, I got the idea for programming them in from that Spielberg flick."

Jubilee clapped her hands. "I loved that movie!"

"Besides, Remy," Bobby said, "You've got to admit, it's a good workout. 'Raptors are smart, fast . . ."

"I just don' like dem nasty claws on de little feet," the Cajun said. "Hard to hit, too, wit' de playing cards."

"It'll hone your targeting skills," Bobby said.

They were interrupted by the arrival of Jean Grey and Rogue. Jean was holding up a little white envelope.

Gambit looked at them with suspicion. "They look like de cat that's jus' eaten de little birdie," he said.

Jean waved the envelope at Jubilee. "Look what we got."

"What?" asked the teenager.

As Jean extracted three tickets from the envelope, Rogue announced, "It's for the skatin' competition on Saturday night. We're making it a girls' night out."

"Cool!" Jubilee exclaimed.

Bobby crossed his arms and chuckled. "This is new. I didn't know you were into skating, Jubes. Isn't that kind of for . . . sissy-boys?"

"Not all the boys are sissies," Jubilee retorted.

Gambit smiled rakishly. "Ah, I know . . . she mus' be in it to check out de guys in dey tight pants. Hey, *chere*, you don' have to go out and see skating for dat. Don't you see enough men in tights runnin' 'round heah?" He struck a beefcake pose.

Bobby, encouraged by this hilarity, iced up. "Hey, you want ice? We got ice!" He created an ice sheet on the corridor floor, and grabbed the Cajun, who was still vogue-ing. They clutched each other with exaggerated drama and improvised a comical ice-waltz. This lasted all of a minute before Gambit's boots slipped and they landed in a heap, sliding for a few feet across the ice.

Jean and Rogue laughed, and even Jubilee had to smile. "Okay, enough of the high hilarity," Jean said. "Now, let's go get something to eat!"

This met with general approval, though as Bobby cleared the ice and everyone prepared to exit, Jubilee said defensively, "You know, I read somewhere that figure skating gets ratings as high as football, so there!"

"I am having the best time!" Jubilee chattered that Saturday night at the ice arena. She, Rogue, and Jean were returning to their seats after an intermission. The final group of skaters, which included Chris Kim, were up next. Jubilee was heavily laden as she and the others climbed over the spectators in their row. She had bought popcorn, nachos, and a souvenir T-shirt.

"We're having a good time, too," Jean said. "We should do this more often, Jubilee."

"It's so great to hang out with you guys. I feel like one of the gang. This is awesome!"

"And to think we're nowhere near a mall," Rogue quipped as they finally settled into their spots, with Jubilee on one side of her and Jean on the other.

"It's like a mall out there," Jubilee said. "There's all those booths in the lobby, selling all that cool skating stuff. Dude, I had no idea those skating dresses were sooo expensive. And I really liked that shiny red velvety one that designer from Delaware had at her booth, too."

Rogue shrugged. "But where would you wear a skating dress?"

Jean smiled enigmatically and passed Rogue a plastic bag. "Give this to Jubilee," she said.

When the teenager received the parcel, she looked into it and shrieked. "Ohmigod! It's that skating dress! Jean, this cost, like, a fortune!"

Jean smiled. "Hey, I have a little extra cash stashed away. Consider it an early Christmas present. And Rogue, she can wear it to go ice-skating. I think the Rockefeller Center rink is open by now."

"You are totally awesome! This is so cool!" Jubilee hugged the bag to her chest.

Below, the Zamboni machine was finished resurfacing the ice, and the announcer said, "The final group of competitors will come out for their six-minute warm-up."

"There's Chris!" Jubilee cried, as he stepped out in his characteristic black satin costume.

"I hope he does well," Rogue said.

"This could be his first step toward the U.S. Olympic Team," Jean said.

Around the rink, enthusiastic fans pulled out American flags, and some had posters saying things like GO CHRIS! and KIM'S THE MAN! He definitely was developing a following.

Rogue pointed out another skater, a dour-looking, pale-skinned blond man, who was circling Chris Kim like a vulture. He had a gaunt face, and wore an ice-blue outfit that matched his cold eyes. "There's the old sourpuss."

"Is it that Rupert guy?" Jubilee asked. "Chris's big rival?"

Rogue nodded. "Yeah. His name's Rupert Smythe. He's English."

Jubilee pursed her lips. "He looks like he's sucking on a lemon."

"Last year he was a shoo-in for world champion." said Rogue. "He's been around for ages. He was in the last Olympics, but he screwed up in the short program and only came in fourth. This

Olympics'll be his last chance to get a medal. They say his knees are starting to go."

"Isn't he trying to do a Quad, too?" Jubilee asked.

Jean put in, "Yes, but it's only a Quad Toe Loop. It's the easiest of the quadruple jumps. Chris can leave him in the dust with a Quad Axel."

"Oh, hey," Jubilee said, "I think Chris is setting up for one now!"

Sure enough, Chris Kim picked up some speed, and effortlessly landed a Quadruple Axel right in front of Smythe, proving the older skater could not psych him out.

Jean suddenly gasped and grabbed Rogue's arm.

"What's up, Jean?"

"I thought I felt a flash of telekinetic energy in the room just now," Jean said in a whisper, "but it's died down."

Rogue raised an eyebrow. "That's interestin'."

Jubilee found it interesting as well, but now something new was going on down on the ice, causing the crowd to murmur. A mature dark-haired woman, coiffed with a beehive hairdo and wearing a fur coat, had left the gaggle of coaches, who had been watching their charges at one corner of the rink. She made her way around to the broad side of the ice. Against this was a long table, where the nine judges and other officials sat. The woman approached a man at the table's end, and handed him a sheaf of papers. He examined the sheets, then passed them to some other people.

Jean observed, "That's Rupert Smythe's coach talking to the competition referee. I wonder if Smythe's developed an injury."

Suddenly all the judges and officials and referees leapt to their feet and stirred to an uproar. They were all looking, not at Smythe, but at Chris Kim, who was trying to ignore the distractions and do his warm-up. Then, the announcer called into his microphone, "*Christopher Kim, please approach the referee.*"

"I don't get it, what does Smythe's coach want with Chris?" Jubilee asked her friends.

She got no answer, but watched, perplexed, as the young skater approached the table. The officials surrounded him; in their dark suits they resembled a murder of crows. Chris began to fidget and wring his hands, giving his own coach a desperate wide-eyed look. The crowd was buzzing as his coach, a white-haired man, went over, only to be engulfed by the inquisitors.

"I've never seen anything like this," Rogue said. "Not even with Tonya and Nancy . . ."

Jean said, "I really don't like the way this crowd is getting."

"Do you think there could be trouble?" Jubilee asked, eyes wide with concern.

"Should we call the other X-Men?" asked Rogue.

Jean sighed. "By the time they get the signal and scramble the *Blackbird* it could be too late. If anything happens, we'll have to handle it first."

Then came the announcer's voice over the PA system. *"Christopher Kim will be withdrawing from the competition."*

The crowd's buzzing grew as the young skater, pale with shock, left the ice. Then he disappeared into a pack of people, who whisked him away into the yawning tunnel that led backstage.

"Oh my God!" Jubilee cried, leaping to her feet. "What happened?"

Rogue pulled her down. "Settle down, sugar. People are riled up enough as it is."

At this point, a woman, who had been sitting a few rows up behind the judges, elbowed her way to the announcer's table. In her hand was a manila envelope. She shoved the announcer aside and yelled, *"Chris Kim is a mutie! That's why he was pulled out! The evidence is on this tape!"* She waved the envelope.

All hell broke loose.

The audience roared. People leapt to their feet.

Then came the ugly anti-mutant remarks:

"How dare he?"

"Who does he think he is!"

"Ice the mutie!"

Needless to say, the pro-Chris Kim banners disappeared. All over the arena people began squirming and getting up or sitting down. The crowd looked like a mass of wriggling creatures, living under a rock that had been suddenly overturned into the sunlight. Their voices rose to a deafening din.

Jean nudged Rogue. "The core of the troublemakers is over there— see them?" She pointed to a block of seats a just a few sections over from theirs. There were some large, burly men there, who did not look like typical skating fans. They were standing and yelling the majority of the diatribes, though others in the crowd were picking up the poisonous rhetoric.

"I don't like the look of them," Rogue said. "I'll bet they're Friends of Humanity creeps, or one of them other mutant-hatin' groups."

Seconds later, the men started to throw garbage toward the ice. Some of the projectiles hit their neighbors in the audience, and these people, already agitated, began to pick more fights. Security guards ran down the aisles and tried to break up the pandemonium, but the original instigators resisted. Elsewhere in the arena, new fights were erupting, while many other spectators crawled over each other to make a run for the exits.

"This is getting out of hand," Rogue said to Jean.

Jean replied. "I'm going to try to calm the crowd telepathically, but these emotions are running so strong, and with all this insanity, it's going to be hard to concentrate."

Rogue nodded. "I'll see what I can do."

Jean grabbed her arm. "Don't fly or do anything to call too much attention to your powers. It'll only fan the flames."

"How can I help?" Jubilee offered.

"Don't," said Jean. "It's too dangerous. You go out to the lobby— we'll meet you there. If they evacuate the building, stay close to the cops."

"But, Jean, there's got to be something I can do!"

The redhead glared at her sternly. "There are too many variables. I want you out of harm's way."

Jubilee pouted and took up her bag with her souvenirs. She got up and began climbing slowly up the stairs to the exit. When she was a few rows up, she turned to watch the scene. She saw Rogue wading into the fray below, trying to separate the combatants in the most agitated section. Someone tore up a seat, and she grabbed it out of his hands, unnoticed by him, before he threw it. Jean was at the edge of the crowd, her eyes screwed shut, apparently trying to get through to people mentally. This seemed to have no effect. A few seconds later, she opened her eyes again, and gazed intently into the morass. Jubilee concluded she had switched to her telekinesis, to try to blunt the blows of the audience rioters.

I hope Chris is okay, Jubilee thought. Her heart began to pound—what if the riot had spread backstage? Now that she thought about it—there was something she didn't like about those big guys who escorted Chris off the ice. They might have been bodyguards . . . or it could have been a trap. After all, the FOH goons had infiltrated the audience. Maybe they had infiltrated backstage security, too!

She had to get back there and save him. Jubilee ran up the stairs and out the doors, entering the outer passage where the refreshment and souvenir stands were. It was a madhouse out there, with people running around, trying to escape the arena entirely, and security guards vainly working to control everyone.

She ran around the circular passage until she found the door leading to the skaters' entrance. A big security guard stood there, next to a sign that read, NO ONE ALLOWED BEYOND THIS POINT WITHOUT CREDENTIALS.

"Darn!" Jubilee said. She remembered now that you needed to wear a special badge on a cord around your neck, with a photo ID, to get into the restricted areas. Only skaters, their coaches, and the officials could get those. In frustration, she punched the plastic bag with her souvenirs . . . and got an idea.

She dashed into a bathroom. In all the commotion, no one was using it. Ducking into a stall, she shucked off her jeans and shirt, and pulled on the new skating dress Jean had bought her. She kept her sneakers—she'd seen skaters on TV wear them backstage before putting on their skates. For a final touch, she wore over the dress the T-shirt with the competition logo. Now she looked like a skater dressed for warm-up, though she hoped no one would notice her bare legs instead of the thick flesh-colored tights that were usually worn. She moved experimentally and found the outfit quite comfortable. Now she understood how Jean could have run around in that awful green minidress during her Marvel Girl days.

Ditching the bag with her street clothes in the bathroom, Jubilee ran back out into the passage. It had been announced earlier that after the men's competition, the ladies were scheduled for a public practice session on the rink. Hopefully she could pass as a skater herself, perhaps having come early to cheer on a male teammate.

She returned to the restricted entrance and its stern doorkeeper.

"Excuse me, honored sir," she said with a fake foreign accent. "I am skater from Madripoor. I lose pass. I must get in. My coach worry!"

The security guard peered down at her from a great height. Jubilee was petite and athletic—she certainly had the right figure for a skater.

"I haven't seen you in the practices before."

"I miss practice. I just come from my country today. Please, kind sir! I lose coach, I lose pass, I must find him!" She put on her best pathetic face, and quivered her lower lip.

It worked. The security guard waved her through.

Yes! the teenager thought as she pelted down the stairs to the backstage area.

The atmosphere down there was like that of people in a bomb shelter during an air raid. They were fairly safe in the restricted area, but they were trapped as a tempest raged outside. Jubilee encountered a small group of female skaters who had already come for the practice, gathered in a huddle and talking in hushed tones. She recognized a couple from the skating tapes. If it had been under any other circumstances, she would have been starstruck and asked for an autograph, but other things concerned her now.

She pulled aside a well-known National champion in the group, a pixieish brunette dressed in a Team USA warm-up suit. "Have you seen Chris Kim?" Jubilee asked her.

"Do I know you?" the skater asked, squinting at her through too much eye makeup.

"Oh yeah!" Jubilee bluffed. "Don't you remember that wacky time we had in St. Petersburg last year?"

The skater knit her brow. Clearly she didn't remember, but she was pretending she did. "Oh . . . sure . . . St. Petersburg. . . . What a party. . . . Um . . ."

"Chris Kim, I'm looking for him."

"Last I saw him, he was being led out by two of Rupert Smythe's bodyguards."

"Led out? Out where?"

The skater shrugged. "I thought it was kinda weird. The safest place to be right now is down here. But I think they were headed to the upper levels. Maybe Rupert has a secret hidey-hole."

"Why would Rupert Smythe's bodyguards be guarding Chris?"

The skater looked at her vacantly and twisted a curl around her finger. "Maybe Rupert lent them to Chris, what with the riot and all. Geez, can you believe Chris is a mutant? He seemed so nice, too."

Jubilee, to avoid throttling the airhead, made her excuses and dashed off. Her fears were being borne out. Clearly, Rupert's coach had been the one behind Chris Kim's disqualification. She, and Rupert himself, could also have been in cahoots with the mutant-haters. The bodyguards could have indeed been part of the scheme, too.

They may be taking him somewhere they can rough him up . . . or worse, she thought.

She darted through the maze of locker rooms and warm-up areas, looking for a stairway or something leading to the upper levels. She finally found an elevator marked ROOF.

Her instincts told her that was the place to go, and she entered the elevator.

Sure enough, when she came out onto a rooftop parking lot, she espied a very distressing scenario.

A few yards away, near the edge of the roof's low surrounding wall, two large men were manhandling Christopher Kim.

Jubilee's eyes widened, and her heart raced, but she remembered what she had learned from Wolverine. Stealthily, she crept along the shadows until she got close enough to hear what they were saying.

One of the thugs said, "So, you're so upset about being called a mutie, and being pulled from the game, that'cher little pretty-boy heart just broke." He shoved Chris toward his compatriot.

"Yeah," the other chimed in, "so you ran up here and decided to end it all by jumping off the roof."

Chris, his hair disheveled, one sleeve of his costume torn, exclaimed, "I can't believe Rupert Smythe would go through all this trouble to expose me as a mutant just to kill me!"

"Actually, killing you wasn't his idea," replied the first thug. "It was ours." He chortled cruelly. "One less mutie in the world. Even if you do *look* human."

"Cute little skater boy? Mutie scum! Heh, heh, heh," The other thug grabbed Chris by the shoulders and shoved him toward the wall.

Jubilee sprang into motion. With a flying leap, she sprang from the shadows, limned with the brilliance of her mutant light energy, which she hurled in tiny, painful blasts at the attackers. The thugs lost their grip on Chris. She charged at one of the thugs, and butted him with her head in the solar plexus. He reeled backward.

Behind her, she heard Chris cry out, "Hey!" Spinning around, she saw to her horror that the other thug had his arm around the skater's neck in a choke hold, and was dragging him closer to the wall. She kicked her first assailant to keep him down, then rushed to the other one. By now, he had hauled Chris onto the ledge and was trying to push him over.

"Yaaah!" Jubilee howled and elbowed the thug in the gut. It connected, but when he doubled over he lost his grip on the skater. Chris wobbled precariously on the ledge . . . then, he lost his balance, as Jubilee vainly hurled herself to try to catch him . . .

. . . but he didn't fall. He just floated there, suspended in midair a few inches past the wall's edge! Jubilee reached the wall and looked down—it was a good four or five stories to the parking lot below. Chris looked somewhat dazed, not really understanding the enormity of the situation.

Jubilee stared a few seconds, dumbstruck herself. He really was a mutant! He was levitating! Then, another thought came to her: *If he realizes what's going on, it could end up like in the cartoons; he'll lose his concentration and he'll fall.* Carefully, so as not to startle him, she reached over and hauled him back to relative safety.

With sudden realization, he blinked, wide-eyed, and turned to peer back down at where he'd just been. He opened and closed his mouth a few times, but nothing came out.

Now Jubilee turned to the thugs, who were still nursing their injuries. "Hello!" she admonished, "you guys have the dumbest suicide plan I've ever heard! If the guy's mutant power is to *levitate*, why would he kill himself by *jumping off a roof?*"

This only provoked them. They snarled and tried to rush her and Chris.

Now, Jubilee had another idea. She noticed Chris was still wearing his skates—he hadn't even had time to put on the plastic guards to cover the blades. Remembering the claws on the feet of the velociraptors in Bobby's danger room program, she yelled, "Kick 'em, Chris!" At the same time, she created more of her light show, which helped keep the thugs disoriented as Chris, fueled by adrenaline, sliced at them with the razor-sharp steel blades.

Howling with pain, nursing long, shallow but painful, cuts, the thugs were almost defeated when Rogue and Jean finally showed up.

"For Heaven's sake," the redhead shouted at her. "Can't you ever follow orders?"

Jubilee ran to her, with Chris in tow.

"She saved my life," Chris said gratefully, as Rogue went to deal with the thugs.

Jean sighed. "Well, there is that, I suppose."

Chris turned to Jubilee. "Are you a skater?"

"Uh, no, actually," she replied sheepishly. "I'm just a fan."

"What you are is a hero!" he exclaimed. "Thanks." He gazed into her eyes gratefully.

"It was nothing," she said, and blushed.

Rogue came up to them, dragging the chastened thugs. "Dang, ain't this somethin'?"

The police had arrived shortly after Jean and Rogue had begun to help quell the riot, and things were now back under control. The arena had been evacuated; the rest of the competition was postponed. Rogue turned the thugs over to the authorities. Down in the restricted skaters' area, people were heading out as Chris, his rescuers in tow, rejoined his relieved coach, George Carson.

"Thank God you're all right!" the middle-aged man cried upon seeing his student. "When those goons surrounded you, I had no idea what had happened to you. I was worried sick!"

"Those guys were in some kind of hate group. They tried to kill me!" Chris replied. "But this girl saved my life." He presented Jubilee. "She's a hero! She held off those two bruisers with nothing but some, like, martial arts moves and . . . what was making those little lights, a flashlight or something?"

Jubilee suddenly felt extremely self-conscious. "Oh, I did what anyone would have done . . ." She scratched the back of her head and shuffled her feet. "Um, I'm with these guys." She pulled over Jean and Rogue.

Carson shook Jubilee's hand gratefully. "Thank you . . . thank you so much."

Jean spoke up. "We were glad to help . . . how did things turn out with this disqualification?"

"Chris . . . I have some bad news," the coach said. "The officials reviewed the tape and documents that were submitted to them. They have an analysis proving that the way you do your jump . . . well, it defies the laws of physics. Is it true? Are you a mutant?"

The youth hung his head. "I think so. I can fly."

Jubilee put in, "Well, not fly, exactly . . . levitate."

Jean whispered to Rogue, "So, *he* was the source of the telekinesis I sensed during the warm-up, after all . . ."

Chris protested, "I never knew I had these powers! This is news to me, too! I was just doing the jump the way I was taught."

"I believe you," the coach replied. "I know how hard you worked to learn the jump. But you must have been using your power without even realizing it."

"Your powers musta kicked in between last season and this one," Rogue deduced. "That happens at around your age."

Chris's eyes swam with anguish. "People hate mutants." He turned to his coach. "Do you hate me, now, too?"

"Of course not," the coach said. "I've known you your entire life. You're almost like a son to me. I could never hate you." He grew somber. "But the skating federation is suspending you from competition. They say your mutant ability gives you an unfair advantage. There's going to be an official hearing." His voice grew soft. "Chris . . . this could become permanent."

"No!" he cried. "They can't . . ."

"This has never happened before in skating," the coach replied, "but with the current climate . . . it doesn't look good. A few years ago, I heard a skiier was disqualified for being a mutant . . . I think he was Canadian . . ."

"But the Olympics . . . !"

Rogue put an arm around the distraught boy's shoulders. "Sugar . . . calm down. Don't give up yet. If there's a hearin', they'll have to make arguments, right?"

"I'll defend you," the coach resolved. "I'll argue your mutant power is a God-given talent, like the talent for figure skating itself."

"That's the spirit," Jubilee said. "And . . . while you're waiting for the hearing . . . you can stay with us."

"What!" Jean exclaimed.

"Where do you live?" the coach asked.

"Upstate . . . Salem Center . . ." Jean replied. "We're at the Xavier School for Gifted Youngsters."

The coach knit his brow. "I've heard the name . . . can't place it, though. I don't really have time to follow much outside the skating world. But it sounds very classy. And Chris is certainly a gifted youngster."

"Um, um . . ." Jean stammered. "I don't know if this is a good idea."

Rogue said, "Actually, it is a good idea. With Chris out as a mutant, the media will go nuts. It's the biggest scandal skating has ever seen. We can keep him out of the craziness for a few days."

"Please, Jean?" Jubilee pleaded. "Chris needs peace and quiet right now. And the mansion's been quiet for a while . . ."

Jean sighed. "All right . . . we'll talk it over with the others. How do you feel about it, Chris?"

Chris Kim said nothing. He just stared into space.

Several days passed: dark, gloomy, rainy days. Chris went to Xavier's mansion, but he kept to himself, staying mostly in his guest room. Jubilee fussed over him like a mother hen, cooking (somewhat ineptly) for him and popping into the room every hour on the hour with some kind of treat. It never quite got through to her when he would tell her he wasn't hungry.

Finally, the results of the hearing came in. Chris took the call from his coach in the study, while Jubilee, Jean, and Rogue waited in the living room.

"I wish Professor Xavier was here," Jubilee said, drawing up her knees to her chest as she sat fidgeting on the couch. "He always knows what to say in these situations."

"He still won't be back from Muir Island for a couple of weeks," Jean said.

Rogue said, "So, I guess y'all heard the news about how they're gonna investigate Rupert Smythe's part in all this. I wonder how much he knew about the FOH plan to start the riot and attempted murder."

Softly, Jubilee said, "I heard the thugs say Smythe didn't know they were going to try to kill Chris."

"Hmm." Jean remarked. "Well, whatever his part, that investigation could drag on for months, and until they have solid evidence, Smythe can still compete. He might make it to the Olympics after all . . . but his knees might not even hold out that long."

"Poor Chris. Maybe this'll work out," Rogue said, and crossed her fingers.

Just then, Chris stepped solemnly into the room. They knew, even before he said anything. And then, he told them, in a small voice. "I'm out. For good. I'll never be allowed to skate again."

He was met with saddened silence. Then, finally, Jubilee came over to him. "Um . . . is there anything we can do?"

Chris shook his head. "I just . . . need to be alone . . ." Then he slunk out of the room.

Jubilee sprang to her feet and headed for the door.

"Don't," Rogue commanded.

The teenager turned back. "But he needs me!"

"Not now," Jean told her "Let him be for a while. He needs to think things through."

Rogue said, "You were the one who said he needed peace and quiet. Give it to him now."

Jubilee sighed in exasperation and crossed her arms, but she slumped back down onto the couch.

Three days passed.

"Wake up, Chris! Today is the first day of the rest of your life!" Jubilee threw open the curtains of the skater's room. The sun, out for the first time in days, streamed in. Chris had spent all this time in his darkened quarters, listening to the rain. Jubilee figured he'd had enough peace and quiet. If he didn't do something, he'd be mired in depression forever. Or worse.

From under the rumpled bedclothes, Chris moaned. "Skating was my life. I can't skate anymore. I have nothing to live for."

With her hands on her hips, Jubilee retorted, "Then don't live for anything. Just live!"

He moaned again and covered his head with the blanket. Jubilee marched over and yanked it back. "Christopher Kim, I did not risk my butt to save yours from those thugs just to watch you sleep the rest of your life away."

"But . . . what else can I do? All I've ever done is train."

"Have some fun."

"Training was fun."

"There's all kinds of fun. Come on, it's a nice day. Look at the pretty leaves outside. Smell the wood smoke. Listen to the birds." She cupped her hand to her ear.

They couldn't hear any birds, but there seemed to be shouting outside.

Jubilee returned to the window. "Cool! Look, some of the guys are playing basketball outside. Let's go play."

"I can't play basketball. I'm too short."

"Maybe, but you have an advantage. You can be Air Kim!"

"Using those powers is what got me into trouble in the first place."

"Well, you can't hide from using your powers. They're part of what you are. Let's go—you'll see, it'll be a blast!" Jubilee grabbed one of his hands, and hauled him to a sitting position.

Perhaps Chris decided it would take less energy to go along with her than resist. He finally consented to dress and go outside with her.

It was no ordinary basketball game. Remy was dribbling the ball, which was glowing with a charge of kinetic energy. Rogue was flying a few feet off the ground in front of the basket. Jean was floating on one side, waiting for the rebound, and Bobby generated an ice sheet under Remy just as he let loose the shot. Remy slipped onto his rear, but he made the basket. The ball bounced insanely upon hitting the ground, discharging a blinding blast. Jean, undaunted, stared at the now-singed ball, which froze in midair. Rogue flew in under it and, rising into the sky, slam-dunked it from three feet above the net.

Chris's jaw dropped. "What the heck?"

"I told you before." said Jubilee. "We're all mutants here. This school teaches us to use and control our powers."

"I . . . I guess I wasn't paying attention before, with everything that was going on."

"If there's one place you can have fun with your powers, it's here." Jubilee grinned. "This is what recess is like for us." She waved her arms to the players. "Hey, can we play?"

"Sure," Remy said. "But if both of y'all join, you gotta be on separate teams."

"Wait," Rogue put in. "I'll join your team and Jubes and Chris can join mine."

Jubilee propelled Chris toward the court, and he joined the madness.

Two hours later, Chris was actually smiling as everyone clattered back into the mansion.

"Way to go, duuude," Jubilee said. "You scored the winning basket."

"I just wanted to jump . . . I didn't think I'd jump that high." In the last seconds of the game, Chris had darted past three flying interfering mutants and made a miraculous slam dunk. He really was Air Kim.

Remy shook his head. "Dey too many people who can fly playin' dis game. I feel like a midget in de NBA."

"Hey, I can't fly!" Jubilee admonished and shoved Remy playfully.

They were in the living room, and Chris suddenly was transfixed by something on the coffee table. He went over to it and picked up a book, then began leafing through it.

Jubilee noticed and broke off her teasing, joining the skater's side as the others left for the kitchen. "What's that?"

Chris showed her. "*Great Works of the Italian Renaissance.*"

"Oooh." Jubilee rolled her eyes and groaned. "I remember when we got that book. Professor Xavier took us to New York, to that big, boring art museum. He made us stare at a bunch of pictures of naked fat women . . . yawn-o-rama!"

Chris looked at the book thoughtfully. "I've been in a lot of the cities where these paintings are displayed," he said. "But I've never seen them. I've been all over Europe and only seen the four walls of my hotel room and the inside of the ice rink. We never had the time or the money to stay a little extra after the competition and see the sights. I always wanted to see the museums. I would read guidebooks and imagine what it would be like."

"Eew. You like museums . . ." Then Jubilee remembered she hadn't thought much of figure skating until Jean and Rogue had gotten her into it. Maybe museums weren't so bad after all. "So . . . um . . . you've never been to the Metropolitan Museum of Art? In New York?"

The skater shook his head. "But I skated once at the Rockefeller Center tree lighting ceremony."

"Well, dude, we're only about an hour away from the Big Apple. We can go to the museum tomorrow. We'll take the train; we'll make it a road trip."

"No way!"

"Way! I've got nothing better to do. Okay, there's some school-work, but Professor X is out of town and I can blow it off. Let's do it!"

"But what about the media? Won't they still be after me?"

"You can go in *disguise*." Jubilee raised an eyebrow and winked.

The next day, Jubilee and Chris sat on a hill in Central Park at sunset. It was still a clear day, but there was a stiff breeze that carried the bite of winter. They looked out at the autumn foliage, which was past its peak—some of the trees were already bare.

"So, how'd you like the museum?" Jubilee asked.

Chris took off his baseball cap. "I had a great time . . . this disguise really worked well. I didn't think I'd look so different just wearing a hat."

Jubilee didn't tell him there was an image inducer hidden in the hat. "I had a pretty good time too. You really know a lot about art."

"I read a lot on plane trips. See, I told you there was more in there than pictures of fat naked women."

"I liked the Egyptian stuff," Jubilee acknowledged. "And those knights in armor . . . and those indoor gardens with the pretty statues . . ."

"The paintings are so much more beautiful in real life," Chris said with a sigh. "The colors just aren't the same in the pictures in books. And to see the sculptures in the round . . . !"

"Hey, Chris . . . now you have the time to go to all the museums you want."

Chris blinked. "Yeah . . . I guess . . ." He jumped with realization. "You know what I could do? I could take the money I would have spent on training this year, and use it to tour Europe. I could see all the great museums—the Louvre, the Uffizi, the British Museum!"

"Hey, that's a great idea! And if you keep moving around, it'll be harder for the press to bug you . . . you should keep the hat, though."

He smiled at her.

Jubilee sighed. He had a very sweet smile, and she hadn't seen enough of it lately. But then she realized he was talking about going away, perhaps for months . . . and she was just getting to know him.

"Chris . . . you can still stay at the mansion right now. We can go to all the museums in New York, and you can learn to use your powers . . ."

He shook his head. "No offense, but . . . I want to get away from the mansion for a while. I've been cooped up in there long enough."

"But . . . but . . . what about . . . um . . . us?" She winced as she realized she sounded like something out of a cheesy soap opera.

"Jubilee . . . I like you. A lot. And . . . I'm really grateful to you for saving my life."

"Oh, no . . . don't tell me . . . you're not . . . into . . . girls . . ."

"No! I mean, yeah, I like girls . . . but . . . you might not believe this . . . I've never dated or anything. There just wasn't time for that while I was training."

"So you have time for it now."

He squirmed. "Um . . . Jubilee . . . I need to sort of . . . get used to my new life, y'know? My whole world has been turned upside down. I have to get my head together before I can get into dating or any of that stuff. I didn't think I'd even start dating till after I got my gold medal."

"That would only have been a few months from now."

"A lot can happen in a few months . . . Jubes, I'm sorry. I don't want to blow you off or anything . . . but you know what I've just gone through."

Jubilee hung her head. "Yeah . . . just a couple of days ago I was really worried you might do something . . . drastic . . . if you know what I mean."

"I really appreciate everything you've done for me."

"It was my pleasure."

"Thanks for saving my life . . . and giving me a new one."

They looked into each other's eyes for a few moments. Then, Chris hestitantly leaned over and kissed her on the cheek.

Jubilee said nothing for a second. Then she jumped up. "Well, we'd better get going. It'll be dark soon."

She pulled him to his feet and led him down the hill.

Dear Jubilee:

Europe is so awesome! I got to see everything this time! The museums are incredible! So are the palaces, and the cathedrals! Everything's so beautiful! I saw the Mona Lisa yesterday. It was unbelievable! To actually stand in front of the real thing after seeing so many pictures of it . . . it made me feel alive. I love this stuff. I think I want to become an art critic!

I haven't been using my powers much, but I don't hate them or anything. Maybe in a few months I'll go back to your school and take some lessons. But I've been in athletics training my whole life, so there's no hurry. My coach is still fighting the federation. I want to win, but at least now my life won't be over if they never let me skate again. I still miss it, but it hurts a little less nowadays.

Thanks so much for everything. I'll never forget you.

Love, Chris

Jubilee read the letter one more time, then folded it up and pocketed it in her yellow trench coat as she headed toward the Danger Room. *I am so over you*, she thought. Besides, she had other things to worry about. Magneto was up to no good again, they'd just gotten back from Genosha, and there was that Legacy Virus . . .

Iceman met her in the corridor, going the other way. "It's all set up in there for your session. Wolverine is waiting," he said. "Oh, by the way—do you still want me to look into converting the pool to an ice rink, now that it's winter?"

Jubilee paused for a moment. Then she said, "Yeah, sure. It's too snowy for rollerblading. No sense wasting that nice skating dress Jean got me."

Okay, so maybe I'm not completely *over you . . .*

"Hey," Bobby said, "I could go skating with you."

"Wouldn't you rather skate with Remy, instead? You two made *such* a lovely couple."

"Nah. He always wants to lead."

They chuckled for a few minutes before Jubilee continued on to the Danger Room.

Such Stuff As Dreams Are Made Of

Robin Wayne Bailey

JEAN GREY SAT at her small writing desk addressing a stack of wedding invitations in the early Sunday quiet. Steam curled upward from a cup of black coffee she held in her left hand, while with her right she dipped the nib of her pen in the well of a Parker Ink jar and scrawled another name on a vellum envelope. With a flourish, she set the pen aside, screwed the lid on the jar, sat back, and sighed.

Her desk calendar still showed the date as December 6th, and she ripped the page away, crumpling it before dropping it into her trash can. So much remained to be done, so many preparations. How would she ever be ready in time?

The morning sun streamed through her window, pleasantly warming her face, a relaxing sensation. She closed her eyes and listened as the opening strains of *Sammy Kaye's Sunday Serenade* began on the NBC Red Network, to which her Philco radio was tuned. The soft music, so deliciously romantic, only added to the sense of contentment that filled her, and she fingered the invitations, wondering if she dared take time to address just one more.

A glance at her wristwatch brought Jean upright in her chair. Only thirty minutes before her work shift began! Slamming back the last of her coffee, she rose and smoothed the wrinkles of her white uniform. Near the room's only door, a rectangular mirror in a wooden frame hung on the wall beside a picture of the American flag. Pausing before it, she twisted her red tresses into a tight bun, checked the gold lieutenant's bars and the caduceus pin on her collar, then pinned her nurse's cap in place.

Outside, a low-flying plane passed, its drone surprisingly loud. Her back to the window now, she caught a fleeting glimpse of the craft in the corner of the mirror, then a sudden bright flash. Sunlight on metallic wing, she assumed, until she heard the explosion that followed and felt the shock of it.

Jean Grey whirled. In the distance beyond her window, fire and smoke roiled up from the area of the men's barracks. Before she could move, another fireball blossomed into the air, vast and scorching. Her window cracked, and the splinters flew toward her. With a scream, she flung herself down, covering her face while her room seemed to buck and tremble.

A moment of tense silence followed. Jean shrugged off broken glass as she got to her feet. She didn't bother to check herself for cuts, nor did she spare more than a despairing glance at the invitations now scattered on the floor. Instead, she snatched up the blue cloak that lay folded on the foot of her bed, flung it around her shoulders, and fled her room.

All the nurses in the barracks were awake, shouting questions, demanding answers, wide-eyed with fear and confusion, in various stages of dress. They congested the hallways. "Get to the hospital!" Jean called as she pushed her way through them. "Be ready for casualties!"

A young army nurse just coming off shift stood petrified in the entrance, one hand still holding open the screen door. "No warning!" she wailed. "No siren! Jean, the sky's full of planes!"

Jean shoved by her and stepped outside. Already, smoke filled the air, and fire heat blew in waves across the field. A second massive explosion knocked her off her feet as one of the hangars exploded and flames engulfed a pair of mustang fighters parked before it.

Overhead, yellow-winged aircraft strafed the men's barracks. Another building, a machine shop, geysered upward in a terrible shower of brick and board and fire. Beyond it, more mustang fighters and cargo ships, all lined up so neatly on Hickam's airfield, folded like balsa toys under the unheralded attack.

Jean heard her name. A sprawling lawn separated the nurses' barracks from Hickam Hospital. A tall man in flight surgeon's uniform ran toward her. Again, he called her name, his expression grim, determined, heedless of the bullets that chewed the ground behind him.

"Scott!" Jean waved her arms, attempting to warn him as she struggled to her feet. He jerked and twitched wildly, then froze for a moment, his shoulders slumping, and looked at her like a little boy who knew he'd done something horribly wrong. Then he crumpled like a broken doll.

A scream ripped from her lips, and something churned inside her mind, something dark and frightening that stirred and came roaring awake, something powerful and angry. It reached out from her, enveloped the yellow-winged plane, seized it in midair, then crushed it like a thing of paper. Fuel erupted, and a second bright sun hung briefly in the sky and then smashed into the earth.

Jean stared at the wreckage on the lawn, stunned, feeling the power, whatever it was, recoil inside her and knowing that somehow she was responsible. But she couldn't think about it now. Instinct and impulse only drove her, and she ran to Scott, threw herself down by his side.

All around her people ran now, but no one stopped to help. On the rooftops, some soldiers were firing back with machine guns or pistols. A plane tried to take off, then veered sharply off the runway as a massive four-engined B-17 attempting to land came screaming through the air, a blazing torch from mid fuselage to tail section. The yellow-winged warplanes swarmed like bees around it, scorching the air with tracers. It smashed into the runway, cracking open, and the forward half skidded to a stop while the rear splintered and burned.

Scott's blood stained Jean's hands as she cradled his head. "Stay with me, Scott!" she begged. "Help's on the way! Don't you leave me!"

With a gasp, Jean Grey bolted up in the bed, her body trembling, drenched in a clammy sweat. Beside her, Scott Summers also snapped awake and slapped the switch on the bedside light. The low wattage glinted on the slender goggles of ruby quartz in which he slept.

"The dream again?" he questioned, his voice alert, concerned.

Jean rubbed her temples as she climbed out of bed, crossed the floor of the room, pushed back the drape over the window, and stared beyond it. The moon shimmered on the lake outside the converted boathouse they called home. A gentle August night wind shivered through the pines. All seemed at peace on the Xavier estate.

"Different," she said as her trembling subsided. She let the curtain fall back into place. "But the same, yes." She turned to face her husband, and despite her unease, she smiled at the way the pillow had mashed his thick brown hair into a crooked coxcomb on one side of his head. The book he'd been reading when he fell asleep lay open on the floor. Without comment, she lifted it telekinetically, closed it, and placed it on his nightstand next to a pair of glasses made from the same ruby quartz as his goggles.

"Almost every night this week," he said, sitting up and drawing his knees to his bare chest beneath the blanket.

"I can't figure why," Jean answered. Remnants of the dream yet lingered, troubling her. She remembered the desk calendar and its glaring date in red letters and numerals: *December 7, 1941*. She knew that date: Pearl Harbor. The Day of Infamy. Yet she'd never had any particular interest in World War II, and no connection at all to Hawaii or Hickam Field. She tried to shrug off the images. "It'll be dawn soon," she said, pushing her feet into slippers. "I'll make some coffee."

With eyes squeezed shut, Scott traded the goggles for his glasses. "I'll fry the eggs," he said.

Scott served breakfast on the dock and as they ate they watched the sunrise through the whispering trees. The dream melted away, and Jean relaxed as the sky brightened. Three weeks married, and she never felt closer to Scott than at this moment, nor more at peace. Peace was a rare and precious thing for the X-Men, for the world feared and hated them, branded them outlaws, mutants.

But that was the outer world. Xavier's estate was a refuge from all that, and she and Scott had it to themselves for the weekend. The Professor, bless him, had arranged a trip to New York City with all the others and a full agenda of museum tours and stage plays. *Consider this an extension on your honeymoon*, he had whispered to her before everyone departed. *Enjoy yourselves.*

With that thought in mind, she took Scott's hand and led him back inside.

The ordnance building went up in a roiling ball of fire and fury. The post exchange followed. Enemy dive bombers pounded the parade ground, the hangars, the barracks. Choking smoke rolled across the lawn, and on the southwestern horizon a blacker, thicker smoke rose over Pearl Harbor.

Jean Grey ran toward the hospital, her blue cloak falling from her shoulders to the grass. Machine-gun fire tore the earth around her, throwing up chunks of the sidewalk's concrete. With a scream, she shielded her eyes and kept on running. She'd be needed at the hospital. Another explosion. An invisible hand smashed her down. Such pain in her ears! Blood on her face! And deep inside her head, something waking, stirring.

Through the pain in her ears, she heard her name. Across the lawn, in the doorway of the hospital, Scott saw her fall, and his face twisted with fear for her safety. Heedless of the danger, he ran to her aid.

A yellow-winged plane, its bombs dropped, strafed across the lawn, and the ground in front of the hospital erupted. Still reeling from the blast, Jean shouted his name.

"Stephen!"

Like a broken doll, Captain Stephen Maxwell sprawled on the grass. For an instant, Jean stared in disbelief and shock. Overhead, the yellow-winged plane climbed away. She screamed again in rage at the enemy that had harmed the man she loved. And it was getting away! She wouldn't let it.

Hot fury churned inside her, and a force unknown yet instinctively familiar ripped outward from her mind. Suddenly she saw the plane with different eyes opened as they had never been before. She saw the face of her enemy within, saw his thoughts even as that force smashed into his brain. In an instant, she tasted his arrogance, felt him recoil as he sensed her impossible presence in the cockpit with him. No, not in the cockpit—inside his head! How she savored his unexpected fear.

She screamed, and inside the plane the pilot screamed with her. The plane's fuselage crumpled, fuel tanks ruptured, exploded. For an instant the blue sky burned with a bright red sun.

Jean ran to Stephen's side. *Stephen? But his name is Scott.* Confused, frightened, she lifted his bloody head in her hands. "Stephen!" she cried as she tried to wipe away the red blood that filled his eyes. Yes, Stephen seemed to fit him somehow better than Scott. His lids fluttered, and he clutched at her sleeve. His lips moved.

But she couldn't hear him. Pain in her ears, and so many other voices in her head, all so loud! The soldiers on the rooftops firing back with machine guns and pistols; the pilots in their planes making cold calculations; the nurses in the barracks behind her so full of terror and confusion; a mechanic in pain half-buried in the rubble of a hangar. The ernest prayers of a B-17 crew in the midst of a crash landing. . . . She heard them. More, she felt their fear, their rage. It all rushed upon her, a sensory tidal wave of chaos.

Stephen's hand clutched at her sleeve, then at her uniform's lapel. He attempted weakly to pull himself up, and suddenly his voice rose stronger, more clearly, over all the others. Except it wasn't his voice. *Jane, I—I wanted to marry you*, he managed. His thoughts seemed to enfold her with a sad, fading tenderness. *I'd have made you a good husband, Jane. We won't have time now. No time.*

His hand slipped, and something tore from her uniform. His fingers curled open, revealing her name tag on his palm and her name: *Jane Somerset, 1st Lt.*

Jean started, shook her head. But that wasn't right, she thought, snatching at the pin, reading the name again. She was Jean Grey!

Another yellow-winged plane dove out of the sun, engines screaming. Enraged, Jean whirled, her red hair flying around her like flame. Her mind opened; her strange new power erupted forth, and in the sky above the hospital, an enemy aircraft exploded even as the finger of its pilot began to tighten on a trigger. Fire and metal rained down; the plane swerved crazily, crashed on the runway in a seething fireball beside the burning tail section of the American B-17.

Jean turned her attention back to Stephen and flung her arms around him. In a manner she couldn't understand, she felt his heartbeat, sensed his diminishing life spark, touched the evaporating chaos of his thoughts, tasted his passion, his regret and terror. "Don't leave me!" she cried, pressing her face to his. "I won't let you go!"

The force inside her uncoiled once more, plunged deeper into his mind, entangled him, entangled them both, and drew them together, bound them. Stephen fell toward a black yawning abyss, and unable or unwilling to let him go, Jean fell with him.

Jean fought her way up from the dream, her breath ragged, heart racing. Scott bent over her, shaking her, worried. "Wake up!" he said. "Jean?" A ray of sunlight streamed through a gap in the window's curtains. She blinked and passed a hand over her eyes.

"That's it!" Scott said softly as he brushed a lock of hair back from her temple. "No more war movies before bedtime."

She pushed herself up on the pillows and forced a smile. "I fell asleep," she answered simply. "Is it afternoon?"

Scott looked at her for a moment, inscrutable behind the ruby quartz lens that hid his eyes. Then he pushed his lower lip out in a mock pout. "You were calling someone's name," he told her, "and it wasn't mine."

"Stephen," she acknowledged curtly. She chewed her lip. "Stephen—something. I don't remember clearly."

She flung the blanket back, and with the barest nudge of her telekinetic power, eased open the closet door on the far side of the room. A pair of black slacks and a green turtleneck sweater floated from the shelves and settled on the bed at her feet.

Scott continued to watch her as he paced to the large double-windows and opened the curtains wider to let in more light. She watched him, too, from the corner of her eye as she dressed. The sight of her husband, naked in the light, stirred her. Her husband! There had been times when she thought she might never have the chance to call him that, and she had wondered if being an X-Man meant ruling out love.

But she had loved Scott Summers as long as she could remember, since their first days as students in Professor Xavier's school. Through dangers both from space and time they had persevered, grown stronger, closer. And she knew now with a perfect clarity that, rather than ruling out love, love was an X-Man's greatest strength.

She shared a subtle rapport with Scott, a small effect of her telepathic power. It let her sense his moods, his thoughts. She sensed his concern as he watched her in silence. "You're thinking of Jason Wyngarde," she said with a quiet shudder.

Adjusting his ruby quartz glasses on his nose, Scott nodded. "And the Shadow King—we have so many enemies. Some of them could strike at you through your dreams."

Jean shook her head stubbornly, frowning, as she pulled on her boots. She'd already thought of such things herself. Rising, she planted a kiss on Scott's lips, turned toward the windows and opened them with the gentlest telekinetic shove. "Don't worry," she whispered.

Effortlessly, soundlessly, she glided into the air and out the window, like Peter Pan on the way to Never-Never Land. Not even the curtains rustled at her parting, and Scott made no attempt to call her back. Past the lake and over the pine trees she flew. Even here, safely out of sight on the Xavier estate, she seldom used her power in such an ostentatious manner, but the thrill of sun and wind on her face chased away the shadow on her spirit and the chill left by the dream.

A squirrel nibbling a walnut near the kitchen door of the mansion chittered and scampered away as she touched ground again. She let herself in and stood for a moment, listening to the silence. With so many

X-Men in residence, so many visitors in and out, the mansion was seldom silent, and this was a rare moment.

Her heels made soft sounds on the bare wood floors as she walked through the halls and made her way to the library. The School for Gifted Youngsters—she still thought of it by that name, though it was now the Xavier Institute for Higher Learning—boasted a wonderful collection of books on every subject, and floor-to-ceiling bookcases lined every wall. It was not to the books she went, however, but to a personal computer on an antique oak desk in the warmest corner of the room where she settled herself.

With a sigh, she turned on the machine. This wasn't quite how she'd expected to spend the afternoon, but she had questions, and a little research might turn up some answers. And if it didn't? Well, there was always the Danger Room. Maybe all she really needed was to work off a little tension.

The afternoon segued into evening, and sunset melted into darkness. Books piled up on either side of the computer as she worked, and when the desk was full, she pulled up a chair and stacked more books there. The lights clicked on, and it took her a moment to notice, so engrossed was she in her research. Scott entered the room with a tray of sandwiches and a pot of coffee. "I figured you could use some help," he said. Setting the tray aside, he picked up one of the books and sat cross-legged on the floor.

"Remind me to marry you someday," Jean answered. Barely glancing from the computer screen, she took one of the sandwiches and continued reading an army web-site entry on Hickam Field.

"I might even ask you," Scott answered with a smile. "Someday."

Smoke rose black and heavy into the blue sky. Percussive shock waves, one after another, shook the ground as the rain of bombs continued to fall. Planes lined up in neat rows near the runway exploded and burned, so much grotesquely twisted wreckage. Hangars exploded; machine shops collapsed into fiery rubble; flames engulfed the hospital's south wing.

Jean screamed and could not hear herself. She clutched her bleeding ears in terror. Yellow-winged aircraft swarmed overhead like angry bees. Torpedo planes dropped their lethal loads. Machine gun tracers tore chunks from the earth. All around her, men and women, soldiers and nurses, ran for duty stations or in panic. On rooftops, some soldiers fired back with handguns. She heard none of it, not the whistle of the bombs, nor the roar of the explosions, not the voices, nor the guns.

Yet, lying on the rubble-strewn ground where the last explosion had tossed her, somehow she *heard*. A cacophony of voices shouted in her head, the volume maddening, so many she couldn't sort them. In the barracks, on the rooftops, even in the planes above—she *heard* them.

Then, through it all, one familiar voice calling her name with a desperate fervor: *Jane! Jane!* And she looked up to see Scott—or was it Stephen?—running toward her. In that moment, she sensed the cold fear that filled him, knew it was for her safety, and it propelled him heedlessly across the lawn to her side.

As if in a dream, Jean watched him run. In slow motion he came, like a character in a Bijou movie, while above him a yellow-winged plane began its dive. As if she had seen it all before, she knew the outcome. Her heart thundered in her chest, blood pounded in her ears, and this time, she fought the pain in her body, and struggled to rise.

The man she loved—Scott or Stephen—would die. She knew that somehow, she had seen it. *Unless I act this time to save him.* She got to her feet, her eyes on the plane overhead. Something uncoiled inside her, something strange, yet familiar. It half-woke and stirred and shivered, and she reached out her hands toward the menacing aircraft.

Its guns spat fire. Pieces of earth flew up, and Scott or Stephen flung out his arms dramatically. For an instant, he stood frozen with a stunned expression on his face; then he fell. *Jean! Jean!* She heard the echo of her name fading in his dying mind.

No longer merely stirring, the sleepy thing inside her shot awake. It saw the yellow-winged craft through her eyes and, raging, lanced outward, following the line of her hand, and crushed the enemy plane with astonishing ease.

Too late! Too late to save her man. But not too late for vengeance. Not this time. She reached upward again with a telekinetic fist, crushed another plane and another. Fury fed the thing inside her; she sent it out again and again, showing the attackers no mercy. Bright fiery flowers blossomed overhead, and the sky became a garden of death, and she rose to soar above it like a shining bird on wings of flame.

*   *   *

"Jean! Jean!"

Her eyes snapped open. In midair, Scott spun like a top. Scores of books flew in circles about him, pages fluttering madly. Cables and cords, a desk lamp, pieces of the computer, a chair, all swirled throughout the library in the grip of a telekinetic tornado.

In an instant, it was over. Everything fell to the floor in a clattering, except for Scott, who made a more colorful sound.

Jean sat up on the brown leather sofa where she had fallen asleep, and the horror of what had happened struck her. Her power had gone out of control—her worst fear. The library was a shambles, books tumbled, shelves destroyed. The west wall was blown completely outward.

Scott crawled up from the floor and hung his arms over the end of the sofa. His brown hair flopped down across his forehead; his ruby-quartz lenses sat crooked on his nose. "Do you ever wonder," he said with an exasperated sigh as he stared at the wall, "what the construction companies in town must think of us?"

She flung her arms around his neck, trembling at the thought that she might have hurt him. She knew now she had to do something about these dreams—these nightmares.

"I felt it, too, this time," Scott confessed. He stroked her hair as he held her. "Through the rapport we share. It's not just a dream, Jean. There's . . . someone."

Jean tried to calm herself and broke free of Scott's embrace. As her trembling subsided, anger replaced it. Too many people had tried to manipulate her in the past, to use her. She didn't like it, and she didn't like the idea that someone might be trying now.

She drew a deep breath, then another, and set even her anger aside as she closed her eyes and gathered subtle mental resources. She sensed Scott behind her, all love and worry, then tuned him out of her awareness.

Not just a telekinetic, Jean Grey was one of the most powerful telepaths on the planet. Opening her mind, she found what she sought—a barely detectible psychic residue hinting at the presence of another unfamiliar mind.

So she was under attack, as Scott had believed, from some unknown foe. Well, the X-Men were no easy prey, she least of all. "Keep the coffee boiling," she told Scott as she lowered herself once more to the sofa. "I'll be right back." She let her body go slack against the soft leather.

Freed from the flesh, her mind moved onto another plane, an astral plane accessible only to telepaths and mystics, where her powers were amplified to new degrees. Now the psychic residue she had detected hung in the air like a tenuous veil of light. She touched it, and it sparkled in response. She recoiled at first, then touched it again, and the sparks seemed almost to dance around her fingers. But already the light was dimming. When she tried to follow it back to its source, back to the mind from which it sprang, it faded completely.

"It's strange."

Scott sat on the arm of the sofa looking carefully down at her. He felt helpless, she could tell, and she didn't need to read his mind to know that. The expression on his face said it all. "Of course it's strange," he answered. "We're X-Men. It's not like we could have a quiet, normal weekend alone."

She patted his hand. "I was angry a moment ago," she admitted. She gestured at the mess the library had become. "But for all this violence, and for all the violence in the dreams, I can't sense any hostility. I don't understand it. Nor do I understand why a psychic trail just fades."

Scott frowned. He rose from the sofa and, if only to feel useful, began picking up and stacking the scattered books. "While you were asleep," he said, inclining his head and giving her an amused look, "and before your little telekinetic storm picked me up and gave me *The Wizard of Oz* treatment, I ran a computer search on the name you gave me."

Jean stood up. "Jane Somerset," she said. "She was an army nurse, a first lieutenant." She folded her arms sternly. "Have you been hacking into military records again, dear?"

"Well . . ." Scott pretended sheepishness. "Nothing turned up there. The army doesn't seem to have computerized their records back that far." He shrugged. "However, a patient named Jane Somerset turned up in the records of the Veterans' Administration. Seems she's been in and out of VA hospitals, mostly in, for the past fifty years."

"Where is she now?"

"Her last discharge was twelve years ago," Scott answered. He touched the temple of his glasses as he glanced toward the ruins of the computer. "I was interrupted before I could learn more."

Jean rose on tiptoe and kissed his cheek. "You're such a good husband," she said. "As a reward, let me help you with the housekeeping." She took the armload of books he had gathered, and turning, telekinetically righted overturned chairs and tables. A lamp returned to its corner on the desk. Books flew about the room again and darted to the shelves.

"Do you think anyone will notice they're not alphabetized?" Jean asked impishly as she sent her armload of books after the others.

"Do you think anyone will notice the hole in the wall?" Scott answered.

"I want to go for a drive," Jean said, changing the subject. "A nice romantic drive in the moonlight. You'd like that, wouldn't you?"

"It's too late to snow me, Red," her husband answered. "What's the plan?"

"More of an impulse," she admitted. "I think Jane Somerset is somewhere near."

Scott frowned. "She'd be at least seventy by now. And why would she attack you?"

Jean took Scott's hand as she urged him from the library. "I don't think it's an attack," she answered. "I should have thought of it sooner. Our first names are almost the same. And there are other similarities, if the images in the dreams are true."

"You're both telepaths?"

Jean glanced at her wristwatch. "It's only eight o'clock," she said, pulling him toward the door. "Let's just drive."

"We might as well go this way," Scott said with a shrug, indicating the massive hole. A broken piece of plaster hung down from the top of the hole. Scott lifted his glasses just a fraction. Scarlet beams of energy lanced from his eyes and shattered the treacherous obstacle, clearing the way. He adjusted his lenses again. "It's closer to the garage."

A half moon floated above the trees in the summer night sky as they drove in their new convertible, a wedding gift from longtime friend and fellow X-Man, Warren Worthington III, along the country lanes toward Salem Center. If Jane Somerset were near, the town seemed a likely starting place, and Jean suggested it.

But Jean paid little attention to the romantic moon or the rush of wind through her hair or the beauty of the night. She closed her eyes. Unable to find a trail, she opened her mind, all her psychic senses, and called Jane Somerset's name. No answer came, nor any sense of a presence. Yet unexpectedly, Jean Grey felt an overwhelming grief and a regret deeper than she could bear.

An image of bombs flashed through her mind. Jean flinched and forced it away. She wasn't asleep this time, and she wanted no more of such images. She concentrated, instead, on other images from the dream, on wedding invitations, on Captain Stephen Maxwell.

As if from a great distance, she heard the sound of bells in her mind. They faded, replaced by a sound like weeping that also faded.

Jean rubbed her eyes and sat more erect in the car seat. "If Jane Somerset is a psi, then she's a low-level one. I don't know why I can't make contact with her. I've tried; I'm trying now. But on the astral plane I got an image when I touched her light. Just a flash of something—a church steeple, I think."

Through the quiet streets of Salem Center they drove past coffee shops and antique stores, restaurants and the lone movie theater. The town seemed a place out of time, tranquil and safe in its storybook isolation.

"Stop," Jean said suddenly, her hand clutching on Scott's right arm.

The Salem Center Congregational Methodist Church rose up on the left side of the street, stark and black without a light in its stained-glass windows. Its tall steeple thrust upward at the moon. Jean felt a shiver of recognition, and opening the car door, got out.

"No one's home," Scott observed.

"Let's walk," Jean insisted.

Hand in hand, they strolled the sidewalk and up the steps to the church doors, which they found locked. With the smallest part of her power, Jean mind-probed the interior. Indeed, it was empty, but a parish house stood at the south end of the church, and the minister, with an armload of groceries, was juggling a key at his door.

"Hi!" Jean called, waving.

Startled, the minister nearly dropped keys and groceries both. "Oh, me," he exclaimed nervously. He peered at them with momentary suspicion, then relaxed. "Can I be of service to you young people?"

Scott introduced Jean and himself and shook hands with the gray-haired reverend. "We were wondering," he said conversationally after they'd exchanged a few pleasantries, "do you know a Jane Somerset or perhaps a Stephen Maxwell?"

"We think they used to live around here," Jean lied sweetly.

The minister set his groceries down and rubbed his chin thoughtfully. "Jane, you say?" He rubbed his chin again. "Why no. We do have a Martha Somerset on our membership roles, a longtime parishoner, wonderful woman, though she doesn't attend services much anymore. Quite old, you know. But no one by the name of—"

Jean gripped Scott's arm. The sound of bells layered over the explosions of bombs filled her head. Her knees buckled momentarily at the unexpected onslaught before she blocked it out. "It's all right," she said, steadying herself. "Just a bit of dizziness."

But the minister's suspicions were once again aroused. Bending, he recovered his sack of groceries and inserted his key into the door's lock. "It's quite late," he said. "Do come back for one of our services. Good night, good night." Then he was inside and the lock clicked shut.

Biting her lip, Jean reluctantly reached inside the minister's mind and seized the address of Martha Somerset. She hated invading people in such a manner, but a sense of urgency compelled her. "I know we're close," she told Scott. "The images are so intense!"

Martha Somerset lived in the oldest part of Salem Center where the homes were all Victorian and stately, though some were faded and in need of repair. Scott parked the car at the curb before such a house, and leaned across Jean to stare at the structure. A few lights burned in the windows, though the hour was late. Getting out, they walked side by side up the cracked sidewalk, past neat flower beds, to a door with leaded glass windows. Scott pushed the doorbell.

An antique little face peered from behind a sheer lace curtain, before opening the door. Her hair was thinning gray, and little flesh clung to her bones. Yet her eyes sparkled, and she regarded them with none of the minister's nervousness as she wiped her hands on a lace apron.

"Martha Somerset?" Scott inquired.

"Yes?" She looked them both up and down.

Jean took Scott's hand, interlacing her fingers with his. "I know it's late," she said apologetically. "But do you know a Jane Somerset?"

The old woman's eyes widened. "Why, Jane's my sister!" She threw back the door and beckoned them into a foyer with flowered wallpaper. An old coatrack stood behind the door, and against one wall, an upright piano. "However do you know Jane?" she asked. "And may I get you some tea?"

Even without her telepathic power, Jean sensed Martha Somerset's loneliness, but also her sincerity and warmth. She liked the old woman immediately. "Is Jane here?" Jean asked. "Please, I have to know."

Now Martha stood back for a moment and examined Jean closely, and her cheerfulness quietly faded. "Oh my, no," she said. "The news isn't very good, I'm afraid. But I'm forgetting my manners. Let me get you that tea."

She ushered them into a sitting room off the side of the foyer and returned a few moments later with a silver tray upon which sat an English brown Betty teapot, china cups, and saucers. She poured three cups and distributed them.

"Jane's been very ill, hasn't she?" Jean said, restarting the conversation. "In and out of the hospital."

Martha Somerset nodded as she balanced her cup and saucer expertly on the palm of her left hand. "I had her transferred from San Francisco to a hospital here just last week," Martha told them. "We grew up here, you know, and I just couldn't afford that expensive place anymore. But the strain of another move was too much, and she's had a stroke."

"But she is here," Scott said, "in Salem Center?"

"Please," Jean said, leaning forward. "I know you have no reason to trust us, but I must see her."

Again, Martha seemed to study Jean. She took a sip of her tea, then set the cup back on the tray. "You hear her, don't you?" she said to Jean.

Scott and Jean exchanged glances. "What do you mean?" Scott asked.

"I used to hear her sometimes, too," she answered. "I took care of her for a while, you know, when I was younger. Maybe *hear* isn't the right word. But I knew when she needed things: another blanket, a sip of water, or when she was awake. She let me know, though she never spoke another word from the day Stephen died, and of course she was quite deaf." Martha shook her head sadly. "She never got over Stephen's death."

Jean said. "They were to be married?"

Martha nodded, her face serious. "She is talking to you. No one in this town but me remembers that. They were going to get married right over at the Methodist church on Christmas Day. But she was an army nurse at Hickam Field, you know, right up from Pearl Harbor." She took a sip of her tea. "I never married, myself."

Jean touched her head. The sound of bells and bombs echoed softly in the back of her skull. An urgency filled Jean. She had no doubt now that Jane Somerset was calling to her. "Please, Miss Somerset," she set her teacup down. "Martha—tell me where she is?"

Martha brushed her hands over the lap of her neat lace apron. "Why, she's up on Harvard Street in St. Anne's Convalescent Home."

Jean rose to her feet. "Let's go see her," she said.

Martha's eyes widened again. Then she slapped her knees. "It's a little past visiting hours" she said, rising. "But I can get us in."

The staff nurse was firm—only one visitor at a time, so Jean went in alone. Jane Somerset lay comatose amid a spiderweb of intravenous tubes; she'd never regained consciousness after the stroke. Jean approached the bed, gazing down at the frail, almost skeletal form on the sheets. Martha had told them much on the drive over.

Deafened by a bomb blast, unable or unwilling to speak or even communicate after her ordeal, Jane had spent most of her life in hospitals and institutions. At first, a brain injury had been blamed, and there was a scar from a wound over her left eye to suggest it, but no such injury could be found. Insanity, some others suggested, or trauma-induced catatonia. Whatever the cause, Jane Somerset had lived most of her life sealed inside her own mind.

But Jean knew the cause. Reaching out, she touched the parchmentlike skin of Jane's hand, and as she did so, she remembered a childhood friend named Annie Richards. Struck by a car, Annie had died in Jean's arms. That tragedy had triggered Jean's still-latent telepathic abilities at a young age. Mind-locked with Annie, Jean had nearly died with her friend—would have died, but for the intervention of Professor Charles Xavier.

But for Jane, there had been no Professor, and for all intents and purposes, on December 7, 1941, she had died with her beloved Stephen.

She squeezed Jane's hand. "I'm here," she whispered.

It was only Jane's unconscious mind, after all these years, that was reaching out in her final hours, trying to make contact with someone, to tell her story. Had she not come to Salem Center, she might have gone unheard. But in Jean, she had found a kindred soul. "I'm so glad to meet you," Jean told her.

An image unfolded in Jean's mind of a desk at a window and wedding invitations piled high, and bells pealed in her ears—wedding bells. There were no bombs in the background this time, just sadness and regret. Through the touch of their hands, Jean felt Jane's life slipping away with a sensation and certainty few others could ever know.

Chewing her lip, Jean slipped from the room into the corridor and down the hall to a waiting area where Scott sat quietly with Martha. The two had obviously struck up a friendship. "There's a place I know," Jean explained, kneeling down beside Martha as she reached out for Scott's hand, "where anything is possible. Will you trust me?"

Martha regarded her without blinking. "If it's for Jane, I'll do anything," she said. "We've both lived a long time."

Jean smiled softly. "Then go to sleep," she said, sending the telepathic command into Martha's brain. The old woman sighed and eased back on the waiting room couch.

She turned to Scott and her smile became mischievous. "Well, handsome, would you meet me at the altar a second time?"

His brow furrowed with suspicion over his ruby quartz lenses. "What are you up to?" When she only arched her eyebrows, he answered, "I'd meet you there a dozen times."

"Great," she said, grinning, "but I won't be the bride this time." Before he could protest, she touched that furrow above his glasses. "Sleep." He slumped back in his chair.

Jean returned to Jane Somerset's room. The lights of Salem Center shone outside the window; she pulled the drapes, and moved to the bedside again to take Jane's hand.

Closing her eyes, she felt beyond the walls of the room for the minds of Scott and Martha Somerset. Then, taking them in tow, she plunged deep into the dormant mind of Jane Somerset, past her sleeping conscious mind, past the layers and layers of her subconscious and deeper still to that very core mind where all that remained of Jane Somerset's self-awareness resided.

Jane Somerset, a young girl in a crisp white nurse's uniform with gold wings on the collar, regarded her with a shy smile. In her mind, time had not passed. "Hello," she said. "I know you, don't I?"

"It's time to get ready," Jean said. "Stephen is waiting; the service is about to begin."

Jane Somerset looked confused, then she brightened. "Stephen?"

"Come with me," Jean said, holding out her hand.

Nervously, Jane Somerset reached out. As their fingers brushed, Jean shifted them to the astral plane where all things were possible to a strong enough mind, and hers was one of the strongest.

Jane Somerset's uniform metamorphosed into a wedding gown, the very one she once had dreamed of wearing. Jean had plucked the pattern from Jane's memories. "He's waiting for you," Jean said, pointing. An organ swelled with the familiar strains of the Bridal March. "There's the music. Go to him now. Be happy."

The astral plane bent to Jean's mind and became a chapel. Scott, clad in captain's dress uniform, waited at the altar, and with him, Jane's sister, Martha, much younger and tearful in the white gown of a bridesmaid.

Scott's thoughts reached out to her, for on the astral plane words were unnecessary. "What role are you playing?"

"What else?" Jean answered, her red hair spilling loosely past her white collar and over the shoulders of her black suit. "I'm the minister."

"Are you sure you remember the words?" Scott grinned.

Jane Somerset arrived at his side, radiant, beaming with happiness. "I've dreamed of this moment, Stephen," she whispered. "Now we have all our lives together."

"Her power was completely latent," Jean told Scott over coffee in the mansion's kitchen. The Sunday afternoon sun was sinking slowly outside the window. It would be dark soon, and their fellow X-Men would return home. She and Scott had spent the day trying their best to clean up the library. "The shock of the attack activated it suddenly, and just as suddenly the trauma of Stephen's death shut it down until, sensing her own approaching death, a small subconscious part of her reached out again."

She grew silent and stared into her coffee. "If the Professor hadn't been there for me when Annie died . . ." She pushed the cup back.

"We've buried a lot of friends, Scott," she said. "I don't think I've felt closer to any of them."

Scott reached across the table for her hand, but the phone rang. Picking up the receiver, he spoke a few quiet words, then hung up. "That was Martha," he said, his voice subdued. "It's over."

Jean gazed out the window at the red sun that hung on the horizon.

Continuity Guide

"Every Time a Bell Rings" by Brian K. Vaughan takes place about a year prior to the second (flashback) story in *X-Men* Vol. 1 #54 (March 1969). In that story, Warren reversed his decision never to use the wings again, and took on the role of "the Avenging Angel," before he was found by Charles Xavier and recruited to the X-Men.

"Diary of a False Man" by Keith R.A. DeCandido takes place concurrently with *X-Men* Vol. 1 #43 (April 1968), the story in which the Changeling died in the guise of Professor Xavier. The final portion of the story takes place shortly after *X-Men* Vol. 1 #66 (March 1970), which is when Xavier revealed his deception to the X-Men.

"Welcome to the X-Men, Madrox" by Steve Lyons takes place between *Giant-Size Fantastic Four* #4 (February 1975), when the Fantastic Four first encountered Madrox and sent him to Xavier's School, and *Giant-Size X-Men* #1 (October 1975), by which time Madrox had decided not to remain with the X-Men.

"Peace Offering" by Michael Stewart takes place between *Uncanny X-Men* #108 (December 1977) and 109 (February 1978), and shortly after *Iron Fist* Vol. 1 #15 (September 1977), which is when the X-Men encountered Iron Fist and trashed Jean Grey and Misty Knight's apartment.

"The Worst Prison of All" by C.J. Henderson takes place between *Uncanny X-Men* #110 (April 1978) and 111 (June 1978).

"Chasing Hairy" by Glenn Hauman occurs while the Beast was still a member of the Avengers, specifically right before *Avengers* Vol. 1 #181 (March 1979).

"One Night Only" by Sholly Fisch takes place shortly after *Uncanny X-Men* #153 (January 1982).

"A Fine Line" by Dori Koogler takes place just prior to *Uncanny X-Men* #224 (December 1987), when Colossus rejoined the X-Men. He, Shadowcat, and Nightcrawler were injured during the "Mutant Massacre," when Mr. Sinister's Marauders led an assault on the Morlocks that left most of them dead or injured. The final portion of the story takes place between *Uncanny X-Men* #227 (March 1988), when the X-Men were believed killed, and the *Excalibur* special.

"Steel Dogs and Englishmen" by Thomas Deja takes place concurrently with *Excalibur* #11 (August 1989).

"The Stranger Inside" by Jennifer Heddle takes place concurrently with *Uncanny X-Men* #243–246 (April–July 1989), when the team was believed dead and living in Australia.

"Once a Thief" by Ashley McConnell takes place in the general vicinity of *Uncanny X-Men* #275 (April 1991), which is shortly after Gambit joined the team.

"Ice Prince" by K.A. Kindya takes place shortly after *X-Men* Vol. 2 #3 (December 1991).

"Such Stuff As Dreams Are Made Of" by Robin Wayne Bailey takes place shortly after the miniseries *The Adventures of Cyclops and Phoenix* (May–August 1994), which chronicled Scott and Jean's rather bizarre honeymoon.

Contributors

ROBIN WAYNE BAILEY is the author of twelve novels, including *Shadowdance* and the *Brothers of the Dragon* series, and numerous short stories. A former officer of the Science Fiction and Fantasy Writers of America, and currently on the board of directors of the Science Fiction and Fantasy Writers Hall of Fame, he writes full-time from his home in Kansas City, Missouri. He claims he learned to read from comic books that his father brought home coverless from the local paper mill when he was a kid, and he's been a lifelong reader of the X-Men's adventures.

Born in a tiny fishing village in Cuba, **KEITH R.A. DeCANDIDO** was smuggled to New York City by a roving pack of gypsy librarians who trained him in their vile and depraved ways. In addition to short fiction in four previous Marvel anthologies (*The Ultimate Spider-Man, The Ultimate Silver Surfer, Untold Tales of Spider-Man*, and *The Ultimate Hulk*), Keith has coauthored a Spider-Man novel with José R. Nieto (*Venom's Wrath*), written the bestselling *Buffy the Vampire Slayer: The Xander Years* Volume 1, and written books, comic books, and short stories in the *Buffy, Doctor Who, Magic: The Gathering, Star Trek: The Next Generation, Xena: Warrior Princess*, and *Young Hercules* milieus. Keith is or has been an editor, critic, TV personality, anthologist, book packager, and musician—the latter as percussionist for the Don't Quit Your Day Job Players, a rock/blues/country band that released its second CD, *Blues Spoken Here*, in 1999. He lives on the Upper West Side of Manhattan with his lovely and much more talented wife, Marina Frants, where they maintain their Web site at www.sff.net/people/krad. Keith would like to loudly and vociferously thank Kurt and Ann Busiek for invaluable research assistance that made writing "Diary of a False Man" possible.

THOMAS DEJA lives and works in New York City. Starting with pieces under the psuedonym "Sergio Taubmann" in the seminal humor 'zine *Inside Joke*, Thomas has been telling stories for ten years. His work includes stories in *After Hours*, *Not One of Us*, *Rictus*, *The Ultimate Hulk*, *Creatio ex Nihilo*, *Bedlam: Bedtime Stories for the Criminally Insane*, and *The Bare Bone Anthology*, and has netted him mention in two editions of *The Year's Best Fantasy & Horror*. His nonfiction pieces in *Fangoria* have been published in two languages, and other nonfiction has appeared in *The Scream Factory* and *Wet Paint*. He continues to serve as associate editor of *Space and Time* magazine, and to contribute to the online novel *The Mandrill at the Side of the Road*.

When not prowling the night as a masked urban vigilante, **SHOLLY FISCH** has spent the wee hours as a freelance writer since 1984. His comic book credits run the gamut from *Clive Barker's Hellraiser* to *Ren and Stimpy*, including stories for *Batman Chronicles*, the *Spider-Man Holiday Special*, *She-Hulk*, and others, plus magazine articles, television scripts, Web site reviews, and more than two hundred pieces for *Marvel Age Magazine*. He also wrote the story "Here There Be Dragons" for *The Ultimate Hulk*. By day, Sholly is a mild-mannered vice president at the Children's Television Workshop. Occasionally, he also manages to spend a few minutes with his lovely wife, Susan, and brilliantly talented children, Nachum and Chana.

When last we left **GLENN HAUMAN**'s biography (previously seen in *The Ultimate X-Men* and *Urban Nightmares*), it was trying to hide from a midget clairvoyant that escaped from prison. Despite the small medium at large, it managed to inform readers that Glenn is still running electronic publisher BiblioBytes (http://www.bb.com). He's received an ACLU Civil Liberties Award for commitment to free speech on the Internet, and may be the last Silicon Alley veteran to have gotten no venture capital. Winning 9–0 in the Supreme Court over the Communications Decency Act, he feels he is now prepared to join ongoing debates in the Science Fiction and Fantasy Writers of America as an active member. He contributed numerous errors to the *Star Trek Encyclopedia* CD-ROM. He lives in a spiffy house in New Jersey with his wife and cat.

CONTRIBUTORS

JENNIFER HEDDLE is an editorial assistant at Roc/NAL, where she works on science fiction, fantasy, horror, mystery, and New Age books. This is her first published story and she couldn't be happier that it's about Rogue, her all-time favorite member of the X-Men. She lives in New York City with a normal roommate and an abnormal cat, and spends entirely too much time obsessing about when Mulder and Scully are going to kiss. She would like to thank the following people for their support: Keith, Michele, Lorie, Laura Anne, Genny, Nic, Allegra, Holly, Cheri, Karen R., Laura, Kristin B., Monique, Sue, Marie, Ed, Lucienne, and all the members of Café UST and the J&Visionaries. She would also like to thank her brother for introducing her to the X-Men in the first place and her parents for always believing in her abilities. Now if she could just figure out a way for Rogue and Gambit to live happily ever after . . .

In his time, **C.J. HENDERSON** has earned his keep as a movie house manager, waiter, drama coach, fast-food jockey, interior painter, blackjack dealer, book reviewer, stockman, English teacher, roadie, advertising salesman, creative writing instructor, supernatural investigator, bank guard, storage coordinator, children's theater director, card shark, film critic, dishwasher, magazine editor, traffic manager, short-order cook, stand-up comic, interview and general article writer, toy sales man, camp counselor, movie booker, street mime, and as a senior editor of legal publications at Matthew Bender & Co., Inc. He now—quite happily—does none of the above. He does write novels, comics, and short stories, however, just to keep himself amused.

K.A. KINDYA works by day as a producer of *Star Trek* CD-ROMs at Simon and Schuster Interactive. (Yes, she's a professional Trekker.) By night, she watches Japanese animation. She was trained as a journalist, and has published nonfiction articles in such magazines as *Archaeology*, *Successful Meetings*, and *Publishers Weekly*. Her first published fiction was a short story for Circlet Press; "Ice Prince" is her second. She is grateful for the opportunity to combine two of her obsessions. One, the X-Men, she has been following for more years than Jubilee is supposed to have been alive. The other is figure skating, whose competitions she follows with an enthusiasm most people reserve for team sports played by large, burly men.

DORI KOOGLER lives on a farm in Virginia with her husband, two children, and two dogs. She is a professional Mom, with a thriving taxi service on the side, and expects to recruit her son into the business in another three years. When she isn't ferrying kids to soccer, ballet, karate, etc., she works on her yarn collection, does advance model testing for TowelBoy Corp., and discusses the fine art of CharacterTorture in many online venues. This is her first professional sale.

STAN LEE is known to millions as the man whose super heroes propelled Marvel to its prominent position in the comic book industry. Hundreds of legendary characters, such as Spider-Man, the Incredible Hulk, the Fantastic Four, the Silver Surfer, Iron Man, Daredevil, Dr. Strange, and the X-Men, all grew out of his fertile imagination. Stan has written more than a dozen bestselling books for Simon & Schuster, Harper & Row, and other major publishers, and he has also served as editor for *The Ultimate Spider-Man*, *The Ultimate Silver Surfer*, *The Ultimate Super-Villains*, *The Ultimate X-Men*, *Untold Tales of Spider-Man* (with Kurt Busiek), and *The Ultimate Hulk* (with Peter David). Presently, he resides in Los Angeles, where he chairs Marvel Films and has served as co-executive producer for Marvel's many motion picture, television, and animation projects, from the *X-Men* and *Blade* feature films to the *X-Men*, *Spider-Man*, and *Avengers* animated TV series. His latest venture is Stan Lee Media, which can be found on the World Wide Web at www.stanlee.net.

STEVE LYONS was born and lives in Salford in northwest England. He has contributed articles, short stories, and comic strips to many British magazines, from *Coronation Street* to *Batman* to *Doctor Who*. He has also written a number of books about TV science fiction shows, including the official *Red Dwarf Programme Guide* and several *Doctor Who* novels. This is his fourth appearance in a Marvel anthology, and—at last!—his first chance to use Madrox the Multiple Man.

ASHLEY McCONNELL is the author of fantasy, horror, and media tie-in novels and short stories, including "Gift of the Silver Fox" in *The Ultimate X-Men*. She lives in Albuquerque, New Mexico, and spends her disposable income on cats and Morgan horses.

CONTRIBUTORS

MICHAEL STEWART is a copyeditor and freelance writer. He currently lives in New Jersey with his wife, Barbara, and their pets. His past work has included children's books, comics, and magazine articles. This is his first time writing about killer mutants, bionic private eyes, and ninja assassins.

BRIAN K. VAUGHAN is a filmmaker, freelance writer for Marvel Comics, and Hollywood stunt driver. More importantly, he once ate an entire box of crayons on a dare, survived swallowing a lit firework, won a bare-knuckle fistfight against the Harvard Marching Band, sneezed over a thousand times in three days, and has casually worked the word "lumpy" into every story he has ever written. Brian's mutant power is the ability to effortlessly turn oxygen into carbon dioxide.

Illustrator **MIKE ZECK** has been drawing comics for more than two decades for most of the major publishers. Some of his Marvel artistic highlights include launching *The Punisher* to stardom with a five-issue miniseries, the *Secret Wars* maxiseries, and the acclaimed "Kraven's Last Hunt" story arc in the Spider-Man titles. With Phil Zimelman, he has provided covers for several Marvel anthologies, and he also drew the illustrations for Tony Isabella and Bob Ingersoll's Captain America novel *Liberty's Torch* and Adam-Troy Castro's Sinister Six trilogy of Spider-Man novels. Mike and his wife, Angel, reside in Connecticut.